ONE
PERCENTER

D.R. GRAHAM

Entangled Publishing, LLC
2614 South Timberline Road
Suite 109
Fort Collins, CO 80525
Visit our website at www.entangledpublishing.com.

Embrace is an imprint of Entangled Publishing, LLC.

Edited by Heather Howland and Vanessa Mitchell
Cover design by Heather Howland
Photography by iStock

Manufactured in the United States of America

First Edition February 2015

embrace

For the people who have always had my back.

99% of bikers obey the law. The other 1% make their own...

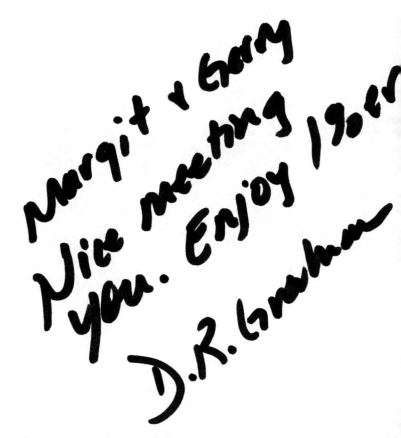

Chapter One

Both sides of my family and their friends file down the aisle of the church in solemn silence. To my left, dark suits, expensive shoes, and conservative dresses. To my right, ripped denim, leather vests, and skanky skirts. Twenty uniformed cops watch from along the back wall with their arms folded across their chests.

My push-up bra is creating way too much cleavage for a real church, but the Noir et Bleu Motorcycle Club tank top is a necessary show of respect. If God is somewhere up there in the rafters, He's probably disappointed with my trashy funeral attire. There's no sign of Him. Maybe He's too scared to be here.

One of my dad's old helmets rests on a chair next to me at the altar. Uncle Ronnie set it there to remind everyone who my father was. As if anyone could forget. My mom is sprawled across the pew in the front row to my right. Her blond hair matted, her makeup smeared, she leans on Uncle

Terry's leg as if she's the one who's dead. It's pathetic. The judgmental whispers from the left side of the church make a tingly feeling creep up my throat. I swallow hard and close my eyes. Too bad that doesn't make the mortification disappear.

The eulogy clenched in my hand is soggy from sweat. I place the curled paper on my lap and wipe my palms on my cut-off jean shorts. Shit. It's too hot in here. If they don't get this over with soon I'm going to pass out and end up a worse mess than my mom.

Leland walks in. Now I can't breathe. The sun silhouettes his face, but the tailored suit and his perfect posture confirm it's him. To avoid eye contact between us, I focus on Auntie Elizabeth sitting in the front pew to my left, as far away from my mom as possible. She's crying into Uncle Blaine's linen handkerchief. He smiles at me and mouths, *Are you doing okay?*

I force myself to nod, even though I'm not doing okay. I stare up at the ceiling to prevent tears from escaping.

The minister sneaks out of a side door and slides onto a wooden bench behind me. My hands shake, partly because his arrival means the service will start soon, and partly because if he sits there during my speech, my ass in my short shorts will be in his direct view the entire time.

My brother's boyfriend, Sam, sits in the third row sobbing. His parents and sister are several rows behind him, but nobody comforts him. I catch Auntie Elizabeth's attention and point at Sam. She leans back and waves him forward to join them.

The door at the back opens and the Gyllenhalls enter.

Aiden stares at me as he walks down the aisle. My entire

body trembles, and I can't swallow. The black jeans, motor-cycle boots, and white dress shirt under a leather vest are his version of dress clothes, and he's even more striking than I remember. His sleeve cuffs are rolled up and his collar button is undone, which gives me a glimpse of a new tattoo on his neck.

He steps aside to let his dad and uncle file into the reserved pew directly behind my mom. Then he continues toward me. The church appears to spin around him as he walks. The faces and stained glass windows circle in a blur of color as if we're inside a kaleidoscope. He takes the two steps up onto the red-carpeted altar, reaches out, and squeezes my hand tightly. His skin on mine makes the spinning stop. My eyes close as he leans down. "Sorry, Ti," he whispers. His right palm slides up to my neck and his lips graze my cheek.

The tears I've been fighting win the battle and drip over my eyelashes.

Chapter Two

FOUR MONTHS EARLIER

A band of four geeky misfits plays barely tolerable Top 40 covers on a stage that could accommodate a symphony. Weird. A country club like this should have enough money to hire musicians with some talent. I roll my eyes at Cooper and jerk a "what gives" thumb at the band. He laughs and shakes his head, maybe because he agrees that the band sucks, or maybe because he can't believe I would notice the one slight flaw in this fairy tale place. As part of the fairy tale, Auntie Elizabeth gave us both Cinderella makeovers for tonight. Cooper looks really handsome in the suit jacket and silk tie that he picked out himself. I'm not sure where he gets his sense of style. It certainly wasn't from either of our parents.

According to the embroidered crest on the napkins, the country club was established in 1937, but the facilities are state of the art—indoor-outdoor pools and tennis courts, a fully equipped fitness center with yoga and spin studios, a formal dining restaurant, and a juice bar café for breakfast and lunch. It's essentially a two hundred acre, five-star resort and spa plopped down in the middle of a neighborhood of mansions. It takes my breath away just to be here.

Balancing a plate in her hand, Auntie Elizabeth joins me in the corner of the ballroom where I'm semi-hiding. Her black dress has an understated elegance that suits her.

"What's with the shitty band?" I ask.

"Shh. The lead singer is the vice-president of the club's son. They might go on a break soon—if we're lucky." She pops a sausage roll in her mouth, chews demurely, and then takes a sip of wine. "Don't let Blaine hear you swearing around here."

"I swore?"

"You said shitty."

I laugh, wondering how we came from the same family tree. "Sorry."

She holds her hand in front of my face. "Gum."

I tilt my head forward and let my gum drop into her palm. I'm pretty sure spitting it into her bare hand is less classy than chewing it, but whatever.

"It's probably going to take a while for you to get used to how everything is done with these people."

"Don't say shitty and don't chew gum. I got it."

She smiles at my weak attempt at humor and links her elbow with mine. "You've been hiding back here long enough. Let me introduce you to some of the girls your age."

"Uh." I glance around the royal caliber ballroom with its tuxedoed waiters and highly polished crowd of socialites.

I don't belong and I'd rather not prance around meeting people who are definitely going to sense that. "It's okay. I'm good here."

"Come on." She drags me across the dance floor to the other side of the ballroom where people are mingling near the windows that overlook the golf course. I'm having a little trouble keeping up because I'm wearing four-inch heels that match the ice-blue strapless cocktail dress she bought me for my introduction to the country club set. Suffocating and treacherous are not my idea of a party outfit, but my old clothes wouldn't have quite cut it. Aiden on my arm wouldn't have quite cut it here, either.

Elizabeth stops in front of a group of girls who all dwarf me and appear perfectly comfortable in their high society clothes. They're about my age and the way they laugh and hug each other makes me think they've known each other since they had silver spoons in their mouths. I wonder how long it will take for them to figure out I was fed with a cheap PBA-laden plastic spoon available at all Dollar stores.

Elizabeth rests her hand on the arm of the tallest girl. "Cara, I would like to introduce you to my niece, Tienne. She's just moved in with us."

Cara smiles and extends her hand to shake mine. "I love your dress. Is that a Lionetta?"

Clueless, I look at Elizabeth who nods that it is. "Tienne is going to be working as an assistant at my design firm while she waits to be accepted into school."

"That's great." Cara sounds genuinely excited. "I'm doing an internship in the same building as your aunt's firm. We can do lunch."

Elizabeth smiles as if she's proud of her matchmaking

skills. "I'll leave you girls to get acquainted." She squeezes my sweaty hand, turns, and heads back across the dance floor.

I shift my weight, twitchy at the thought of socializing with these girls. I subdue the urge to flee and force a smile. "Sorry about the forced introduction. My aunt's a little overly enthusiastic."

"No need to apologize." Cara lifts her foot to adjust the ankle strap on her pumps, and her long brown curls cascade over one shoulder like she's in a shampoo commercial. She points at the girls beside her. "This is Reese Birming, Haley Cooke, and I'm Cara Livingstone."

Reese wears her shiny black hair in razor sharp angles that accentuate her bony features. Her skin is olive brown and it almost shimmers when she moves. I didn't know girls could actually look like that without Photoshop. She catches me staring and doesn't appear flattered. Blushing, I blink and shift my attention to Haley. She resembles a doll. Her ginger hair doesn't move when she turns her head, and her glassy green eyes never seem to blink. Her skin is pale as porcelain and it looks like someone painted her cheeks rosy and added five freckles on each side. They're perfect.

This isn't going to go well. All the binding party dresses and pinchy shoes in the world aren't going to hide who I really am, or fool girls like this into believing that I belong here. I can't even think of anything to say.

Fortunately, Cara carries the conversation seamlessly past my lack of small-talk skills by asking, "What are you planning on studying? Interior design?" She seems genuinely interested. The other two are waiting attentively for my answer, too.

"No. Performing arts. I want to be an actor." I brace myself for their reaction, since I don't fit the image of a typical theater person. But they don't laugh like I expect.

"Are you in any shows?" Haley asks.

I tuck my hair behind my ear and shift my weight again. "I'm auditioning for one in a couple of weeks."

"Let us know when tickets go on sale. We'll come watch."

"Um." I study each of them, wondering if they're being fake friendly. It seems like just friendly-friendly, unless they're better bullshitters than every other person I know. That's unlikely, since I grew up with professional bullshitters, but I can't tell. "Okay."

"Your brother is adorable," Reese says. "How old is he?"

"Sixteen." I glance at the lobster and caviar stocked buffet table where he is mingling with a group of teens. He fits in here perfectly.

"Ooh. A bit too baby-faced for me." She chuckles and nudges Cara with her elbow, "but Cara likes her boys young."

Cooper isn't any of their types, or more accurately, none of them is his type. I laugh at the irony, but I don't want them to ask what's so funny, so I stifle it and take a sip of my punch.

Cara checks Cooper out. "Mmm. He is my type if he were a few years older, but I'm going after Leland this year."

Reese sits back on the edge of the windowsill and glances at a group of guys by the bar. They are all under twenty-five and dressed in tailored suits. They seem like dull, pretentious corporate types, but at least gossiping about boys will distract the girls from asking me personal questions. "I wouldn't waste your time on Leland," Reese says. "He told my brother that he'll never date a girl from the country club."

"Is he looking over here?" Cara whispers.

"Yes. Don't look now."

The only one who looks our way is tall and has dark wavy hair. He's cute in a clean-cut way—squeaky-clean-cut. Someone should tell him he'd be sexier with a couple of tattoos or a scruffy beard. He smiles and lifts his eyebrow slightly before rejoining the conversation with his friends.

"Tienne," Reese hisses as if she's scolding me. "I said not to look."

"Sorry." I finish my punch and get rid of my glass on a table nearby as they exchange country club gossip. More of the clean-cuts in suits shoot casual glances our way as if we're the topic of their conversation. I guess they're typical guys despite the atypical attire. Maybe everything about the two worlds is the same beneath the surface.

I stare at my fresh manicure. The country club spa didn't have my preferred black or blue polish, so I let the aesthetician choose. She went with a pale, rose-petal pink, and I have to admit it does look pretty.

"Where did you go to high school?" Reese asks, interrupting my admiration of my nails.

"Um." Shit. I can't tell them I graduated from James Owens. Its claim to fame is stabbings in the hallway, epic brawls in the stands at the football games, and the lowest graduating rate in the city. "I went to public school."

Haley is the only one who has a slight reaction to the mention of public school. The expression flickered across her face for less than a second, so I can't tell if it was judgy or just surprised. "Which one?"

Okay. The temperature in the room skyrockets and the sweat dribbling from my armpits threatens to ruin the damn Lionetta. Exit strategy time. "It was a really small school. On the other side of the city. You probably wouldn't have heard of it." I extend my arm to shake hands with each of them. "Nice meeting you all. If you'll excuse me, I need to use the restroom."

"Let's catch up for lunch on Monday," Cara says. Her smile is as sweet as my favorite Barbie doll when I was little.

I say something noncommittal about her invitation, but try to imitate her pleasant smile before I leave. It's possible that I look more like Chucky than Barbie.

I can feel their stares. Is it completely demented that I would be more comfortable in the middle of a bar fight with beer bottles flying past my head than at a country club dance worried what the popular girls are saying behind my back as I walk away? This is so not my scene.

The restroom has marble counter tops, dark cherry wood cubicle doors, and I bet the gleaming toilets have never had someone's head passed out in the bowl. If Aiden were here he would point out that classing up the bathroom doesn't make your shit smell any less. That might be true, but this place sure is chic. And there is free moisturizer, little individual-sized mouthwashes, and real cotton towels. Maybe I could get used to this part.

After freshening up and giving myself a lecture that sounds more like a death threat than a pep talk, I head back into the trenches and make a beeline for Cooper. He's talking to a thin guy with super-styled light brown hair. He looks about sixteen, same as Cooper. "Hey."

"Hey. Sam, this is my sister, Tienne." Sam extends his hand and smiles in an easygoing way that makes me instantly like him. "Tienne, this is Sam Livingstone."

"Relax," Sam says and wiggles my hand to make my entire

arm loosen up. "The trick to fitting in is to look comfortable."

"That's easy to say for someone who is the heir to Livingstone Enterprises."

Sam laughs. "Is that what my sister told you?"

"No. That was my attempt at trying to sound like I know what I'm talking about. You're an heir to something, right?"

"To the financially floundering Livingstone Funeral Services franchise." He points at me in a mock cautionary way. "Keep that to yourself. If Cara finds out that I told you, I'll be in need of those services."

I like his charisma; definitely a good match for Cooper. "Your coffin should be complimentary at least," I joke.

"You would think, but not even family members get a discount in a Livingstone franchise anymore." He looks down at my dress as if he's checking me out, but just says, "Nice Lionetta."

"Thanks." I raise my eyebrows in a question at Cooper and he smiles, which I take as a hint. "I'm going to leave you two boys alone. Nice meeting you, Sam."

"Likewise."

As I walk away, my tiny crystal-encrusted purse vibrates. I lean against the posh wallpaper and pull my phone out. It's a text from Aiden, thank God. I need a dose of something familiar to boost my self-esteem.

How's the high life?

Apparently shit is a swear word and chewing gum is a crime

Meet me outside in 15

I check the time. Although it feels like we've been here all night, it's only been an hour. Elizabeth will be disappointed if I bail this early.

I can't leave

Just want to give u something. Will only take a minute

I could use the break. Nobody will notice.

K

My aunt walks over to me. "What are you grinning about?" she asks as she tickles my waist.

"Nothing. Are you having fun?"

"I must be." She tips her glass and gulps back half of her wine. "My face hurts from smiling so much. Are you having fun?"

Fun? No. This doesn't meet any of my criteria for fun. Necessary for Cooper's sake, yes. Tolerable, barely. "Sure. Thanks for inviting us."

"Why is your lip doing that nervous thing? Were the girls horrible?"

"Not too bad." I mean that, but it doesn't matter. I'm only here so Cooper can make friends. Me, I just want to fly under the radar. "I'm not really their type."

"Maybe you'll find out that you have more in common with them than you think. My goodness, you've been hanging around with hoods for so long you probably don't even know what normal people are interested in."

Wow. Low blow. I frown and run my fingers through my hair. I know she and Blaine don't approve of the people we grew up around, but she's never actually said it out loud before. The wine must be lowering her inhibitions.

My hurt must show, because Elizabeth rushes to say, "I'm sorry, that came out wrong. What I meant was — "

"Don't bother." I cut her off and stare at my Manolo Blahna-something shoes wishing I was actually born to wear fancy things. "I know what you meant."

"No," she blurts. "I… It's just that your mom, well, she wasn't always the way she is now. When she was your age, she was planning to go to school to study acting, too. Then she met your dad and — "

"Yeah." I hold my hands up in surrender, hoping she's not tipsy enough to get into it with me here. "I know how the story ends."

"Tienne, what I'm trying to say is that you're beautiful and talented and intelligent just like she was."

Was. Her attempt to fix things is making it worse. "I look forward to ending up just like her, too."

"You know I didn't mean that in a bad way. You aren't going to end up like your mom if you make different choices than she did. You can achieve whatever you want in life, whether it's acting, or interior design, or something else. That's all I meant."

I know she means well, but it doesn't matter how she dresses it up if no one buys it. "Excuse me, I need to go outside." I start to turn away — away from this conversation, these people, the reminders that I'm not as good as they are.

Elizabeth's shoulders drop as if she feels that she's just failed at her first attempt at parenting. She tucks her hair behind her ear and stares at her empty wine glass. "Sorry. I don't know the right things to say."

Shit. I didn't mean to make her feel bad. It's not her fault that my mom is the last person on Earth I want to be compared to. It's also not her fault that I don't know how to take a compliment. I sigh and fidget with the handle of my purse. "You don't need to apologize. That was the most encouraging thing a parent-type figure has ever said to me." I step in and hug her. "Thanks for believing in me."

She smiles and squishes up her nose like a happy chipmunk.

I'm glad I'm the reason she did the chipmunk face, but before things get too mushy, I wave and spin around. "I'll be right back." When I reach the archway to the lobby, I look back over my shoulder. She's watching me in an adoring way. I wave again, then head outside. This must be how kids with normal parents feel.

I can hear the rumble of Aiden's bike for a good minute before he actually pulls up to the steps in front of the country club. On his cut-off leather vest are the colors of the Noir et Bleu Motorcycle Club, same as his dad, his uncle, three of my uncles, and my dad when he was still alive. Aiden is so not what you would expect to see at a prestigious place like this, but the tattoos and scruffy facial hair is definitely a sexier look than any of the stiffs inside. He hangs his helmet from the handlebar and grins. I make my way down the stone steps to the curb of the roundabout in a sultry walk.

"Wow. Nice dress. I hardly recognize you." He winks.

"This old thing," I tease, relieved to know that the prissy dress doesn't completely destroy my sex appeal. I swing my leg over and straddle the tank with my back facing the handlebars. He makes a sexy sound in his throat as I hook my knees over his thighs and ease my hips up closer until our chests touch. His hand slides up under the skirt of my dress. He runs his fingers along my thighs until he reaches the fabric of my underwear. Then he kisses me.

When we finally break to breathe, I whisper in his ear, "Maybe I could sneak away for a while."

"I don't want you to get in trouble on your first day." He glances at the cedar beams and slate walls of the building. "Nice club."

"Yeah." I wink and run my hands up under his T-shirt. "A little more refined than the club you're used to."

His right hand slides out from underneath my dress, and he reaches into the inside pocket of his leather jacket. "I have something for you."

"Really? It's not my birthday. Let's see, is it the anniversary of our first kiss? No. Our first date? No. The first time we, uh, you know. No. Hmm, I don't think it's an anniversary. What's the occasion?"

"The occasion is that I love you."

"Oh, well, that is a good occasion."

He hands me a box that looks like it might have jewelry in it. My eyes narrow and search his face to see what he's up to. He looks super serious. "Ti, I know I've told you before, but I want you to know that I really love you. Not like I'm just saying it. Like, I really love you. For real."

"I love you, too." My heart beats in a weird jerky rhythm like a person who can't dance. I open the box. There is a big freakin' diamond ring in it. My mouth drops open to swear, but no sound comes out.

The expression in his eyes seems more nervous than I have ever seen him look before. "I'm going to marry you one day. I want to make sure you're okay with that."

"I, uh. What?" Stunned, I take the ring out of the box. My hands shake as I slide it onto my left ring finger. It fits perfectly. Is he on crack? This is crazy. "Gylly, I'm only eighteen."

"That doesn't matter."

"But I want to go to school."

His fingers lace between mine and he rotates my hand to angle the diamond to catch the light. "You can be married and go to school."

I blink at least ten times, letting the shock sink in. "What's the rush? Are you worried that I'll meet a sexy rich guy who will sweep me away?"

I'm joking, but his eyebrows angle into a frown as if there is some truth to that fear. "I don't want you to ever doubt how I feel about you."

"I don't need a ring to remind me of that." I hold my hand up and admire the diamond next to my perfect manicure. Black nail polish would have looked hideous. Eighteen? Maybe it doesn't make a difference how old I am. It's going to happen eventually. "Did you steal it?"

He laughs. "No. I bought it."

"Really?" The way it sparkles against my skin is mesmerizing. "It's beautiful, but I can't wear it around your friends. They'll steal it."

"Nobody is going to steal it, and you can't wear it at all if you don't say yes." I smile and wrap my arms around his neck. He rests his forehead on mine and whispers, "What do you say? Do you want to be with me forever?"

Forever with Aiden is exactly what I want, what I have always dreamed about. My eyes fill up with tears, so I close them and nod. "Yes."

He kisses me again and this time something charges

through my entire body. My fingers dig into his neck and pull him even closer to me. Both his hands are back up my skirt. I let my head drop back so he will kiss my neck. He makes his way down toward my collarbone and looks up. "I really like this dress."

I laugh, but then the sound of someone clearing his throat startles me. I glance over my shoulder. Shit. Uncle Blaine is at the top of the stairs with his arms crossed. I blush as I tug down the hem of my skirt to cover my exposed thigh. For someone new to 'parenting,' he sure has the you're-in-trouble look down pat.

"Uh, excuse the interruption. Tienne, there is someone I would like to introduce you to inside."

"Okay. I'll be right there."

Blaine doesn't leave. He stares Aiden down as if he had assaulted me or something.

"Sorry," I whisper to Aiden.

Unfazed, because he has never cared what other people think of him, Aiden says, "Don't worry about it." He kisses me one more time on the cheek before I swing my leg to step back off the bike.

"Thanks for the gift." I wink and hold my hand in front of my waist to flash the ring without Blaine noticing.

Aiden nods with a grin and starts the bike.

I love you, I mouth.

He reaches over, tugs the fabric of my skirt, and pulls me tight to his body. His hand reaches up to clutch my hair and ease my head forward until his lips are hovering next to my ear. "I love you more."

Mmm. I can feel that right down to the core of my being. No lame corporate type is ever going to be able to compete with that. He's definitely got nothing to worry about, ring or no ring.

He slaps my ass before he revs the bike and takes off.

When I turn around, Blaine is still frowning. His disappointment is obvious. "Making out with an outlaw biker right in front of the country club isn't going to look good on the application for membership."

I shake my head, angry that Blaine would assume Aiden is scum just because he doesn't wear tailored suits or drive a Range Rover. "You knew who I was when you invited me here."

"I thought you left that life behind."

I shrug and bite my lip because as much as I want to tell him what I really think of his elitist discrimination, I don't want to ruin everything for Cooper.

"Don't you want a fresh start where you can be whomever you want to be?"

I spin the ring around my finger and shift my weight to my other foot, refusing to accept that I need to change who I am as a condition to having a better life.

He sighs at my lack of a response. "If you want the life your parents chose, that's fine. I'm not going to stop you. If you don't want that, then you're going to have to make some changes. Nobody here can tell just by looking at you that you came from the motorcycle club world, but these people won't accept you if you keep dating a guy like that. I don't want him around here or the house, so make a decision."

I close my eyes to press the restart button. He has done so much for Cooper and me that he absolutely didn't need to. What is my problem? Why can't I just be grateful and respect their world? "Sorry, Uncle Blaine."

"It's okay. Just don't let it happen again." He turns and reaches his arm forward to open the door. "Are you coming?"

"Um, I need some fresh air if that's okay."

He nods without looking at me and steps back into the country club. The rumble of Aiden's bike gets quieter as he speeds away. I had no idea he was even thinking about marriage, let alone saving for a ring. The diamond is so beautiful, but I can't wear it here. To avoid a million questions from Auntie Elizabeth, I slide it off and tuck it into the tiny zippered pocket in the lining of my purse before heading back inside.

A drink would be good right about now.

Nobody is watching the booze behind the bar, so I steal a bottle of whiskey and skirt around the edge of the ballroom. The only private spot I can find is outside on the balcony that overlooks the golf course and a forest.

It's too dark to see what kind of trees they are, but since the inner city neighborhood where I grew up only had concrete playgrounds and school fields where people let their dogs crap, I wouldn't know a pine from a cedar anyway. I can, however, confirm with absolute certainty that the woods-scented air freshener from the gas station does not in any way resemble the real thing.

The first swig from the bottle makes me cough. The next one goes down smoother and calms the emotions swirling in my stomach. The burn of the alcohol surges through my bloodstream and my arms and legs start to tremble. It is the same shaking I get before I go onstage. Deep breaths usually help, but they're not helping right now. With my next inhale I catch a whiff of something I recognize. Maybe I don't know anything about nature, but I do know that smell.

Either someone just lit up, or there's a resident skunk on the golf course.

When I squint, I can make out the outline of a guy sitting on the railing of the balcony. A pothead wearing a suit. They keep my family in business, so I knew they existed, but I've never seen one before.

"Getting shitfaced at your first event isn't going to look good on the membership application," he quips.

"I have connections. My uncle's the president of the club." I take another gulp. The alcohol is making me feel more like myself, which isn't a good thing since my mouth is likely to get me in trouble. I resist the urge to say more, but it lasts all of five seconds. "I hope you have connections, too, because smoking up probably doesn't look that good either."

"It's medicinal." He chuckles. "I'm already a member, but if I weren't I would be able to earn some compassionate votes."

He thinks he's hilarious, and is obviously bullshitting, so I shoot back, "Oh? So, you're dying of cancer?"

"Something like that."

Not finding him particularly funny, I say, "That's too bad."

I chug more whiskey and cough again. He doesn't say anything, but it seems like he's staring at me. He can spare the judgment, or the ogling, whichever one is the cause for the scrutiny.

Once the effects of the alcohol kick in fully, I throw the bottle, along with the rest of its contents, over the railing, assuming it will land on the grass of the golf course. Instead, it smashes on the concrete below. Oops. The sound makes me cringe a little before I attempt to strut toward the door. So much for my smooth exit.

"You don't have to leave. I was just joking."

Joking about cancer, drugs, and my lack of suitability for country club membership. Not exactly amusing. I keep walking.

"Tienne," he calls after me.

I stop, curious how he knows my name, and also because I need a second to steady myself. I turn to face him and strain to recognize his face. "Do I know you?" I ask.

He laughs and lifts the joint to his lips, still only a silhouette. "Don't you remember? Our eyes met from across the room and you were totally coming on to me."

I roll my eyes to blow him off, whether he can see me in the dark or not. Then I walk away. Even if I were single, he'd have to step up his game significantly. He'd also have to get a tattoo. And a bike. Not that I'm interested. Because I'm not.

Chapter Three

Inside the country club, the band screeches out notes that don't seem to go together. Only one elderly couple—likely too deaf to hear the music—dances. Everyone else stands well clear of the speakers. Cooper and Sam are still talking. It looks as if they're hitting it off. I don't want to interrupt, so I search for Elizabeth. The whiskey has made my legs numb and the four-inch heels are impossible to walk in. Eventually, I give up and lean against a marble pillar.

Elizabeth finds me instead. "Tienne, there you are." She clutches my arm for balance. "I've had a little too much wine. I need you to drive the Mercedes home and I'll get a ride with Blaine."

"Uh, that's probably not a good idea." Now we are both leaning against the pillar. Good thing it's here.

"Why?"

"Hmm." I stare up at the crystal chandelier, searching for a reason other than that I stole and chugged a bottle of top-shelf booze. "Because I don't drive stick."

"It's an automatic."

I remove my shoes for safety. "I don't remember the way."

"Yes you do."

"I didn't bring my glasses?" It comes out more like a question than an answer.

"You don't wear glasses." She frowns and leans in to smell my breath. "Where did you get alcohol?"

"The bar. It was the easiest thing. I just walked right up and helped myself. I don't know about this club of yours." I shake my head, mockingly at first, until I realize that maybe they don't lock up the booze because they usually deny entrance to bottle-stealing people like me.

"Cut it out." She almost manages to sound annoyed. "If you don't want to be here just say you don't want to be here and go do what you want to do."

I sigh and look around the room. "What's the point of trying? The people here won't accept me once they find out how I grew up."

"Just be yourself and let them judge you based on who you are now, not who you were. It takes time. You've only been here for an hour and a half. Have some patience."

I exhale and close my eyes. Who I am now is still who I was then. I'm just standing in a different room. A way nicer room. If I learn how to fit in to this world it would definitely set me apart from my mom. Unfortunately, it would also set me apart from everything else in my life. "Eighteen is too young, right?"

She gets rid of her empty wine glass on a nearby table. "For drinking? Legally, yes, it is too young."

"No. I mean for knowing who you are and what your

future is going to be."

"Yes," she sounds amused, but sympathetic. "Eighteen is also too young to know all that."

"But it's not too young to get married."

The way her expression turns uneasy makes me think she suspects it's not an idle statement. She takes a moment to wave politely at a woman across the room, but when she faces me, she's serious. "Your mom got married at eighteen. You tell me if you think it's too young."

I turn away to avoid the question and the apprehension in her eyes. From across the room, the pot smoker's gaze meets mine, and he heads in my direction, as if he's been looking for me. He is wearing a charcoal suit, and his wavy dark hair is slicked back except for a small curl that has escaped over his forehead. Although it is not a style that would earn him any street cred, it's kind of working for him in a boy-next-door way. Elizabeth realizes I'm distracted and glances over her shoulder. The guy walks right up and shakes her hand. "Mrs. Montgomery. Nice to see you. How's the fundraising for the hospital coming along?"

"Wonderfully. Have you met my niece, Tienne, yet?"

He raises his eyebrow and smiles in a way that most girls likely find charming. "No, not formally." He extends his hand to shake mine. "Leland Crofton."

His expression is the one that guys always get when they assume they're going to score. Whether he thinks I'm cheap or that he's God's gift, it pisses me off. To give him the hint that he's wasting his time, I make my hand feebly limp as he shakes it. "Of the Crofton Airlines Croftons or something?" I ask in a disinterested way.

He scans my face as if he's trying to get a read on me.

"The Crofton Construction Croftons."

"You're a liar. Those ridiculously soft hands haven't done a day of construction in your life."

He glances at his palms and shrugs. "My dad's haven't either. He's more the visionary—high-rises and highways all over the world."

"Impressive," I say with more than enough sarcasm to deliver the sentiment. "It's always nice to hear about companies that are committed to reducing our carbon footprint."

Elizabeth gives me a warning glare, but Leland goes on, ignoring my tone and her discomfort.

"It just so happens that high density buildings can be eco-friendly if built properly. That's actually part of my job. I find ways to make our projects more sustainable."

"That's wonderful," Elizabeth chirps, to smooth over my bad manners.

He grins as if he thinks he's gained some sort of advantage by impressing my aunt. I wrinkle my nose like I smell his bullshit. "Were you smoking marijuana or did you have a run-in with a skunk?"

"Tienne!" Elizabeth gasps.

He can tell I'm challenging him just to amuse myself and he confidently fires right back, "Actually, the truth is that I was out on the balcony." He pauses and I wonder if he might admit to smoking pot just to call my bluff. Instead he says, "A skunk was startled by a noise that sounded like breaking glass. I didn't realize it had permeated my clothes. My apologies."

Okay, he has more game than I gave him credit for. Not that I am actually going to give him credit.

"Oh, I can't even smell it." Elizabeth says. She places her

hand on his arm and smiles at me with a mix of encouragement and caution. "Excuse me. I'll let you two get better acquainted."

As she walks away, he steps closer and studies me as if waiting for my next sassy comment. Around us, the party continues. No one is dancing, but the band's lead singer is still moving in awkward contortions that only Mick Jagger should ever attempt. A waiter walks by with a tray of glasses filled with wine, so I snag one.

Leland watches me take a sip. "Go to dinner with me."

"No." I adjust my skirt even though it is already hanging perfectly.

"Why not?"

"Well, for one reason, I don't respond well to being told what to do." And if I were wearing my regular clothes, you wouldn't even be asking me out right now.

"Will you please allow me the privilege of taking you out to dinner?"

"No."

"Ouch." He straightens as if ready to defend himself. "I asked nicely."

I exhale slowly and attempt to be more polite. "How you said it is not my only reason for saying no."

"What are your other reasons?"

"I don't date guys who do drugs."

"I'll quit." He answers too quickly to be sincere.

I shake my head and lean against the pillar again. "That's what they all say. I don't date liars either."

"I'm serious. I just smoked my last joint."

"You must be desperate to make a promise you can't keep just so you can get a date with someone you don't even know."

"I'm not desperate. I'm motivated."

Normally, if a guy is chatting me up, Aiden instantly slides in next to me to signal that I'm not available. If Aiden doesn't notice right away, one of the club members lets him know pretty quickly. It feels weird that I'm still standing here all by myself. No Aiden. No one to act as his eyes and ears. No pressure to be who I have always been. I sneak a glance at Leland and finish off the glass of wine before I say, "Don't quit killing your brain cells on my account. In my experience, guys who belong to clubs are trouble."

"I'll quit the club too."

"Although we both know you're full of shit, even if you did quit the club, the answer would still be no."

Another waiter circles past and takes the empty glass for me as if he read my mind and knew I was searching for a place to put it down. Leland laughs and runs his hands through his hair as if he can't believe how difficult I'm being.

"What's wrong, Mr. Crofton? Don't girls usually say no to you?"

"No, they don't."

"How incredibly arrogant of you to say."

"I'm joking." He removes his suit jacket, drapes it over the back of a chair, and loosens his tie. Okay, maybe suits can be somewhat sexy. Aiden would look amazing in a suit, not that he'd get caught dead in one, and not that he would appreciate that I'm noticing how some other guy looks in one. "What would it take to convince you to go on a date with me?"

There is nothing in the world that could convince me. "What do you care? I heard that you don't date girls from the country club."

When he moves so we are standing more shoulder to shoulder, a hint of his expensive cologne wafts over me. "How did you hear that? Were you asking the girls about me?"

"No, I was not asking the girls about you." I open my purse and check the time on my phone, hoping that he'll take the hint I'm bored with him and go hit on someone else. "Your name was mentioned in a tedious conversation in which I was merely a bystander."

"You're not technically a club girl."

I chuckle. "No, not a country club."

He gently slides my phone out of my hand and drops it back in my purse, capturing my full attention. "I can tell that you're not like all those other boring girls."

I tilt my head and arch my eyebrows in a consolatory way. "Too bad I can't say the same about you."

"Are you implying that I'm boring or girly?"

I glance at his silver tie, charcoal trousers, and black dress shoes. His skin is clean-shaven and definitely moisturized. His teeth are perfectly white and his fingernails are shiny like they were recently manicured. He also smells like something I would like to bathe in. "Both."

He laughs. "Are you single?"

"Nope, but that wouldn't matter."

"Why? I'm not your type?"

My eyes scan his lean build, pausing on his lips for longer than I intended. "Nope."

This time, he reaches for a drink from the waiter. He offers to get me one too, but I shake my head. "What is your type?" he asks.

"The opposite of you. No offense."

He chuckles. "You're mean."

"I said no offense."

He smiles in a mischievous way. "Is your hostility genetic or hormonal?"

Oh, no he didn't. "Definitely genetic, and if you value your life you won't refer to me as hormonal again."

"So, you're abrasive toward everyone and it's not just me who you find repulsive?"

"I'm nice to a few people."

He sips his wine slowly. "What would I have to do to become one of those people?"

I frown, surprised he's still trying. Most of the guys I know would have walked away by this point. "Well." I step into my shoes, which still leaves me a head shorter than he is. "Although your flirtatious banter is somewhat more entertaining than staring at the wall, I'm not interested in going on a date or having a quickie in the coat room. If you have a different topic of conversation that is a little more thought provoking and doesn't revolve around the agenda of you getting yourself laid, I may be persuaded to continue standing here to get to know you strictly as a fellow member of the club. If you've got no other material, I'm outta here."

I thought that might finally offend him, but he waves a hand like he's erasing the last few minutes. "Okay. Sorry. Let's start over. Where are you from?"

"East of here."

"That's fairly vague. It makes it difficult to have a cordial conversation if you don't participate"

"Your problem. Not mine." I flick my hair over my shoulders. Oops, that might have come across as flirty. How do I undo a hair flip?

His eyes linger somewhere around my collarbone for an

extra beat before coming back to meet mine. Shit, he definitely took it as flirty.

The accidental signal seems to put him at ease and he asks, "What do you do?"

Hands at my sides. No hair flipping. No head tilting. No lip moistening. "I'm starting on Monday as an assistant at my aunt's interior design firm, but I'm hoping to go to school to study acting."

"Acting?" he scoffs. "Do you have any idea how hard it is to make it as an actor? A design career is more practical."

"Really? That's your angle? Squashing a woman's dream?"

"Sorry." He winces, then smiles in a sheepish way. "I'm sure you'll knock them dead on Broadway one day."

I roll my eyes at his attempt to backpedal.

He taps his lips and looks up at the ceiling as he thinks. "Okay, give me a second to come up with a charming conversation starter."

"Aim for a non-insulting one. You're never going to reach charming."

He chuckles and glances across the room at his buddies who are probably aware of how much time he has already spent wheeling with no results. He turns his back to them, maybe to avoid the distraction or the pressure. "Okay. Let's try something completely different. If you could be reincarnated as a wild animal what would it be?"

"A honey badger."

He seems surprised and slightly impressed. "They're vicious."

"I'm aware of that."

"Is your hair naturally blond?"

"What do you think?"

He glances over at Cooper who also has white-blond hair and says, "Yes. It's beautiful, by the way."

"Thanks," I mumble and tuck it behind my ear, wondering why he's wasting his time.

He watches Cooper, who appears to be telling Sam a hilarious story that requires bold hand gestures. "If you were forced to choose between saving yourself and saving your brother, who would you choose?"

"My brother. In a heartbeat."

"If you could use the club funds to bring in a band that actually has some talent, which one would you choose?"

"Aerosmith."

He shakes his head like he doesn't agree with my taste in music, but doesn't challenge it. "Do you have a nickname?"

"Yes, but only certain people are permitted to use it." People like Aiden. I open my purse and unzip the pocket to peek at the ring. The light from the chandelier catches the diamond and makes it sparkle.

"What do they call you?"

"If you were one of the people authorized to call me by my nickname, you would already know it." I zip the pocket back up and check my phone to break whatever the vibe is that we have going. I've humored him way longer than I should have, and I'm starting to feel guilty about how Aiden would react if he knew I was letting a cute guy chat me up.

"Do you have any questions for me?"

"Nope."

He chuckles at how uncooperative I'm being. It's a pleasant laugh, though, so he must not mind my attitude, or he finds the game amusing. "What's a quality you admire in your mom?"

"Nothing," I say without hesitation. Okay. This conversation is definitely done.

He looks shocked for a second, but then his expression shifts to intrigued, and he keeps going. "What does your dad do for a living?"

God, take a hint. "My dad's dead. He was murdered two months ago, in case that was going to be your next question."

He actually flinches and shifts backward as if my words have physical impact. "Are you serious?"

I look away from him and my gaze falls on Cooper. I immediately regret blurting that out about our dad without thinking. Shit. The gossip will definitely filter down to Cooper and could ruin his chances to reinvent himself. Why did I do that?

Across the dance floor, Cara, Reese, and Haley glare at us as if I'm trespassing on their territory. One more reason I should have wrapped this up ages ago. "Listen, Landon, it—"

"Leland," he corrects me.

"Right, Leland. It's been nice chatting, but I'm bored and a little bit drunk. The country club girls are giving me the fuck-you vibe because Cara has the hots for you. If any of them is stupid enough to say something confrontational to me, it might get ugly. So, I'm going to go."

"Can I get your number?"

"No."

"Can I at least offer you a ride home?"

"Do you like how your face looks right now?" He frowns, confused by the question, so I clarify. "If my boyfriend finds out that you gave me a ride home, he'll rearrange your face." I reach up and lightly slap his cheek. "You've got a cute face, so it's probably best if I just catch a cab."

"You think I'm cute?" His boyish grin is kind of adorable, and it makes me smile. "Excellent. I made you smile. I think we've made enough progress for one evening. I will sharpen my conversational skills for when we next meet, Miss Montgomery."

"Desrochers."

"Tienne Desrochers, you are the most interesting person in this place."

"That's not saying much."

He laughs and kisses the back of my hand as if I'm a princess or something. For some reason my cheeks feel as if they're flushing. He looks up and his face turns serious. "Sorry to hear about your dad."

Okay, well, that was unexpectedly sweet, but we're done here. If I stay any longer the cracks in my façade are going to open up and spew the real me all over the place in an ugly mess. "See ya."

I miss Aiden, and the more I think about it, the more sure I am that we need to discuss this whole engagement thing. I stumble a little as I walk over to Cooper. He's at the dessert table eating a brownie. I reach over and grab a couple strawberries. "Will you be all right here if I take off?" Dumb question. Obviously, he'll be all right here without me. He's the one who belongs.

He nods and asks, "How are you getting home?"

"I'm going to catch a cab to Gylly's place. Will you tell Elizabeth for me?"

"Sure." He steals a glance at the group of teens who came back into the ballroom from the balcony. Sam's gaze meets Cooper's and he excuses himself from his friends before making his way in our direction.

"Sam seems nice," I say.

"Yeah." Cooper smiles, looking embarrassed that his feelings are so obvious.

"This place suits you, Lucky Boy. Have fun."

"It could suit you too if you want it to."

I look around at all the nicely dressed members and smooth the fabric of my dress. "Maybe." I kiss his cheek, leave him with Sam, and call a cab on the way to wait by the front door.

The driver pulls up to the curb after only five minutes of waiting. In my old neighborhood, we had to sit around for at least twenty minutes and usually call twice. Sometimes they never showed at all. I guess they were busy shuttling around big tippers from the country club.

In the cab, I slide the ring back on and spin it around my finger. I think I need to give it back. Not because I don't want to be with Aiden forever, but because I'm too young, and I really don't want to follow in my mom's footsteps. Waiting would be the better thing to do, right? He's going to take it the wrong way, though. How am I supposed to tell the love of my life that I don't want the engagement ring he gave me? Oh God. I'm dizzy. I roll down the window and lean my head on the doorframe.

"You're not going to get sick, are you?" the driver asks over his shoulder.

"It's hard to say."

"Aim it out the window."

He drives a little faster, obviously to get me out of his cab before I vomit. I don't feel like puking. I feel more panicky.

I pay and step out of the cab. Then I take my heels off and carry them as I walk up the driveway and along the path to the front door. Maybe I shouldn't bring up the ring tonight. I just want to sink into the familiar warmth of his arms and let the sound of his heart ground me back in reality.

After knocking, I lean my forehead on the siding and wait for Aiden to answer. The door opens a crack and he pokes his head out. "Ti. I didn't know you were coming by." He sounds genuinely surprised, but not necessarily in a good way.

"Is it okay?"

"Of course."

I wait for him to swing the door open and invite me in, but he doesn't.

"Have you been drinking?"

"Just a little bit."

He smiles and steps out onto the front step closing the door behind him. He's shirtless and only wearing jeans. "Do you want me to give you a ride home?"

I kiss the TDAGF tattoo on his left pec. It stands for Tienne Desrochers and Aiden Gyllenhall forever. I slide my hands over his abs. "I was hoping I could stay here."

"Uh." He runs his hand through his hair to push it back out of his eyes. "Tonight's not a good night."

"Why?"

"My dad said some guys might be crashing here tonight. Let me get dressed and I'll take you to your aunt's."

He looks twitchy. Aiden never looks twitchy. "What's going on?"

He shakes his head. "Nothing. Wait here. I'll be right back." He opens the door a couple inches and slips back into the house. Before he has a chance to shut the door and hide whatever is making him act like he's done something he shouldn't have, I kick it as hard as I can. "Ow! God damn it, Ti."

Aiden clutches his wrist. I kick the door again and it slams into his shoulder, knocking him back. Sitting on the couch is Leah, the girl he dated before me. Her eye is black and her lip is swollen. She's smiling at me like a boxer who just got his ass kicked but won on a technicality.

I throw my purse and shoes on the floor and sprint across the room. Rage throbs through my veins as I jump over the end of the couch and pounce on her. Momentum sends us both crashing to the carpet. I grab her hair. She tries to squirm away and we knock into a lamp. It shatters.

"Bitch!" I scream as I straddle her chest and punch her. Before I can throw another punch, Aiden grabs me by the waist and peels me off her. I kick and scream, trying to get at her, but he's too strong. My fingernails claw at his forearms. He doesn't seem to notice. "You're fucking dead, Leah."

"Ooh, I'm scared. What are you, five foot nothing and sixty pounds?" She sits back on the couch. "You're wearing a fucking princess dress, for Christ's sake."

"Get out of here, you stupid filthy whore!"

"Ti. Calm down." Aiden spins me around and tries to restrain me in a hug. My knee slams him in the nuts and he drops to the floor. He groans and reaches out to grab one of my legs, but I stomp on his hand and pick up my pumps to throw at Leah. The first one hits her in the back of the head. The second one hits her right in the mouth because she was dumb enough to turn to face me. Furious, she climbs over the back of the couch to come at me. "Sit down, Leah," Aiden growls as he slowly stands. "Ti. Outside."

I pick up my purse, swing the door open, and run down

the path. He chases me. Even though the adrenaline fuels my getaway, his legs are way longer than mine, and he catches up before I even make it to the driveway. His fingers clamp around my upper arm and he spins me around.

"Ti, what are you doing?"

"What am I doing? What the fuck were you doing? Am I psychotic, or did you not just ask me to marry you?"

"I did. She came over because she needed my help."

"Yeah, I'm sure she did. If it was so innocent, why were you trying to hide her from me?"

"Because I knew you would freak out on her, and you did."

"I freaked out because you were trying to hide the fact that you have a whore at your house on a night when you didn't expect me to come over."

"Ti. You know me well enough to know that's not what's going on."

"Do I?"

"Yeah, you do. What's this really about?"

I blink back tears as I stare at him. This is about him. This is about me. It's about not wanting to get married at eighteen and trapped into a life that I can't get out of. It's about everything. I don't know what it's about. "We're over. Don't call me." I run down the driveway and hit the sidewalk at a full sprint. Once I reach the end of the block, I slow down and check over my shoulder. He's standing barefoot on the sidewalk in front of his house watching me.

"Ti. You're overreacting. Come back."

I take a deep breath, then turn the corner and walk away. My hands are shaking so badly that it's a struggle to take my phone out of my purse to make a call. It rings repeatedly and I can barely breathe as I wait. "Uncle Blaine." I start bawling.

"What's wrong, sweetheart?"

Everything. I can't imagine my life without Aiden, but I can imagine it with him, and it's not good. "Will you pick me up in front of my old house, please?"

"Of course. Are you all right?"

"No."

"What happened?"

I exhale and glance down the street I grew up on. All the shitty old houses with the chewed-up lawns and beat-up cars out front. "I don't want my mom and dad's life. I want a fresh start."

"I'll be right there."

Chapter Four

The sun floods my bedroom, ruining my attempt to crawl under a rock and die. Ever since Uncle Blaine picked me up last night, my phone has been dancing across the top of my dresser every few minutes with calls, texts, and voicemail alerts. Hopefully the battery will die soon.

There is a soft knock on my door. I don't answer.

"Ti." Cooper pushes the door open. "I brought you some tea." He places the teacup on my bedside table and flops on my bed beside me.

"Thanks," I mumble into my pillow.

He gently lifts my hair from my face and studies me more closely. "Gylly called and asked me to check on you because you haven't been answering your phone."

I groan and roll over. "I'm fine. Tell him he can go fuck himself."

"Why? What happened?"

"He was with Leah when I got there last night. I don't

want to talk about it."

Cooper pulls me in to cuddle. Now his phone is going off. He reaches into his jeans and mutters something that I don't quite hear.

"Who is it?" I ask.

"Uncle Terry."

"It's probably about Mom." I slump down to hug my pillow. "Go ahead. I'll survive."

"She'll likely survive, too."

"My money is on me over her."

"It might be nothing serious." He moves to sit on the edge of my bed and rests his elbows on his knees as he talks to Uncle Terry. "Yeah... When?... How bad is it this time?... Okay... Which hospital?... I'll be there as soon as I can... Uh, no. Ti isn't around...Yeah, see ya." He hangs up and looks over his shoulder at me. "It's the same old shit over again. What do you want me to do?"

"Go. I have theater this afternoon anyway."

He stands and cocks his head. "Are you absolutely sure something was going on between Gylly and Leah?"

Instead of answering, I bite my bottom lip. I want to say yes, but I can't force myself to say something that isn't true. "Thanks for the tea."

He nods and turns toward the door. Before he steps into the hall, he turns back. "I almost forgot; a delivery came for you."

"Send it back to Gylly."

"It's not from Gylly." He points at me in a see-you-later way. "It's in the kitchen if you feel like dragging your ass out of bed." He leaves and quietly closes my door.

I mope around until I get hungry enough to get out of

bed. I attempt to freshen up a little in the bathroom, but it's a lost cause. My face looks like complete shit. I wouldn't even be surprised if there is a bird living in the nest of hair at the back of my head. I shuffle down the kitchen staircase in case Elizabeth and Blaine have people over for Sunday brunch or something. The house seems quiet, so I don't think anybody's home.

There's a massive vase full of three dozen sunflowers on the counter. I've only gotten flowers one time, when I was six and Aiden was eight. He picked a dandelion out of the school field and gave it to me. That doesn't really count. This arrangement must be from Uncle Blaine. He seemed really worried last night when I was crying so hard that I couldn't tell him why I was crying. He's sweet. Blaine and Elizabeth would be good parents. I've wondered a lot why God let my shitty parents have two kids and won't let Blaine and Elizabeth have any.

I open the card and read,

Tienne,

It was a pleasure to meet you last night. I asked your brother what your favorite flowers are. Hopefully he wasn't playing a cruel joke on me by telling me something that you hate or are allergic to.

Leland Crofton

I'm still staring at the card as Blaine and Elizabeth come in through the back door. Elizabeth has a canvas bag of groceries slung over her shoulder and Blaine is carrying a bouquet of six sunflowers. His mouth drops open when he sees the huge arrangement on the counter. "Ah, man. Someone beat me to it." He frowns at his own bouquet as if it's pathetic in comparison.

"Yours are a nicer color," I reassure him and search the cupboards for another vase to arrange them in. "Thanks."

"Ooh!" Elizabeth squeals. "Who are these from?"

Blaine looks concerned that this might be Gylly's attempt to win me back. "They're from Leland Crofton," I tell them, trying to make it into no big deal. "He just wanted to say that he enjoyed meeting me at the country club last night."

Blaine opens the fridge to unload the groceries. His smile seems a little smug, as if he might have had a hand in some behind the scenes matchmaking scheme.

"Wow. Leland Crofton. Nice work, Tienne." Elizabeth is nearly jumping up and down.

I roll my eyes, embarrassed. "I'm going to have a shower."

"I'll bring your new outfits up for you to try on."

"What? Thank you, but you didn't need to buy me work clothes. I have some skirts and dress pants."

"You need an entire business-appropriate wardrobe."

So, if outlet store deals aren't going to cut it, that's a pretty good indication I won't be able to cut it either. There's no way I can pay Elizabeth and Blaine back for everything they've done, and it's overwhelming to be showered with gifts I don't deserve, let alone opportunities I didn't earn. "It's not necessary. I'm only going to be there temporarily."

"Maybe not. If the acting thing doesn't work out you might choose design as a career option to fall back on."

I nod and chew on my bottom lip. "Fall back plan" sounds

a lot like a nice way of saying "when you fail."

She waves her hands as if to erase what she said. "You'll need corporate clothes once you make it in the theater industry, too. You want to fit in, don't you?"

"Yeah. I guess." I glance at Leland's sunflowers. They're beautiful, and it is flattering to know that someone would go to the trouble of asking what my all-time favorite type of flower is. I sniff them before I head upstairs. I grab my phone off the dresser before climbing back into bed. The voicemail box is full and I leave it that way so Aiden can't leave any more messages. I delete all the texts without reading them and turn the phone off. This is the first time in my entire life that I have faced the future without Aiden right next to me. I feel as if I'm standing on the edge of a bridge and I'm supposed to jump, but I'm not sure if there is a bungee cord attached to me or not.

Cooper doesn't get home from the hospital until ten o'clock. When he knocks and comes into my room, he's already dressed for bed.

"How is she?" I ask, trying not to care.

"They're keeping her in overnight to monitor her. She went into cardiac arrest this time, but Uncle Ronnie was there, so he called the ambulance. She seems fine now."

"Are they going to put her in detox?"

He shrugs and climbs into bed next to me, which he does every time Mom is hospitalized. It has happened more times than I can remember. "Yeah, but she won't stay in treatment."

"I know." I give him one of my pillows and lay facing him. "You don't have to take care of her, you know. She never took care of us."

"I want to."

I smile and brush his bangs away from his eyes. "Have you got your outfit picked out for your first day at a fancy private school?"

"Flat front trousers and an argyle sweater. How about you? What are you wearing to your first day at a corporate job?"

"Frumpy skirt and grandma blouse."

"Sexy."

I laugh. "Night, Lucky Boy."

"Night, T Bear."

Chapter Five

Cooper and I roll up at Tisdale High School in Elizabeth's Mercedes. Apparently, she's giving it to us and Blaine's getting her a new one. It's too much generosity for my brain to process, so I'm just going to pretend we stole it. Cooper's leg jiggles nervously as he sits in the passenger seat watching students go by. Half of me wants to walk in with him and stay until he gets settled. The other half of me wants to push him out onto the curb because it's already eight thirty and I'm going to be late for my first day of work.

"It will be fine," I say in a chipper Auntie Elizabeth voice.

He sighs and adjusts the leather strap of his bag over his shoulder, but still doesn't get out. Groups of teens lounge on the manicured lawn and on the front steps to the school. Four parking spots down, three guys pile out of a Cadillac SUV. I recognize the light-brown styled hair.

"Hey, isn't that Sam?" I roll down the window and wave. "Sam! Hi."

"Ti," Cooper mumbles an embarrassed objection.

"What? He's sweet," I say, totally innocently. "He'll show you around and introduce you to people."

"I'm sure he doesn't want—"

Sam hustles over with a smile on his face.

"What were you saying?" I shove Cooper's shoulder.

"I'm sure he doesn't want to be my tour guide."

Sam opens Cooper's door with a sweeping arm gesture. "Welcome to Tisdale."

I tickle my brother's waist. "Looks like maybe he does. Have a good day."

Cooper gives me a quick hug before he gets out of the car. He looks over his shoulder once before they reach the steps of the school. I wave, then sigh. His entire life I have always been by his side when he had to do scary things. A knot of guilt bangs around my chest like it's a pinball machine because I'm letting him face this alone. After he disappears, I half expect him to come running right back out the doors like he did when he was little. But he doesn't.

I check my phone for the map to Elizabeth's office. As I pull out of the school parking lot, I realize that I'm even more nervous than Cooper was. It takes only ten minutes to drive to the high-rise office building, but finding the gate for the underground parking takes almost as long. As I'm getting out of the car, Cara Livingstone pulls up in a clunky Jetta and parks in the stall beside me. Not exactly the wheels I would have expected from a country club girl.

"Hi," she says as she steps out and closes the rusted out door.

The last time I saw her it felt like she was shooting "I hate you" daggers my way for talking to Leland. Today, she seems friendly again. She either has the worst memory, or she's a "let bygones be bygones" kind of person. Or, she's fake as hell and waiting for the opportunity to slay me. My money is on the last one.

"Are you ready for your first day?" she asks.

"Um." I study her, still not sure if I should prepare myself for a backstabbing. "I hope so." I wait as she collects her purse and blazer out of the backseat. "Which company do you intern for?"

"A media company on the tenth floor," she says as we walk toward the elevators.

"That sounds cool."

She shrugs. "It would be better if they paid me. I'm hoping the experience will help me get a scholarship so I can go to school. You are so lucky to have your aunt's connections." She calls the elevator. "I saw you talking to Leland on Saturday night."

All right, here we go. I can take her, but brawling in the parking garage before even showing up for my first day at work would be idiotic.

"How did that go?" she asks hesitantly.

"Fine, I guess." We both step inside the elevator. Unfortunately, we're all alone.

She presses the buttons for both our floors. "Did he ask you out?"

I debate whether I should tell the truth and commit social suicide on the first day, or lie and guarantee my social ranking. I decide to go with the lie. "No. He was talking about you."

"Really? What did he say?"

"He was just saying that you're really nice."

Cara smiles. When the elevator doors open on the tenth floor she says, "Have a good first day."

"Thanks." Okay. That went not too badly. Nobody got stabbed. Conflict resolution is apparently less violent with people who aren't from my neighborhood. Good to know.

She steps out and holds her hand against the door to prevent it from closing. "Are we still on for lunch?"

Wow. Nobody got stabbed *and* we're still lunch buddies. "Yeah, sure."

"I'll meet you at the café downstairs at one o'clock."

"Okay." I smile at how easy it is to interact with normal people as I carry on to the nineteenth floor. I step out into the lobby of Elizabeth's interior design firm and immediately smell the white roses on the reception desk. Everything is white—the leather furniture, the marble floors, and the textured wallpaper. A receptionist greets me and leads the way to Elizabeth's office. She's seated at her desk talking on the phone when I arrive. She waves me in and points at a chair, indicating that I should sit down while she finishes her call. She hangs up a minute later and smiles. "Are you ready?"

"I think so."

"Gum." She hands me a tissue across the desk.

I spit my gum into the tissue and drop it in her wastepaper basket.

Elizabeth presses a button on the phone. "Erica, Tienne is here. Would you please give her a tour of the floor and show her to her office?"

"I'll be right there," Erica says.

"Cassidy is my assistant. She's going to meet with you and go over everything she needs you to do. Try your best to figure things out on your own, but if you get really stuck you can call me."

"Okay. Thanks, Elizabeth. I really appreciate the job."

"Don't forget that it can always be more than a job. If you like it, it can be a career. Make the most of it."

I nod and stand because the woman who I assume is Erica has just popped her head in. Her outfit is definitely not an outlet store find, and her hair and makeup look professionally done. Is that a thing? Do people have personal aestheticians working on them every morning? No wonder Elizabeth insisted on buying my wardrobe. I'm way out of my element here.

At one o'clock, I sink into the chair across from Cara in the café and exhale for what feels like the first time all day. "I can only spare about twenty minutes," I tell her.

"They're keeping you busy already?"

"Busy is an understatement."

"Don't worry. I felt the same way when I started. You'll catch on quickly."

"I'm not so sure. I know nothing about style. I don't want to disappoint my aunt, but honestly, I'm probably not the best person to do this job."

"You want to be an actress, right? Fake it until you make it. That's what we all do." She opens a lunch bag and pulls out a homemade sandwich.

"I didn't bring a lunch. I have to buy something. Can I get you a drink?"

She shakes her head. "No thanks. They charge like six dollars for a tea."

Hmm. I guess Sam wasn't joking when he said their family business wasn't doing that great. "It's on me."

She smiles. "Okay, thanks."

I head to the counter to order a quiche, then sit back down and wait for the girl to bring it out to the table. I hand Cara her tea. "You think six dollars is a lot for a tea, you should see how much money this client is spending on her baby's nursery. The crib alone is worth five thousand dollars."

"Yeah, your aunt has some really wealthy clients. You'd be set if you wanted to follow in her footsteps."

I frown and sip my tea. Ever since I hit the fifth grade my main focus was to avoid my mom's footsteps. Acting has always been the one thing I'm really good at, so I assumed that was how I would get out. Making it on Broadway is a long shot since, unlike almost all of the people in my theater group, I didn't attend a performing arts high school, and I didn't have the advantage of acting coaches or summer drama camps when I was growing up. Those types of things weren't really high on the list of necessities when I only had ten dollars to buy a week's worth of groceries for Cooper. It had never occurred to me that following in Elizabeth's footsteps would be an easier option.

The café girl slides the plate with my quiche in front of me. I take a bite then say to Cara, "Our brothers seem to be a good match."

She nods approvingly and smiles. "Yeah. They look cute together."

"Is Sam open with everyone?"

"No. How about Cooper?"

"No. Our mom doesn't know." I take another bite, swallow, and casually ask, "Why are you interested in dating Leland?"

"Besides the obvious facts that he's sexy, single, and not gay?"

I shrug, hoping to look nonchalant.

"He was named one of the top twenty-five up and comers under twenty-five by the *Madsen Business* magazine. He was a really good student. Well, until he blew off school in his graduating year. He's already pulling a salary in the high six figures at his dad's company."

"Why did he blow off his senior year?"

"I don't know. There were rumors that he was having some personal issues. He partied too hard for a while, but he's turned himself back around." She sips the tea, then smiles. "And he plays tennis, which is one of my passions." She bites into her apple and places it back down on the table as if she's lost her appetite. "He never talks to me, though."

"He definitely knows who you are. Maybe he's just shy."

"He talks to you."

I nod, not sure how to respond.

"Would you go out with him if he asked you?"

"Uh, no. He's not really my type." I tuck my hair behind my ears. I'm worried that she's not going to buy it, so I add, "Not that he would ask."

"He seemed interested."

"No. He was just being friendly. I'm pretty sure he's into you." I stand, partly because I'm afraid she's going to see through me, and partly because I really do need to get back to work. "I should get going. I have to go on a home visit with my aunt's assistant and pretend that I know what I'm doing."

"Look on the bright side. At least you get paid." She holds up the expensive cup of tea as proof that there are perks.

"True."

"Hey, I think Sam is going to invite Cooper over for a hot tub and a barbeque at our house tonight if you want to come too."

Cooper, me, and two non-snobby, non-rich rich kids having some burgers sounds like something I can handle. "Sure, if Cassidy doesn't make me work all night."

Chapter Six

It's after six o'clock when I arrive home from work. Cooper is walking up the sidewalk as I pull into the driveway. I don't know if he notices first or if I do, but Aiden is sitting on his bike across the street. He's gripping the handlebars and I can see the tension in his muscles from here.

Conflicting emotions keep me in the car until Cooper opens the door for me. "Go talk to him," he says as I get out.

"No. I'm not talking to him and neither are you. Just get in the house."

"At least give him a chance to explain. You've been best friends since birth and dating for almost three years. Are you sure you want to end it over one issue?"

"It's not just one issue." I shoot Cooper a look and point at the door to signal him to get in the house.

"Why don't you want to work it out?"

Because I love him to death, and if I talk to him I'll get back together with him, but I don't want that life, so I need to stay away from him. "He cheated on me, Cooper. Why do you want me to just take that like I'm a stupid whore?"

"Look me in the eye and swear to me that he cheated on you."

After a long hesitation, I still can't say it. Cooper waves. Aiden nods to acknowledge him and, when I still don't move, Cooper gives me a stern look. "What's really going on?"

Overwhelmed, I shake my head and run up the path to the front door. When Cooper comes into the house, he studies me. "What?" I demand. My blazer entraps me in a suffocating hold as I flail to remove it. Outside, Aiden's bike revs loudly before he takes off.

"I didn't say anything." Cooper slides his school bag off his shoulder and drops it in the closet.

"I know what you're thinking and you're wrong," I snap.

"Really? What am I thinking?" He heads to the kitchen and I follow.

"I don't know." God, this is frustrating. I wish I did know what he thinks, and what Aiden thinks, and what I think, for that matter. "What are you thinking?"

"Nothing." He opens the fridge and grabs the filtered water pitcher. "What are you thinking?"

Forget it. This is stupid. I want to forget. That's the whole point. "I'm thinking that I don't want to talk about this anymore."

He pours two glasses full. "Talk about what?"

Gah. Stop it. That's so annoying. "Aiden. I don't want to talk about Aiden." Because it feels like my heart is disintegrating. "All right?"

He tips his glass back and eyes me after he takes a sip. "It's not fair to make him into some horrible guy in your mind if he didn't really do anything wrong."

I sit on a stool and tear a paper napkin to shreds. "Who says he didn't do anything wrong?"

"You kind of did when you couldn't say anything at all."

My gut clenches in response to a dreadful terror feeling that just swept through. "Regardless of what he was or wasn't doing with Leah the other night, he's a gang member, Cooper."

He shrugs and washes his glass. "So is pretty much every person we know."

"Exactly. And we don't need that shit in our lives anymore, no matter how much we love the people who bring that shit into our lives. I don't want to talk about Aiden. You're going to make me cry. Change the subject."

"Fine. How was your first day working in the corporate world?"

"Hard." I slide my arms across the granite and clunk my forehead down.

"Sam invited us over for a hot tub. Do you want to come?"

I turn my head to glance at him. "Do you think I made a mistake with Aiden?"

He chuckles, obviously because I was only able to stop talking about him for thirty seconds.

"What? Do you think I did?"

"I can't answer that for you, Ti. Are you coming with me to Sam and Cara's?"

"Yeah, fine." I sit up. "Do you think I made a mistake with Aiden?"

"Either you love him or you don't. It's that simple."

I sigh.

He smiles and circles around the kitchen island to hug

me. "Don't worry about it right now. Go get your swimsuit."

I sigh again, then head up to my room to change into a bikini. Aiden sent five texts today. The last one is: *I'm going to give u some space. Call me when ur ready to talk. Love u 4 ever.*

I decide not to delete that one.

There are about ten people at Cara and Sam's when Cooper and I arrive. They live in a large, older Cape Cod style house with a gorgeous kidney-shaped pool in the backyard. More people flood out onto the deck behind us. I didn't realize it was going to be a whole big party, and I suddenly wish I hadn't come. Concocting an excuse to leave would be easy, but Cooper and Sam seem happy sitting at the edge of the pool talking and laughing. In their Burberry bathing suits, they look like an ad from a men's magazine. I'm wearing a sixteen-dollar turquoise string bikini I bought at Walmart two years ago. It looks good on me, but if anyone asks who the designer is, I'm going to have to make something up.

"Hey, Tienne." Cara waves from the hot tub. "Come join us."

Before I have a chance to go over, the gate opens and a bunch of guys enter the backyard. The last one is Leland. He's wearing khaki cargo shorts and a light pink polo shirt like he's Ralph Lauren's grandson. He smiles when he sees me, so I glance over at Cara to check if she noticed. Shit. From her pinched frown, she definitely has. To do damage control, I walk to him and stop when we are inches apart. "Thanks for the flowers. I told Cara that you're into her, so act like you are and give her a longing, love-struck gaze."

I glance up to see if he's going to do it. Unfortunately,

he couldn't be looking at me with more intensity if he tried. "Why did you tell Cara that I'm into her?"

"I have my reasons," I say. "Just do the look."

He glances over my shoulder and flashes the cutest shy-guy smile at her. "How's that?"

"Not bad." I place my hands over the fluttery feeling in my stomach. "I'd probably fall for it."

He produces the same smile for me before I turn away and speed walk over to the hot tub. The warm water laps up over my shoulders as I slide down next to Cara. She lowers her eyelashes in a flirty way and glances over at Leland. He's staring at us intently, so I lean my head back on the edge of the hot tub and close my eyes.

The other people in the hot tub talk about tennis, sailing, and polo. I've got nothing to contribute. I just listen to how they all speak—worldly, educated, and kind of stuck up. After about fifteen minutes of feeling out of place, I climb out to get a drink from the posh outdoor bar. Two athletic guys are sitting on stools, with their backs up against the bar, facing the pool area. I walk up unnoticed, pick up the knife that is sitting on the wooden cutting board, and cut myself a wedge of lime.

"Livingstone and the new kid look like a pair of homos."

"Do you think they're faggots?"

"How would I know? I'm not gay."

The one guy shudders like it disgusts him to imagine two men together. "If I ever see homos kissing or holding hands or something I'll kick their asses."

"Yeah, I'll help you. Fucking queers make me sick."

Normally, I don't waste my time on enlightening ignorant losers, but the fact that he threatened violence rubs me the wrong way. I can't let that slide. "Hey, boys," I say in a sweet voice.

They both turn around and smile at me. The one on the right rests his elbows on the bar. "Hi. I haven't seen you around before. What's your name?"

I wink at the guy who is closest to me. He glances at my chest and leans in eagerly as if he expects me to whisper my name in his ear. I grab his hair and slam his head against the bar. Then I press the point of the knife up under his chin. He angles his head back to try to get away from the blade. My muscles tense and the point presses in harder. "My name is Tienne and you better be careful who you're calling a faggot."

"What the hell? You're crazy, bitch!" the guy gasps as he struggles to lift his face off the stone bar. The other guy stares at me in complete shock.

"Yeah. Don't forget it." I let go of his hair and jab the knife into the butcher block.

They both step back cautiously as if they've enraged a cougar, but then the bigger of the two puffs his chest and postures as if he plans to somehow defend his manhood.

"Is there a problem?" Leland asks from behind me. "Are these guys bothering you, Tienne?"

I wait for one of them to admit that they felt threatened by a tiny girl pointing a knife at them. Neither one of them says anything, so obviously they realize how lame it will sound if they accuse me of being a freakishly strong, homicidal pixie. They both walk away.

Leland slides his arm around my waist. "Are you okay?"

"Sure." I glance around to see who else may have witnessed my anger management issue. Fortunately, there isn't anybody paying attention.

"What was that all about?"

"They said something they shouldn't have. Hopefully it doesn't happen again."

He grins and looks me up and down. "Did they say something about how good you look in that bathing suit?"

"Nope." I twist so his arm will drop away, then head toward Cooper and Sam. I sit beside them and dip my feet in the pool. "Hey, guys. Don't look right now, but I had to educate the two homophobes standing by the arbor."

Cooper doesn't look, but Sam does. "Jocks," he says and takes a sip from his cup. "They're not that receptive to being educated."

"When she says educate, she means threaten with a knife." Cooper shakes his head as if he's partly annoyed that I've already started trouble and partly touched that I stood up for him. "Was that really necessary? We're trying to be normal, remember?"

"Sorry." I sigh. Maybe if I could learn to keep my Noir et Bleu genetics under control, defending Cooper wouldn't cause more damage than not saying anything at all.

Sam looks unsure whether to take Cooper's comment about the knife seriously or not.

"Maybe we shouldn't hang out together in public," Cooper says to Sam.

Screw those assholes. Pulling a knife on them was dumb, I admit, but my brother should be allowed to hang out with Sam if it makes him happy. I shake my head at Sam in a pseudo-apologetic way. "I'm going to do something that is likely going to be quite uncomfortable for you so that you two can hang out without any rumors. Do you trust me?"

He checks with Cooper and shrugs. "I guess."

I move to straddle his lap and press my chest against his. "Just close your eyes and think of somebody else." He smiles and closes his eyes. I run my fingers into his styled hair and lean in to give him a hot kiss. He places his hands on the small of my back, but doesn't move them. We both almost start laughing, but I hold it together to make sure that everyone gets a good show. When I eventually pull back, he chuckles.

"You're not too bad at that," I say to Sam and wink at Cooper. Cooper chuckles as if he thinks I'm a very entertaining lunatic. Over in her lounge chair, Cara sits with her mouth hanging open. The two homophobes look pretty surprised, too. Leland's expression, though, is hard to read. We definitely caused a reaction, I'm just not sure it was the reaction I was going for. Regardless, it's time to close the curtain on this show. "Well, Bro, I might have reached my quota of poor decisions for one day. We should probably go."

"Yeah," Cooper agrees and stands. He's not embarrassed—we've dealt with way worse—but he does seem disappointed to cut the evening short.

I step closer and whisper, "You can stay if you want. I'll come back later and pick you up."

He blushes, torn between wanting to hang out to flirt with Sam and not wanting to bail on me. "Are you sure?"

"I'm absolutely positive." I kiss his cheek. "Call me whenever you're ready."

"Thanks." Cooper sits back down at the edge of the pool.

"Don't even mention it." I lean over in a sexy way to give Sam one more kiss. "See ya."

"Your sister's a little bit nuts," he says.

"You don't have to tell *me* that."

Sam's smile definitely has a hint of a Cooper-crush in it. It's so cute. I pull on my T-shirt and jean shorts over my wet bathing suit. On the way out I thank Cara for hosting, but she appears to be too stunned to really respond. Leland is standing next to the gate and I have to pass him to leave. I walk by without looking at him, and for some reason I feel bad. The staged kiss was to convince people that Sam isn't gay. I didn't think I would care what Leland thought about it.

Shit.

I push the gate back open, and poke my head in to see if Leland is still standing on the other side. He is, and he looks as if he's not sure how to act. I wave him to join me on the outside of the gate, which he does. "The Sam thing wasn't what it looked like," I say.

He smiles. "You're worried about what I might think?"

Flustered, I shake my head. "No, I don't know, it just wasn't what it looked like."

"It looked like you were giving a gay guy a cover story to keep the homophobic assholes off his case."

"Oh, okay, then it was what it looked like. Do you think it will work?" I slide my hands into my back pockets, which stretches my T-shirt over my chest and definitely catches his attention.

"Uh, yeah." He chuckles. "So, do I have to be gay to get a kiss like that?"

"I kiss straight guys better than that."

He angles his face up at the sky and whispers, "Thank you." He looks back at me and takes a sip from his plastic cup.

I have to admit that it's fun flirting, but that's not why I came back to talk to him, exactly. "Can we keep that incident at the bar quiet?"

He smiles. "If you go out to dinner with me."

"At what point does persistence cross the line into stalking?"

"I think once there is some form of hiding in the bushes involved."

Okay, he's kind of funny. I'll give him that. "When do you predict you'll cross that line?"

"If you don't agree to a date by Friday, people might start calling me Peeping Tom."

"You obviously don't consider a boyfriend a deterrent."

He stretches his arm past my ear and rests his palm on the house. "I would, but I heard that you and your boyfriend broke up on Saturday night."

I steal the cup out of his hand and take a sip. "How did you hear that?"

"I was playing tennis at the club on Sunday morning and I ran into your uncle. I asked him about you, and he kind of let it slip that you might be recently single. That's why I figured it would be okay to send you the flowers." He leans in closer and whispers in my ear, "Was it okay?"

Whoa. This is moving too fast. The last thing I need right now is a rebound with a sexy Tommy Hilfiger grandson look-alike who actually has more game than I thought. Flirty time is over. "You seem like a pretty decent guy, Landon, or Leland, or Peeping Tom—whatever you want to call yourself."

"But?"

"I have so much baggage I need a U-Haul to lug it around. My dad died only two months ago and they still don't know who did it. Living with my aunt and uncle and getting used to their lifestyle is a huge adjustment since I've been living in a polar opposite way for the past eighteen years. I'm in over my head at my new job, and I have a really important play audition coming up. My mom is in the hospital. And to top it all off, less than forty-eight hours ago I broke up with my boyfriend of almost three years. I need time to focus and figure everything out without complicating my life with a new guy."

He nods and looks down at his leather sandals. "I'm a good listener if you just want to talk."

I exhale slowly. Surprisingly, it does feel better to talk openly about it, but it's probably not a good idea since I hardly know him. "Thanks, I might take you up on that offer once I've settled in. I need some time, though."

"That's fair." He doesn't sound like he's just trying to wheel me anymore. I don't know how to respond to that, so I just stand motionless, except for my heart that is jerking around in a slightly alarming way. After a moment, he leans in and kisses my cheek. "Take all the time you need to sort out your baggage."

I'm shocked that he seems as if he sincerely wants whatever is best for me. It makes me feel the way I do when I have to perform a solo, self-conscious and adoring the attention at the same time. "Thanks for understanding." I take a step back, then turn to go. Part way down the path, I look over my shoulder. He's watching me go, and I find myself smiling at him. God, he's cute. And so not what I need in my life right now.

Unfortunately, complications seem to be my thing.

Chapter Seven

My first three weeks at the design firm have been all about learning how to act like a young businesswoman and pretending that I can see the difference between "Cloudy Sky Blue" and "Silver Mist on the Lake Blue." My free time is spent either at the country club with Cara learning how to act like a wealthy member, or at the theater learning how to be good at all the acting I've been doing in my real life. It's not that hard to fit in at the country club. Just smile a lot and pretend like I'm interested in what they're talking about. Fitting in at work is a little more difficult because I actually have to prove that I can handle the assignments, plus I have to combat my genetic predisposition to dropping f-bombs when I screw up.

Cara and her friends aren't exactly what I would call cool, but they're not lame either. We mostly lounge around at the indoor pool, work out at the fitness center, or gorge on the Sunday brunch buffet. Cara and I also eat lunch together during the week. Leland and I have run into each other a couple times at the club, but he's been cool about giving me my space. He just says hi and smiles before heading to the tennis courts.

My mom bailed on treatment, as usual. She's home, and Uncle Terry is living there for now. Cooper visits her almost every day. I don't really know why he wastes his time. She's never going to change. I haven't seen her since we moved out, and the guilt that I feel about that is buried so deep now I barely notice it.

It's Gylly's twenty-first birthday today. I've been missing him a lot, but if I call I'll have to start back at step one of trying to get over him. Up until today, I've been pretty good at convincing myself that it's better if I don't cave in and go back to him. All I have to do is compare my aunt and uncle's lives to my mom and dad's lives and my resolve becomes iron clad. Today, though, I've been crying on and off since I woke up, and I can't think of one reason why it's better if I don't call him.

There's a knock at my door. "Hey Tienne," Elizabeth sings cheerfully as she pops her head into my room. "Blaine and I are going to the club for that fundraiser dance. Would you like to come with us?"

"No, thanks. I'm not in the mood to go dancing."

She steps into my room and sits on the edge of my bed. "What's wrong?"

I start crying. Shit. I hide my face in my hands and suck in deep breaths to make the emotion stop.

Her hand gently touches my leg. "I hope this isn't about Cassidy being hard on you at work. She can be demanding, but she told me you're actually catching on faster than she anticipated."

"It's not about work. Cassidy has been great."

"Did something happen in theater? Did you get cut from the play?"

I shake my head and swipe my palms across my cheeks.

"What's up?"

"It's Gylly's birthday."

"Oh, is she an old friend of yours?"

"He."

"Jilly is a guy?"

"Not Jilly with a J, Gylly with a G, as in Gyllenhall."

"Oh. Aiden." She looks down at her lap. "Are you going to go see him?"

I hug my pillow to my chest. "I don't want to see him. I mean, I do want to see him, but I don't want to see him. Does that make any sense?"

"Yes." She closes her eyes and smiles as if she's remembering something. "If it were easy to stay away from guys like Gylly, your mom probably would have married Chet."

"Who's Chet?"

"He was a guy we went to school with. His father was an investment banker and his mother's family owned an insurance chain. He was incredibly sweet and treated your mom really well, but she couldn't stay away from your dad. Your dad was as handsome as Cooper and he could talk his way into and out of things even better than you do." She chuckles. "There is nothing more dangerous than a bad-boy with charm."

"Gylly's not really like the rest of them."

"That's what your mom always said about your dad." She raises her eyebrow in a cautionary way. "Gylly's father is the president of the Noir et Bleu, isn't he?"

I nod and tap my thumbnail against my teeth, fully aware of what that means for Aiden's career path.

She sighs and waits for a while to see if I have anything else to add. What else is there to say? It is what it is. She stands and leans over to kiss my forehead. "I think Cooper's friend, Sam, is dropping by later to pick him up for the dance. If you change your mind, you can tag along with them. It might be good to have a distraction."

"I'll think about it."

She leaves and I try to read through the part in the play I'm auditioning for, but I can't focus. I can't stop thinking about Aiden. There has not been a year since I was born that I wasn't at Aiden's birthday party. It feels incredibly strange to know that his friends are probably all over at his dad's house and I'm not there. I should be there. As his friend. There is no reason why I can't still be nice to him. Strictly as his friend.

I shower and dress in some of my old clothes: tight black pants, a low-cut black sleeveless top, and black boots. The ring Gylly gave me is in my bedside table drawer. I look at it every night before I go to sleep, but I haven't put it on my finger since he gave it to me. I don't want to wear it, but for some reason I don't want to see him without it either. I string it onto a necklace, then walk down the hall and lean on Cooper's open bedroom door.

He's sitting at his desk using his laptop. He looks over his shoulder and smiles when he sees my outfit. "Are you going to see Gylly?"

I shrug, because I honestly don't know what I'm doing. He nods and presses his lips together. I'm not sure if it's because he thinks it would be a bad idea to go see Gylly, or if he thinks it's about time. "It's his birthday," I say as I pick at the paint on the doorframe.

"I know. I called him this morning."

"Really?" Wow. "What did you say?"

He chuckles, as if it's a stupid question. "Happy birthday."

It feels weird that Cooper knows more about what's going on with him than I do. *Nobody* has ever known more about Aiden than I do. "What did he say?"

"He asked if you were doing okay."

More importantly, "Is he dating anyone?"

"I don't know."

I twirl my hair around my fingers. My head is screaming at me to change and go to the dance. "What should I do?"

"Whatever your heart wants you to do."

"But what if my heart wants what isn't good for me?"

"Aiden is like family. That's all I know. You have to figure out the rest."

Yeah, family. And it's his birthday. "How do I look?"

"Smokin'. How do I look?" He stands and spins around. He's wearing expensive tapered trousers, leather shoes, a gray dress shirt, and a motorcycle-styled canvas jacket.

"Very GQ. The girls are going to go crazy."

He laughs and poses like a model.

God, I adore him. He is the best brother in the world. He might possibly be the best human being in the world. I walk over and hug him around his waist. "Love you, Lucky Boy."

"Love you, T Bear. If you don't go see Gylly, come by the dance."

"We'll see. Don't get a ride with anyone who has been drinking."

"Yes, Mom."

I chuckle as I wave and then leave the house. The drive to our old neighborhood takes fifteen minutes. I didn't intend to stop at our old house, but somehow I end up here, watching my mom through the kitchen window. She seems a little twitchy, but at least she's up and doing things. It looks as if she's cooking dinner. Uncle Terry is at the kitchen table reading a newspaper. She must have asked him something because he folds the paper down and smiles at her before answering. She laughs and looks pretty for a second.

Terry is the second oldest of the four Desrochers brothers. My dad was the eldest. Terry is probably most like my dad in looks and personality. He has three kids, ages eight, eleven, and thirteen. His wife tells everyone they're divorced, but he stays with them when he's in town and she doesn't ever date anyone else. Terry takes really good care of them. They have an estate in the country about thirty minutes away from here with horses and ATVs. They also go on expensive holidays to Europe or the Mediterranean every year. I guess if my mom weren't a junkie we would have had the money to do things like that.

I watch them for a while before driving over to Gylly's place just one street over. I park three houses down. There are about twenty bikes and five trucks in the driveway and on the front lawn. The music blasting from the house is mostly Metallica, Ozzy Osbourne, and a few Aerosmith songs that might have been thrown in for my benefit despite my absence.

I sit in the car for two hours listening to the music. Every once in a while bursts of cheers or laughter rise up. More bikes turn the corner and I sink down in the seat as they ride right past me toward his house. My hand is resting on the door handle, and eventually I pull it. The door opens a crack. The evening air swirls in, carrying with it the notes of the music and the familiar voices of my old life.

After a long hesitation, I close my eyes and lean back on the headrest, then click the door shut. My phone is sitting on the passenger seat. I pick it up and touch the screen to open a picture of Aiden. My finger hovers as I debate whether I should call. The screen eventually turns black. I throw the phone back on the passenger seat and turn the key in the ignition.

The corner store, where we used to hang out when we were kids, is down the street. Seeing it brings back a lot of memories. I pull into the parking lot and stare at the phone booth. I used to use it all the time before I got my own cell phone. I know it's a bad idea, but I get out of the car and lean against the booth. It takes ten minutes to muster the nerve to pick up the phone and drop in the change. My entire body trembles as I dial his number. Each ring lasts an eternity. I gasp like a goldfish out of its bowl.

Finally, Aiden answers. "Yeah," he shouts over the music.

I freeze. His voice is beautiful. Shit. I'm crying. It feels like I'm going to choke.

"Hello," he says, his tone gentle. "Hold on." I hear him walking, then the music is muted as if he went into a bedroom and closed the door. "Ti?"

My crying gets heavier and I cover my mouth so he can't hear my sobs.

"Ti. Talk to me."

All I can make is a weird whimpering sound.

"Don't cry, babe." His voice is holding back emotion and there is a pause before he asks, "Where are you? I'll come get you."

I shake my head and wipe the tears off my cheeks with my palm.

He's silent for a long time before he exhales slowly and clears his throat. He never cries, but I can tell he's struggling to keep it together. "I miss you, Ti."

Tingles spread over the surface of my skin. My heart races like I was just chased down a dark alley. Struggling for oxygen, I lean my forehead against the phone. What was I thinking? I can't be near him and not be with him. My mouth opens to speak, but nothing comes out.

Some guy yells in the background at the party. "Gylly! Where the fuck are you, man? We want to have the cake." Zeke barks. Oh, I miss him too.

"Come over, Ti. It won't feel like my birthday if you're not here. We don't have to talk about things. I just want to see your face."

I bite my fingernail for a second and then clench my eyes shut. I want to see his face, too. So badly. There is nothing I want more, except a life that isn't an exact replica of my mom's.

The sound of the music gets louder again as if the door opened. A girl's voice says, "Come on, sexy, everybody's waiting for you."

"I'm on the phone."

"With who? All your friends are here."

"No, they're not. Give me a minute." The music is dull again, so she must have closed the door. "I love you, Ti. Thanks for calling," Aiden whispers into the phone.

I listen to him breathing and commit the sound to memory. Eventually, I reach up and slowly press my finger down on the lever to hang up. When the buzz of the dial tone echoes in my ear, I whisper, "I love you, too. Happy birthday."

"Damn, bitch. Say what you gotta say and get gone. I gots bizness to do." A skinny meth head is standing outside the phone booth yelling at me.

"You want to use the phone?" The pitch of my voice is way too high. "You've got some important 'bizness' to do? Here you go." I slam the earpiece against the booth like a crazy person. It smashes into pieces and the internal workings of the receiver fly through the air.

"Hey, what the hell?"

I hand him the plastic remnants dangling from the cable. "Don't tell me what to do."

I get in the car, then peel out and drive toward the country club. I can't even see properly through the tears. The lines on the road are blurred. When I get to the club parking lot, I climb out of the Mercedes, but lean against the hood instead of going inside. Hearing the crappy band playing makes me feel like I don't want to be anywhere. I don't want to be home. I don't want to be at Blaine and Elizabeth's. I don't want to be at Gylly's. I really don't want to be at a lame country club dance.

"Hey," a voice comes from behind me. Leland stands near the driver's door of my car. "What's wrong?"

I hug my body and sniffle back the last of the tears. "I don't want to talk about it."

"Do you want to go for a drive?"

"Yes." Definitely. Take me away.

He reaches his arm out to hold my hand, which I don't resist, and leads me to his Audi. He opens the passenger door for me, then jogs around the back and slides into the driver's seat. "Do you care where we go?"

I shake my head.

He smiles and starts the car. The radio is on softly. He smells good. He looks good too. He's wearing dark trousers and a V-neck sweater. Aiden doesn't even own a sweater.

"So, you're having a bad night?"

I nod and bite at my lower lip, not sure how to elaborate.

"The band at the club is brutal, but I wouldn't get too upset over it."

I smile a little bit. His joking mood is exactly what I need right now. "Sorry if you were looking forward to the dance. You can take me home if you want to go back."

"I wasn't looking forward to the dance. I was looking forward to maybe seeing you."

Ah, very charming, Mr. Crofton. "It's pretty late. Were you trying to be fashionable?"

"No. I had an emergency at work."

"A sustainability emergency?"

He chuckles. "I guess it wasn't exactly a life or death emergency, but I had to take care of it before I left. Do you want to talk about why you were crying?"

I stare out the passenger window and tap my thumbnail against my front teeth as I debate about how much I want to tell him. Part of me feels like talking and getting it off my chest. Part of me wants to sweep it all into the U-Haul and forget about it. Finally I say, "There are aspects of my old life that I miss, but they're not good for me, so I have to say good-bye to them. Sometimes it's really hard, and it hurts a lot."

Leland doesn't say anything, but I can tell that he's listening.

We're driving away from the city on a country road, so I ask, "Where are we going?"

"It's a surprise."

"An attempt at being romantic kind of surprise, or a shack in the woods with torture devices kind of surprise?"

He laughs. "I'm attempting to be romantic."

He's sweet. "If I see any evidence of a shack, I will stab you in the eyeball with my metal nail file and steal your car."

"Noted."

My phone buzzes with a text from Cooper wondering if I'm okay. I respond with a quick "yes" so he won't worry and put my phone away. "Do you have any brothers or sisters?"

He smiles and glances at me. "No. It's just me."

"Why are you smiling like that?"

"Because it's the first time you've asked a question about my family. It almost feels like you're trying to get to know me."

"Mmm. Don't get used to it." I roll my eyes and grin, enjoying the easy feeling that I get when we banter. The station on the radio is also relaxing. It sounds like jazz or something. "Is this the kind of music you like to listen to?"

"I like to listen to all sorts of music. This is the type of music that I play."

"Play on what?"

"The piano."

"Hmm." I wrinkle my nose to tease him.

"What? You don't like the piano?"

"The guitar or the drums are cooler." I grin at him in a smartass way and he laughs. "Seriously, though, Cooper likes jazz. Is that what this is?"

He nods.

"Cooper would probably like talking to you about it. He doesn't know a lot of people who are into jazz."

"Definitely. Maybe I could show him my vinyl collection someday. Is your mom doing better?"

Whoa. That abrupt change in subject was a quick way to destroy the easy mood. I shrug and look out the window. "She's out of the hospital."

"What was wrong with her?"

I glance at him. He appears genuinely concerned, but I'm not ready for that kind of get-to-know-you conversation. "I don't want to talk about it."

He nods as if he wants to be respectful, but doesn't fully understand why it's an issue. He turns the car onto a side road that is bumpy and dark. A sign points to Marin Lake. I've heard of it, but never been. My family didn't do things like picnics or days at the beach.

"Isn't it kind of dark to go to the lake?"

He shrugs. "I like it here at night. It's peaceful."

"So, you bring girls up here all the time?"

"No. I come here by myself." He parks the car near the shore, then looks over and stares at me for a while as if he's contemplating something. "Okay, fine. I brought one girl up here and we made out in my dad's car. That was years ago when I first got my license."

"Are you thinking that we're going to make out?"

"Well, I'm not going to turn you down if that's what you want to do, but I actually had something else in mind."

"Really? What's that?"

He opens the door and steps out of the car. I watch as he pulls his sweater over his head and unbuckles his belt. He hops around to take off his shoes and trousers, then walks toward the lake with just his boxer briefs on. It's a bit more forward than I would have expected, but the view is nice, so I'm not complaining. He waves for me to join him. I step out of the car and wrap my arms around myself as I walk to the shore. He drops the briefs and wades into the water.

"Nice ass," I shout.

"Thanks. I work out."

"I see that."

"Are you coming in?"

"Uh, it's a tad cold to be skinny-dipping."

"Nah, the water is basically the same temperature all year round." He leans back and glides along the water.

"Really? Why does it sound like you're gasping for breath?"

"Well, it might be a little cold when you first get in. Woo! Just a little cold." He swims around for a while, so I sit on a log. The water does look serene and inviting. "Come in." He gestures for me to join him.

"I'm not skinny-dipping with you. I barely know you." A branch snaps behind me. I spin and search the darkness for movement. "What was that?"

"Probably just a raccoon or something."

"Let's go, Leland. I don't like the thought of wild animals lurking in the darkness waiting to attack me."

"Come in the water. I'll protect you."

"No. I'll just sit in the car."

"What if it's a bear? A bear will tear right through the soft top and eat you up."

I glance at his Audi convertible and change my mind—not because I actually believe him—but because being alone in the car with my thoughts about Aiden would hurt worse than being mauled by a grizzly. I remove my shirt, kick off my boots, wiggle out of my pants, and pop open my bra. I leave my underwear on and run into the water holding my arms across my chest. Leland laughs at me. I swim close to him, but not so close that we are touching.

"All right, you got your excuse to come in the water and you're safe from bears." He steps forward and places his hands on my waist. His fingers tighten, but he seems to be trying to keep a distance between my naked body and his.

"I didn't need an excuse," I tell him. "If I had wanted to come in the water I would have just come in."

"And you did. So, what does that say?" His mouth hovers close to mine. The warmth of his breath caresses my lips. He moves one of his hands and slides it up along my jaw toward the back of my neck. There is only a dim light coming from the moon, but it's bright enough to see that he is staring at my lips. His eyes reflect the moon as it bounces off the ripples in the water.

I lick my lips and wait but, instead of kissing me, he smiles, spreads his arms out, and swims away. Impressive. Those are some top notch moves. If he had a tattoo, I'd have to admit that this scenario is slightly appealing. "You're a tease, Mr. Crofton."

He laughs. "We haven't even been on a date. You didn't think you were going to get any action without agreeing to a date first, did you?"

"It's a bit insulting when you were embracing my mostly nude body, and instead of kissing me you go for a swim. Even Sam kissed me when he had the chance."

"Agree to a date."

Hmm. That's bordering on bossy, which for some demented reason I find attractive. "Don't tell me what to do."

"Oh yeah. Would you please agree to go on a date with me?"

Good. He's assertive, but also willing to concede. This could potentially work, depending if there is a spark. "Kiss me first. I need a sample of what I'm getting myself into."

He obediently swims toward me and stands up. The water streams over his chest and makes him look shiny in the moonlight. "So, it's all right for you to tell me what to do?"

"Yes. That's how it works."

He rests one hand on my waist, one at the side of my face, and leans in until our lips press together. He doesn't try to touch my exposed body. His hands remain politely where they are. He opens his mouth a little and kisses me with more urgency—the urgency of someone who has been waiting almost a month to do it. I'm not sure if it's him or the skinny-dipping, but it's a really good kiss. There is definitely a spark.

I kiss him back and let my hands explore his upper body a little. Another snapping sound comes from the forest, so I break our kiss to whip around. I wait for a bear to thunder out of the trees and plunge into the water to get us.

Leland laughs. "So, about that date, do we have a deal?"

With my hands on my hips—not that he can see them beneath the water—I stare at him as if he's under inspection. "That performance warrants one date, but you're going to have to take it up a notch if you plan on having a second date."

He smiles and salutes me.

It's a bit cold, so I glide through the water in a breaststroke to stay warm.

"Do you think it's romantic here?" he asks.

"Yes." I turn over onto my back and float in the direction of the shore. "When is this agreed-upon date going to occur?"

"Well, I can't this weekend because my parents are hosting a Crofton family reunion at our cottage. I would invite you along but, trust me, meeting my family on the first date is not going to work in my favor."

"Anything is better than my family."

"Was your dad Albert Desrochers?"

"What?" I tense and drop my feet to stop floating.

"Okay, don't be mad, but I was curious when you said he was murdered. I researched it a bit."

I'm not sure what to think about him snooping. I mean, it's my own fault for blabbing about it in the first place. It's normal that he would be curious about someone he wants to date. He probably should have asked me, though. Then again, to be fair, I wouldn't have answered if he had. I guess we would have talked about it eventually anyway. I don't know. "What did you find out?"

"The newspaper articles said he was shot and it was assumed to be gang related." He stops swimming and stands in the water chest deep. "It said he was a high-ranking member of an outlaw biker gang."

"Imagine that." And, this evening is over. Apparently, I don't appreciate the snooping. I wipe the kiss off my mouth with the back of my hand and wade out of the water toward my clothes. What was I thinking? "Take me home."

Chapter Eight

I get dressed and then sit in the car, pissed that what happened to my dad is going to follow me wherever I go.

A few minutes later, Leland slides into the driver's seat fully clothed, starts the engine, and turns up the heat. "I don't care who your dad was."

"I didn't ask if you did."

"I also found some articles about how he was charged with murder, but only convicted of manslaughter."

My hands tug at the hem of my shirt. I doubt the article mentioned that the reason my dad only did three years in jail was because the motorcycle club paid off the judge. "I don't want to talk about my dad."

"Is that your mom's wedding ring you wear on your necklace?"

I rest the palm of my hand over it. "No."

"It looks too modern to be your grandmother's."

I raise my eyebrows and press my lips together to show

my utter dislike of this topic of conversation.

"Is it yours?"

I don't answer. Instead, I fan out the wet ends of my hair and stare at the strands as if they're under a microscope.

He chuckles. "You weren't joking when you said you needed a U-Haul."

"Nope. You don't even know the half of it." I toss my hair back over my shoulder and slouch toward the door. "Let's just go."

"We haven't set a date for our date yet."

"I'm not going on a date with you. We come from completely opposite worlds, and I'm not interested in being your pet project, your excuse to piss off your mommy, or your experimental phase in slumming it."

"Do you have a serious self-esteem issue or something?"

"Uh, no. I respect myself enough to not be used by someone who thinks he's better than me."

"I don't think I'm better than you."

I roll my eyes, irritated that he thinks I'm stupid enough to fall for that. "Take me home."

"Don't tell me what to do," he says, trying to tease me.

"Ha-ha." I pull out my phone to call Cooper to see if he and Sam will pick me up. Leland places his hand over the phone and stops me. "I told you," I warn him, "I carry a metal nail file. Unless you want to be blinded, I suggest you take your hand off my phone."

He seems more confused than offended. "Why is it so hard for you to believe that I might actually like you?"

"Because guys from your world only like girls from my world for one reason."

"Where'd you learn that, the motorcycle club?"

"Fuck you." I yank on the handle, kick the door open, and take off running down the dark dirt road. I can hear him close my door and turn the car around. The headlights scan the forest and eventually the beam lands on me, so I pump my arms and run faster. My lungs are not used to working so hard. Ow. He drives up beside me and rolls the window down. After a few minutes, I slow down to a walk—partly because my boots are not designed for running and partly because I'm getting dizzy from the exertion. He doesn't say anything. The only sound is my gasps and the gravel crunching under the slow rolling tires.

"How's Wednesday night?" he asks quietly.

I cross my arms and keep walking. When we are almost at the end of the dirt road, I finally stop and face him. "What else did you dig up about me in your research?"

"Nothing. But I assume that your mom is an alcoholic or a drug addict and that's why you don't want to talk about why she was in the hospital. I'm also pretty sure that your brother is into Sam—and since I saw you pull a knife on that guy at the party, I'm going to assume you would hurt anyone who hurt Cooper. I'm also thinking that your ex is an outlaw biker who you're trying to stay away from, but it's not easy since you're still in love with him and possibly married to him."

I sigh and stare out at the darkness for a while. That was unexpected. I don't know whether to be impressed or annoyed. "Very observant."

"Would you like to get back in the car?"

"No, and I would appreciate it if you didn't tell all your friends at the country club about my past. I don't want people to treat Cooper differently because of things that have nothing to do with him."

"I'm not going to tell anyone, and you might be interested to know that everybody there has secrets they don't want anybody else to know."

Something about the way he said that makes me believe him. "Everyone?"

"Everyone. Get in."

Honestly, the idea that everyone has skeletons in their closets makes me feel better. I slow down to let the car pass me, then walk around the back. It stops rolling and he leans over to open the passenger door from the inside.

"Are you going to stab me in the eyeball?" he asks as I slide in.

Not fully recovered from getting my back up, I stare out the window instead of answering. I had a school counselor who tried to teach me cool-down strategies to use when I got angry. Unfortunately, I never quite mastered them.

We don't speak as he pulls back onto the highway and heads toward the city. The radio still plays jazz softly. The drive feels long because of the silence. It's almost one o'clock in the morning when we turn into the mostly empty country club parking lot. He pulls up next to the Mercedes and looks at me as if he's trying to assess where we stand. "I would still like to take you out and get to know you better, if you don't mind."

"Why?"

"Because you're interesting."

I study his face, trying to sort out my feelings.

"You want a fresh start, right?" he says.

"Yes."

The corner of his mouth angles up. "And you like me a

little bit, right?"

"I don't know." I stare out the window at the trees that line the golf course. There are a million reasons why dating Leland would be good for me. The most compelling reason is that I obviously need something to prevent me from going back to Aiden. I glance at Leland, wondering if he could maybe be that something. "Wednesday doesn't work for me," I finally say. "I'm auditioning for a play on Wednesday."

"Which play?"

"*West Side Story*." Ironically.

"How about next Saturday?" he asks.

"Okay."

He smiles and seems genuinely excited.

"Thanks for the drive."

"Anytime." He narrows his eyes in jest. "If you get the part of Maria, I don't want to be your Tony because I'm pretty sure that dude dies at the end of the play."

"I probably won't get the part. I don't have the training that everyone else has, and I've never done a professional play before." I grab the door handle.

"Hey." He reaches over and holds my elbow. "You'll be perfect for that part."

More than you even realize. I turn and abruptly lean over to kiss him. He seems a bit shocked and doesn't react at first. When he recovers and kisses me back, I pull away and get out. "See you next Saturday. Don't be late." I swing the door shut and walk over to the Mercedes. He waits to make sure I get in okay and lets me pull out in front of him. He follows me until I turn onto Elizabeth and Blaine's road and then honks before continuing straight.

As I park in the driveway, my phone buzzes with a text

from Gylly: *What's his name?*

I glance out the back window wondering if he'd been following us. I can't see him, and I probably would have heard the bike if he had been. *None of your business.*

It kinda is my business.

Not anymore. Stay away from him.

He doesn't write again and I'm a little worried that's not a good sign. I walk up the path, open the front door, and throw my purse and keys on the foyer table. I head upstairs and knock on Cooper's door.

"Yeah."

He's lying in bed reading. "Hi." I step into his room and close the door behind me.

"Hi. Elizabeth and I made apple crumble when we got home from the dance. I saved you some. It's in the fridge."

"Thanks. How was the dance?"

He makes a face as if it's a stupid question. "It sucked ass."

"Did you see Gylly hanging around here or the country club at all?"

"No. Why?"

"Just wondering."

He sits up and places his book on the bedside table. "Did you go to his birthday party?"

"I sat outside his house for like two hours, but couldn't make myself go in. When I tried to call him, I went mute. Eventually, I went to the country club to meet up with you and ran into Leland in the parking lot. We went for a drive."

"And that drive culminated in you needing a shower?"

"What? No."

"Why is your hair wet?"

"Oh. We went skinny-dipping."

"Ooh." He pats the bed to invite me to hang out and gossip.

"We only kissed." I move to sit on the edge of his mattress. "Speaking of kissing, do you know Sam as well as I do yet?"

"Maybe." He smiles and rolls onto his back with his arms bent behind his head.

"Good job." I fidget with the corner of his bedspread and stare at my feet. "Have you told Sam about Dad and everything?"

"No, but he knows Mom was in the hospital because she overdosed."

"Leland kind of knows everything and he still wants to go on a date with me. Why do you think that is?"

"Because he likes you."

"But, why would a guy like Leland like me?"

Cooper chuckles and pulls me in for a hug. "Because you're awesome."

I show him the texts from Aiden. "Should I warn Leland to run if he hears a motorcycle?"

Cooper thinks about it for a while, then shrugs. "Call Digger. He'll make sure that Gylly doesn't do anything stupid."

"Good idea. I love you." I stand and kiss his forehead. "Have sweet Sam dreams."

He laughs and throws a pillow at my face.

"Night." I throw the pillow back at him.

On the way to my room, I call Aiden's dad. His real name is Randy, not that anyone calls him that. "Hey, Digger, it's T

Bear. Did I wake you?"

"Nope. What's up?" His voice is raspy.

"Uh, I don't know how much Aiden has told you, but he and I are kind of not together anymore." I close the door and cross the room to sit on my bed.

Randy coughs like the two-pack-a-day smoker that he is. "Why?"

"I'll let Aiden tell you that part."

"I hope it's temporary. He lives for you. You know that, right?"

I clench my eyes shut and pretend I didn't just hear that. "The reason I'm calling is because I've made some new friends at Elizabeth's country club, and I'm—"

"Are you banging someone?"

Classy. "I'm going on a date with someone and I don't want anything to happen to him. Make sure all of your guys, including Aiden, stay away from him, or I will call the police."

He coughs again. "If this country club fucknut hurts you in any way, it won't be Aiden he'll have to worry about 'cause I'll take care of that shit myself. Got it?"

There was a time when a promise like that would have made me feel special, but it's hard to be grateful for that kind of love now. "Yeah. Whatever. Thanks. I gotta go."

I hang up and flop down on my pillow. Even the ceilings in this house are nicer than the ones at my house. Nice, but kind of boring. My ceiling at home has a yellowy water stain in the corner from when the roof leaked. It has glow in the dark stars that Cooper and I jumped on my bed to stick up there. It also has a pinkish splatter near the door from when I threw a Slurpee at Gylly's back and it exploded everywhere.

I miss that shit.

Chapter Nine

On the Saturday of my date with Leland, I wake up already sick with nerves. Cooper is going to visit Mom, so he pops into my room before he leaves. He places a cup of tea on my bedside table and tilts his head with concern. "Why are you green?"

"I have a date with Leland tonight."

"It's not like you to get nervous."

"It's not like me to go out with classy guys. I'm worried he's not going to like me once he gets to know me better."

Cooper walks over to open my closet. "If he doesn't like the real you, he's not worth getting worked up over." He slides the hangers one at a time to sort through all the outfits Elizabeth has bought for me. I haven't even worn most of them and the store tags are still attached.

"It's not just about Leland; I need to figure out how to be accepted by people like Leland if I want to leave my past in the past."

"People will judge you by who you are now. Not who you were."

Who I am now? I don't feel like I've changed. I wear nicer clothes, live in a bigger house, and drive a Mercedes. I'm still Tienne. "What if who I am now is not good enough?"

"He asked you out, didn't he?"

I frown and tap my nail against my tooth. Why did I agree? This is not going to end well. In fact, it might not even start well if my nerves get any worse.

"Do you know where you're going?"

"No."

"Okay." He pulls out a tailored black dress that tapers in at the knee and has spaghetti straps. "You can't go wrong with this and these." He hangs the dress on the back of my closet door and bends over to pick up a pair of black pumps. "Wear your hair in a twist and stick to pink lipstick since you don't know where you're going."

"What does the destination have to do with the color of my lipstick?"

"Just trust me." He walks over to my dresser to lay out earrings. He picks our Grandmother's pearl necklace too, but then notices that I'm still wearing the gold chain with Gylly's ring on it and puts the pearl necklace away. "Is it all right if I tell Mom that you got the part of Maria in the play?"

"No. I don't want her to know."

He runs his hand through his hair, frustrated that I haven't forgiven her yet, or maybe just tired of dealing with her all by himself. "She's been doing pretty good lately. She'll want to be there."

"Sorry, Coop. I don't want her showing up and making

a scene like last—oh, shit." I bolt out of bed and run into my en suite bathroom. I barf three times, then stand up and wash my mouth out in the sink.

Cooper is in the doorway smiling sympathetically. "Better now?"

"Yeah." Sort of. "Thanks for picking my outfit." I brush my teeth and talk around the brush. "Are you doing something with Sam tonight?"

"We're thinking of just making sushi here and downloading a movie or something."

"Cool. If my date sucks, I might be joining you." In other words, I will definitely be joining you. "I promise I won't kiss Sam."

He laughs, but then his smile fades.

"What's wrong?"

He exhales heavily and leans his back against the wall. "Do you think it would be a bad idea to tell Mom about me?"

"Tell her that you like boys?"

"Yeah. Sometimes I feel like I'm lying because I'm keeping secrets. It's uncomfortable when I talk about Sam and she asks whether I'm dating any nice girls. Maybe it's time to tell her."

"I don't know. A couple of the members have done time for gay bashing. Mom's so unpredictable. What if she gets super high and tells someone?"

He rubs his forehead.

"Don't get stressed. You'll give yourself premature wrinkles." I wrap my arms around his waist and lean my ear on his chest. "I'm okay with it. Sam's okay with it. Auntie Elizabeth's okay with it. Uncle Blaine's okay with it. It doesn't matter if Mom's not." I give him a squeeze before I walk over and sit on my bed cross-legged. After a sip of tea I point at him. "You know, the more I think about it, the more I think she better be okay with it. You've done more for her than she ever did for us. She needs to thank her lucky stars that she even has a son who gives a fuck and is willing to check in on her every day to make sure she's not dead."

"It would be nice to know that she accepts me for who I am."

"Yeah, well, there are a lot of things that would be nice in life, but sometimes we need to just be thankful for what we do have."

He smiles and sweeps his hands over his outfit. "Like unlimited designer clothes."

"I was thinking more along the lines of tuition for college. The people who are going to be involved in your future accept you. Who cares what the people in your past think?"

"Mom's going to be in my future. She's going to get healthy and be a part of both our futures."

"Keep dreaming, Lucky Boy."

"Do you think Dad would have been okay with it?"

The answer to his question is unequivocally "no," but I say, "Yes. You were his son. He loved you no matter what." I desperately want him to feel like he can be proud of who he is and, if she weren't stoned, I know Mom would want that for him, too. "Mom will love you no matter what. I was just worried about the guys in the club hassling you, but I guess you don't need to worry about that anymore."

Cooper seems relieved and hugs me before he leaves. His footsteps are soft as he makes his way down the stairs and out the front door. A few seconds later, Elizabeth appears at my open bedroom door. "It was nice of you to tell him that."

I smile. "Do you eavesdrop on all our conversations?"

"Just the juicy ones. Do you want to go for a run with me?"

"Yes, that is exactly what I need right now." I change into shorts and a running top, then sit back on the bed to put on socks and running shoes. She's leaning on the doorframe waiting, so I walk over and hug her. "Thanks for everything—the clothes, the place to live, the car, the job, and the normal life. I don't know how I'll ever be able to thank you enough."

She squeezes me tightly and whispers, "Just be happy. If you and Cooper are safe, and happy, and healthy, that will be thanks enough." I soak it up until she shoves off and says, "First one to drop has to make lunch."

"You're on." We take off running through the house and down the stairs. Blaine is washing his SUV in the driveway and waves at us as we run down the path onto the sidewalk. It looks as if we're in a commercial for something. I don't know what the commercial is for, but it seems like something that other people might want to buy.

Chapter Ten

It's ten to seven. I'm sitting in the front living room trying to remember how to breathe. I've never been on a real date. Gylly has picked me up on his bike or walked over to my house, but it wasn't ever like a formal date. Breathe. Oh, shit. What if Leland stands me up? I'll feel like a complete idiot since Blaine, Elizabeth, Cooper, and Sam are all here and know that I'm waiting.

My hands are sweaty and my legs are shaking. Okay, forget it. I'm not going. I stand and head toward the staircase. I'll just change into comfortable clothes that suit me so I can fifth-wheel with everyone.

The doorbell rings and I freeze. This really shouldn't be that difficult. Why is my body malfunctioning? My mouth feels like I licked up a bottle of white glue and it's solidifying into a thick paste.

Elizabeth comes flying out of the kitchen. "Oh my God, he's here. Okay, don't freak out."

"Too late."

Sam, Cooper, and Blaine all stick their heads around the corner, looking like a grinning totem pole. I flap my hands at them to make them disappear, but they don't. Elizabeth opens the door and I can hear her greet Leland, so I turn around slowly. He's checking me out in a way that Uncle Blaine is definitely not going to like. He has a bouquet of sunflowers and, for some reason, the sight of him makes me want to cry—a happy kind of cry like Miss Universe as they pin on her crown. The rollercoaster of emotions is making me dizzy.

One side of Leland's mouth turns up in a sexy way as he says, "You look beautiful."

I glance over at Cooper. He encourages me with a smile, so I take a deep breath and face Leland. "Thanks."

He hands me the flowers and offers his arm to escort me. I give Elizabeth the bouquet and she grins at me like the crazy lady who used to do story time with scary puppets at the public library where I took Cooper when we were kids. "Have fun," she sings as we walk down the path toward Leland's car.

After opening the door for me, he jogs around the back. I steal a glance at him as he slides behind the wheel. He's wearing a black suit and black tie with a white dress shirt. He looks dressy enough to get married. "Are you okay?" he asks as he turns the key in the ignition.

I open my mouth to answer, but no sound comes out, so I just nod.

He looks like he wants to laugh at me, but when he realizes that I'm actually struggling, he tries to ease the mood with an easy question. "Are you hungry?"

An easy question. Yes or no. Unfortunately, my brain still won't form words. He runs his finger across his eyebrow and takes a deep breath. I knew this was going to suck. He already regrets it. Shit. Calm down. Stop being ridiculous. It's a date. "I'm really nervous," I finally blurt out.

"I see that. Why?"

"I don't know." Actually, I do know. It's because you're way out of my league and when you figure that out, you won't be able to get away fast enough. "It's just that I've never been on a fancy date before. I don't want to embarrass you or anything."

"It's only a restaurant. Order, eat, pay. It's pretty straight-forward."

He's right. It's not that complicated. Why am I trying to make it harder than it is? "Okay." Let's do this.

As we drive through downtown, he asks how rehearsals are going for the play. I try to respond with more than one word answers, but the conversation is not flowing well. I'm totally off my game, and I think he knows it.

"Why are your hands shaking? Are you afraid of bridges?"

"No."

"Are you afraid of me?" His tone is teasing and I like that he's trying to lighten my mood, but it's not working for some reason.

"I don't know what my problem is."

He moves his hand to rest it on my knee. "Maybe you like me."

Yeah right. That's a good one. "Or maybe I caught the hantavirus."

He laughs and relaxes, relieved that I've finally loosened up. "Now, that's more like the Tienne I know."

He takes the turnoff to Mount Scott, which makes my apprehension flare up again because I didn't know there was a restaurant out this way. I went to Mount Scott once on a school ski trip, but we were on a bus and I wasn't really paying attention. My friends and I didn't have proper ski clothes, so we got borderline hypothermic and spent most of the day in the cafeteria.

We park at the base of the mountain and he holds my hand as we walk to the gondola station. Two other formally dressed couples get on the fancy, streamlined silver gondola with us. They're older and smile at us as if they think it's cute to see two young people playing grown-up. The operator gives us a few safety instructions before the car lurches and rises up the side of the mountain on suspended cables. As we ascend, I catch peeks of the scenery through the trees. The view of the city's twinkling lights is mesmerizing. Once we're gliding over the treetops, it's quiet except for the hum of the gondola. The air temperature drops as we get closer to the top. When I shiver, Leland takes off his suit jacket and turns me around to face him before he drapes it over my shoulders.

"Thanks."

The gondola bobs as we pass by a tower and the movement throws me against his chest. He holds me in close. We eventually glide into the station at the top of the mountain, swaying for a few seconds after we stop. Leland holds my hand as we exit and walk with the other couples along the path to the restaurant. The air is fresh and scented like Christmas. Well, not at our house. Our parents never bothered with a Christmas tree, but Randy did and that's why Cooper and I always spent Christmas at the Gyllenhalls'.

Every inhalation I take makes me miss Aiden, so I hold my breath as we walk. When we reach the steps, Leland lets the other couples go ahead. It's incredibly silent, and I swear I can hear my heart beating.

"Thanks for agreeing to this," he whispers. His hands move to my face. They feel cold on my skin. Then he presses his lips to mine. The surge of warmth makes my knees a little bit weak and I find myself pulling his body closer. He kisses me for a while and runs his finger along the curve of my cheek. "You probably almost turned Sam straight when you kissed him."

"You should see what I can do when I'm not nervous."

"Mmm." He raises his eyebrow seductively. "I can't wait."

We climb the steps and he holds open the door to the lodge-type restaurant. The maître d', who is dressed in a tuxedo, seats us at a reserved candlelit table next to the timber-framed window. There is a harp player in the corner strumming tranquil notes. The restaurant hangs off the side of the cliff with the entire city sprawled below us. The different perspective is fascinating. Leland points out the bridge, the airport, and the football stadium. We look for our houses, but the twinkles are too small to make out. My eyes shift one street over and my hand reaches for the ring hanging from my necklace. I wonder if Aiden's home. I wonder who's there with him.

"What are you thinking about?" Leland asks softly.

"Nothing." I drop the ring and it nestles against my skin. "It's beautiful here. Thank you for bringing me."

He reaches over to hold my hand. "I'm glad you like it."

His eyes sparkle in the candlelight and he smiles in the shy-guy way that I like. "Have you been here before?"

"No. My parents come here every year for their anniversary." He thanks the busboy who just filled our waters and brought a basket of bread.

I choose a slice of the warm sourdough. "Are you close with your parents?"

"Not really. We're cordial I guess."

"Why?" I ask before I take a bite.

He shrugs as if he would rather not talk about it. "We're just different. They've never really understood me and eventually gave up trying."

I finish my bread and take a sip of water to give myself time to come up with a different topic. "Do you like your job?"

He frowns and tears off a slice from the loaf. "No. Not really."

"What would you rather be doing?"

"Wow, you almost never ask me questions, and now you're throwing all the tough ones at me at the same time."

"You know everything about me, but I don't know anything about you." This could be fun. "Well, I actually know a few things about you because Cara raves on about you."

"What did she say?"

"She seems to think you're pretty hot shit."

He touches my cheek. "What do *you* think?"

"I don't know enough about your personality to judge yet, but I think you're okay looking."

He laughs. "Yeah, you're okay looking, too."

"So far, I also think you're sweet. I like that you do things like open doors for me, give me your jacket, and pull out my chair. That could all be just an act, though, so I guess I'll have to get to know you better before I form my opinions."

He nods with a hint of determination as if he has vowed

to himself to convince me that it's not an act. "What impresses you most in a guy?"

"I only need two things. He needs to be honest and to be there for me when it matters the most."

"Are you always honest?" he asks as he hands me a menu. "No."

He laughs. "You seem to like your double standards."

"Take it or leave it." I poke his arm playfully. "That's how I am."

"Well, nobody's perfect." He winks and wraps his fingers around mine.

I glance down at Aiden's street again.

The waiter arrives and Leland lets me order first. Then he chooses a wine from the wine list. Everything about this place makes me feel so refined.

Our conversation flows easily and he makes me laugh a lot. Before the food arrives, my phone rings. "Sorry." I'm still laughing as I pull it out of my purse to turn it off. Panic hits me when I notice who it is. He knows I'm on a date. He wouldn't be calling unless it was important. "Excuse me." I stand and rush over to the hall that leads to the bathroom to answer it. "Hello… Why? What happened?" Shit. I knew it had to be bad. "Okay, I'll be there as soon as I can."

When I return to the table, shaking, Leland stands. "What's wrong?"

"I need to get to the hospital."

Chapter Eleven

The hospital waiting room is full of people I don't know. As soon as Leland and I arrive, I scan the room looking for Blaine, Elizabeth, and my brother, but the first person I recognize is Cara. Although she has obviously been crying, a flash of something other than worry crosses her expression when she notices Leland's fingers laced around mine. I drop his hand and give her a hug. "How's Sam doing?" I ask her.

"We don't know yet. My parents are waiting for the doctor to come back with an update, but he was unconscious when the ambulance arrived."

That doesn't sound good, but I say, "I'm sure he'll be okay," to reassure her. Then I walk over to hug Cooper. "Come with me." Leaving Leland with Blaine and Elizabeth, I pull Cooper out into the hall. "Who did this?"

"I don't know." He buries his face in his hands. "We went for ice cream with Blaine and Elizabeth. Sam went outside to answer a phone call and when he didn't come back after like ten minutes, I went to check on him. I found him unconscious next to the ice cream shop. There wasn't anyone around when I got there. Whoever did it took his phone and wallet."

"Do you think it was just a random mugging?"

"I don't know. Someone might have seen us holding hands when we walked from the car to the shop." He shakes his head and breathes heavily. "I shouldn't have done that. It was stupid."

"It's not your fault. You should be able to hold hands if you want to."

"Should be able to and should are two different things."

"Where did it happen?"

"The Double Dip on Forty-Ninth."

I pull out my phone and text Gylly: *Cooper's boyfriend was jumped and robbed outside the Double Dip on 49th while they were with my aunt and uncle. He's in the hospital. Find out who did it, please.*

On it. After a pause, a second text comes through. *How was your date?*

None of your business. I fire that one off angrily, then remember he doesn't have to help me. He will because that's how he is, but he doesn't have to. I quickly write another: *Thanks for helping Cooper.*

I stuff my phone back in my purse. "Gylly's going to try to find out who did it. Let's go back inside."

Cara glances up at me as I walk in and then she stares down at her fingernails. Leland is sitting next to Blaine and Elizabeth with his elbows on his knees. He smiles with concern in his eyes before he moves over to let Cooper sit next to Elizabeth. She's holding her arms out to give Cooper a hug. I take a deep breath and sit beside Cara. I might as well treat it like ripping off a Band-Aid and get it over quickly. "Sorry about Sam."

She nods.

"I'm sorry about Leland too. I should have told you that he asked me out on a date."

"Yeah, you should have." She folds her arms across her stomach and sighs. "I knew he liked you the minute he saw you."

"Sorry," I say.

"Don't be sorry about that. I don't care if he likes you. I care that you lied to me. You're not supposed to treat friends like that."

"You consider us friends?"

"Yes. Don't you?"

"Uh, I don't know. Besides the people at theater, I've only ever had guy friends. The girls in my old neighborhood were all backstabbing bitches. I don't even know how to be close friends with a girl."

"Evidently." She nudges her elbow against my arm. "I still like you, though."

I laugh. "I didn't expect to make friends when I came to live with Blaine and Elizabeth, but I'm glad I met you. Can we start over?"

"Yes." She smiles, but it is strained with worry for her brother. I know exactly how she must feel. She glances over to see if Leland is watching us. He's talking to Blaine, so she whispers, "Where did he take you?"

"The restaurant on top of Mount Scott. It got cut short, though, when Cooper called to tell me what happened."

"Is he a good kisser?"

That's an understatement that makes me smile a little bit, then nod.

"Oh my God! You're so lucky."

A doctor pokes his head into the waiting room and asks for the Livingstones. Two people who I assume are Cara's parents stand and meet the doctor out in the hall. Cara squeezes my hand and then joins her parents to get the update.

While they're gone, my purse vibrates with a text from Gylly. Who needs the police when the Noir et Bleu are on the case? Shit gets done and it gets done fast. *Two homeless tweakers jumped him for the cash. Mickey got the wallet and phone back. He'll drop them off at Sam's house. How is he?*

Not sure yet. How did Mickey find out so fast?

Eyes everywhere. Don't forget it.

The fact that they even need constant surveillance to protect the people they care about says everything. I don't want Noir et Bleu eyes watching me. *Tell those eyes to stop watching me. We're not together anymore. Don't forget it.*

There is a pause before he responds. *Hard to forget that. The gaping hole in my chest that was left when u ripped my heart out kind of reminds me every time I breathe.*

Oh my God. I close my eyes and cover my mouth with my hand. Shit. I didn't need to know that. Pretending that I walked away because he cheated allowed me to delude myself into believing that it was his fault. Knowing for a fact that it crushed him opens a floodgate of guilt that slams into my gut. The phone nearly drops out of my fingers as I buckle over and rest my forehead on my legs. How could I do that to him? He must hate me. It takes a long time for me to recover enough to sit up and write him back: *I'm sorry. I never meant to hurt you. Thanks for helping Cooper.*

I press send and turn my phone off. That's all I can manage before the room starts to spin. Someone wraps his arm around my shoulders, holding me up. "Tienne, what's wrong?" It's Leland. He sounds panicked. "Elizabeth, there's something wrong with her. Her nose is bleeding."

Their voices blend into a strange jumble. Then everything goes black and I hear nothing but silence.

When I come around, I'm in a hospital bed with a doctor leaning over me, flashing a penlight into my eyes. Her forehead creases and I assume it's not only because she has a naturally serious personality.

"What's your name?"

"Tienne."

"When's your birthday?"

"May twenty-first." She writes on a chart, then removes the blood pressure cuff from my arm. She would be good at poker. I can't get a read on her at all.

"Have you taken any narcotics this evening?"

"No."

"Are you on any medications?"

"Birth control."

"Have you fainted before?"

"No, but I do get nosebleeds when I'm stressed."

"Have you been more fatigued than usual?"

"Sometimes." Should I be worried? "But my dad died a few months ago. We moved to a new house, I started a new job, and I'm rehearsing for a play."

She slides the clipboard into a slot on the end of the bed. "Okay. I need to run some tests. Do you want someone to stay in here with you?"

"My brother."

She nods to a nurse who walks out, presumably to get Cooper.

Jesus, why is she acting so serious? It was a nosebleed. "What do you think is wrong with me?" I ask.

She pats my knee awkwardly, as if her supervisors told her that's how to convey a bedside manner, but she doesn't fully get it. "Let me run some tests. You don't need to worry."

Cooper rushes in and looks so grateful that I'm awake. "You scared me, T Bear."

"Sorry." I reach my arm out to comfort him, and he clutches my hand into his chest. "The doctor is going to run some tests, but I feel better now. I'm sure it's nothing." He closes his eyes in relief for a second and I ask, "How's Sam?"

"Good." He smiles. "He needed stitches near his eyebrow and he has a concussion but, other than that, he just has bruises. They're going to release him tonight." He looks over at the nurse who is drawing blood from my arm. "Okay, don't get mad, and keep in mind that there is a needle in your arm, so don't try to hit me." He cringes a little. "I called Mom."

"Coooooooper."

"Sorry. I didn't know what was wrong with you. Uncle Ronnie is bringing her down."

That is the last thing I need right now. "You know I get

nosebleeds when I'm stressed. You didn't need to call her."

"She's our mom."

"Great. Whatever. She probably won't even show up."

Cooper sits on the side of my bed and rests his arm across my shoulder, which makes me feel better. "They'll all be here. You know that." He laughs. "Sorry."

It's not funny. I shake my head and punch him lightly in the ribs. "Yay! I guess Leland is going to get to meet the whole fam damily." I groan.

"You like him, don't you?"

"I should, shouldn't I?"

He shrugs as if he's not sure. "You still love Gylly, don't you?"

Yes. I love him so much that the guilt of turning my back on him with no explanation just landed me in the emergency room. I close my eyes and bite at my bottom lip. God, why does everything have to be so hard?

Cooper chuckles. "You seem to have gotten yourself into a little bit of a pickle."

"A pickle? I think it's more of a shit show."

"Wait until Mom gets here with the entourage. Now that'll be a shit show."

"Can you smuggle me out the back door?"

"Nope. Not until we know what's wrong with you."

"Nothing's wrong with me. Gylly sent me a text that upset me and I guess I got overwhelmed. I'm just tired. By the way, Mickey took care of the guys who jumped Sam, and he got his wallet and phone back."

"Really? How?"

"I don't know. Gylly said they have eyes everywhere. Whatever the hell that means."

"Oh Jesus." He bolts up.

"What?"

"Your nose is bleeding again."

I cup my hands up near my mouth to catch the blood, but it dribbles through my fingers and onto the bed sheets. Cooper darts out through the break in the curtain and returns a few seconds later with the doctor. She's frowning again.

The doctor doesn't release me until the morning. Cooper stayed with me all night, and we walk into the waiting room together. Our mom and uncles are sprawled out asleep on the far side of the room. Uncle Blaine is asleep sitting up. Elizabeth's head is resting on Blaine's shoulder, but she's awake, so when she sees us, she springs to her feet and hugs me. Leland is also awake. He stands when Elizabeth bounces past him. He smiles, but he has dark circles under his eyes and his hair is curled out in wonky directions. He waits until Elizabeth lets go of me, then he steps in and hugs me so tightly, it almost hurts. "Are you okay? What did the doctor say?" he whispers in my ear.

I glance over at my mom and all three of my uncles in their cuts and grungy jeans. Ronnie's and Terry's legs are stretched out, their heads rested back against the wall. They are both snoring, and their round bellies rise and fall with each breath. Len is slouched to the side with his elbow on the armrest and his head propped up on the heel of his hand. His knuckles are all scraped open and his hand is bruised. Len is the youngest Desrochers brother, only fifteen years older than me. He's not bulky like his brothers. He's muscular in a lean way and not quite as tall as the rest of them, but he's tougher than all three put together. I've heard stories. Even my dad didn't mess with Len.

My mom is stretched across two chairs with her head resting on a folded leather jacket. Her hair is pulled back in a ponytail and she almost looks like me in her jeans and white sweater. I don't want to talk to any of them right now.

"Can we just go?" I whisper to Leland. At the same time, I notice that Cara is still here.

She smiles in a way that seems like she feels sorry for me as she walks over to hug me. "I'm glad you're feeling better."

Maybe it wasn't pity that I saw in her expression. It feels like she actually cares. "You didn't need to stay all night."

"That's what friends do."

"Thanks." I swipe away a tear that came out of nowhere. Geez, it's going to take a while to get used to having a friend who is actually thoughtful and caring. "Please don't tell anyone at the country club or at work about—" I point at my family.

She smiles and squeezes my hand. "Don't worry about it. I'm going to head home to see if Sam is awake, but call me if you need anything."

"Thanks, Cara." I give her another tight hug before I turn to Elizabeth and whisper, "I'm going to head home, too. We can talk about what the doctor said there."

Elizabeth raises her eyebrow, disapproving of my plan to give my family the slip. "You can at least say hello to them. They've been here all night."

"No thanks. I think we've all had enough drama for one night." I pull Leland's hand and tiptoe toward the door.

Elizabeth unleashes a huge fake sneeze and then sings, "Tienne, darling!"

My uncles all wake up with a jolt, and my mom opens one eye slowly before pushing up from the chair. "T Bear." She stumbles a little as she stands. "How's my T Bear? Wow, you look so fancy in that dress." She spreads her arms and wraps them around me. I stand stiffly as she half hugs me and half hangs off me. She feels like a skeleton with skin and she smells like cigarette smoke. "What did the doctor say?"

"She said I'm totally fine. I was just stressed and dehydrated and a little anemic. Sorry to drag you all down here for no reason." Ronnie bends his towering six-foot-five frame down to kiss my hair. Then Terry lifts me off the ground in a gentle bear hug and presses his beard against my cheek. It scratches. Uncle Len isn't very touchy feely, so he pats his hand on my shoulder briefly, then moves to stand near the wall. He's the only one who smells like he's showered recently.

"Who's this?" my mom asks and rests her hand on Leland's arm.

"Leland."

Terry, Ronnie, and Len are always overwhelming, but they amp up the intimidation as they glare at Leland, probably because they don't approve of me being with anyone who isn't Aiden. Leland shifts his weight, then rubs the back of his neck as he stares at the floor, avoiding eye contact with them. My mom is joyfully oblivious to all the silent threats. She says, "We should all go out for breakfast."

Only in my nightmares. I tug Leland toward the exit. "Uh, no thanks. I'm really tired. The doctor said I need to get my rest, but you all should go for breakfast. Leland can drive me home. Okay. Nice seeing everyone. Bye."

This time we make our escape. We walk quietly to the elevator. Once we're inside, the mascara tears roll. "Sorry you had to see all that shit."

"See what?" Leland asks. "A family that loves you?"

I wish it were that simple. I choke back the emotion and lay my hand over the ring to hold it against my heart. Sometimes love isn't enough.

Chapter Twelve

For the four weeks after the whole hospital incident, work and play rehearsals kept me almost too busy to stress out about my mom and Aiden. Unfortunately, I'm still exhausted because Cassidy has me working eight to six, and I have to be at the theater five nights a week and four hours on Sundays.

Leland has been nagging me to follow the doctor's orders and find some relaxing activities, so I finally agreed to go to yoga at the country club while he's playing tennis.

He parks in front of Elizabeth and Blaine's house and hops out to open the passenger door as I walk down the path to meet him. Before he lets me get in, his lips touch my cheek and he asks, "How are you feeling?"

"Fine." It's flattering that he cares so much, but I'm not dying, and I'm not made of glass. "You can stop babying me." Seriously, it's been a month.

He takes my yoga mat from me and, after I'm seated, shuts the door. I watch out the back window as he stores my mat in the trunk and then walks to the driver's side. He smiles and rests his hand on my knee as we drive. "Are you excited that the play is only a week away now?"

"Excited and nervous, I guess. There are going to be reps from a few performing arts schools there on opening night."

"That's great. Is your mom going?"

"No. I don't want her there. Elizabeth and Blaine are coming, though."

He parks the car in front of the valet at the club and we get out. Instead of turning toward the tennis bubble, he walks with me toward the yoga studio.

"What are you doing?"

"I suddenly feel like taking up yoga."

I chuckle. "It's not as easy as it looks."

"That's okay. I'm just coming for the scenery. I might not even try."

"The best spots are at the back if you're only here for the view."

He glances at my butt. "Good to know."

We enter the studio, he borrows a mat from the equipment room, and rolls it out directly behind mine. I do a couple of stretches to purposely give him a bit of a show. He sits down and leans back on his palms to watch. When I do a triangle and look back at him from between my legs, he mumbles, "Jesus. I'm coming with you to every class from now on."

"Shh. No talking in yoga." I place my hands flat on the mat and back up into a Downward Facing Dog.

He moans.

"No noises either."

"Okay, I have to go then." He stands and bends over to

kiss my cheek. "I'll meet you out front at noon."

"And then you'll take me out for lunch?"

"Absolutely." He slaps my ass, then leaves.

After the class, I shower and head to the lounge. Cara is already at the juice bar flirting with the bartender when I show up and sit on the stool next to her.

"Hey." She hugs me with one arm. "Brent's making fruit smoothies. Want one?"

"Sure."

He's cute, right? She mouths as he works the blender with his back to us.

Broad shoulders, longish surfer hair, tight ass. Definitely cute. "I thought club staff weren't allowed to date members."

"Yeah, well, it doesn't look like I'll be a member for much longer."

What? She's my only friend. She can't leave. "Why? Are you moving?"

Her cheeks blush and she folds up a cocktail napkin into increasingly smaller squares, maybe hoping that if she takes forever to answer I'll forget the question.

"Did you get into school somewhere?" I press.

"No." She lowers her voice and turns to face me. "My dad told us that he won't be able to afford the dues anymore after next month."

Oh. That's shitty. "I'm sorry. I know how much you like it here, but we can hang out somewhere else."

She sits up straight and transitions from depressed to perky better than an actress could. "Let's talk about something more pleasant. Did you take a class?"

"Yeah. Yoga."

She shoves my shoulder. "Why didn't you tell me? I would have come with you."

Brent slides the smoothies over the counter to us and winks at Cara before leaving to serve an elderly couple at the other end of the bar.

"I'm positive that Leland will be forcing me to go again, so I promise to ask you next time."

"Good." She sips her drink, then spins around on the stool and leans back against the counter. "Is he here?"

"He's playing tennis. We're going out for lunch once he's done."

Her forehead creases and her expression turns serious. "Is it all right if I ask you a personal question?"

"About Leland?"

"No. About your family."

The smoothie thickens in my throat and slows to a halt. "I guess. What do you want to know?"

"Was your dad like your uncles?"

I try to gauge her expression. She's focused on the cup in her hand, giving me no clue to her thoughts. "What do you mean?"

"They were wearing patches on their vests. I assumed that meant they were in some sort of gang."

I shoulder-check to see if anyone can hear her. I don't care that she knows, but the people at the club won't be quite as accepting.

"You don't have to tell me," she says. "I was just wondering what that must have been like for you and Cooper growing up."

Instead of telling her that it sucked, that it still sucks, I shrug.

She spins back around and rests her elbows on the counter. "Sorry. I didn't mean to pry."

"You don't need to apologize. I just don't know what to say. When I was a kid, I used to draw my dad as a Ken-doll-looking guy with short hair and no tattoos. But he wasn't. He was who he was."

"At least you must have felt safe knowing he could protect you."

"No. Not really." Not at all. Safe was not a feeling I experienced growing up. I was terrified that my mom would OD overnight, so I rarely slept more than two hours in a row. I was paranoid that Cooper would get hurt or lost, so I never went anywhere without him. I was convinced that the bad guys my dad did business with were going to come after us, so I obsessively checked the locks on the windows and doors. I also had chronic nightmares about my dad being in a fiery motorcycle crash or being stabbed in a fight. It wasn't any better when he was home, either, because the truth is, I was scared shitless of my dad. Cooper used to draw him as a giant with flames coming out of his ears and dead people on the floor around his feet, and it was pretty much accurate. Nobody except Cooper and Aiden know all that, and even though Cara is sweet to care, she wouldn't understand.

After polishing off the rest of the smoothie, I stand, then reach over to hug her, hoping that she's not too offended that I didn't open up more. A huge part of me wants to be candid but, even if I knew how, it would likely end up in a tear fest and this isn't the place for that.

"I need to get going. Leland is meeting me out front."

Her eyes scan my face with concern. "I didn't mean to upset you."

I force my mouth into a country club smile and pat her arm, wishing I was able to be the type of friend she deserves. "You didn't. It's fine. I'll see you at work. Good luck with Brent."

The valet has already brought the car around and Leland is leaning on the door waiting for me. I kiss him and smile. "You're still thinking about the Downward Facing Dog, aren't you?"

"Yes. I would definitely like to see that again. Maybe we could try naked yoga at my place after lunch." He opens the passenger door for me and checks my reaction to his comment.

I smile although I'm terrified he's not joking. Who am I kidding? I know he's not joking. It's been almost a month and the most we've done is make out on his couch fully clothed.

He grins, excited about the false hope I just gave him, then hustles to get behind the wheel.

Once we're on the road, I realize I need to quit leading him on. It's going to piss him off, but I say, "Um, this would probably be a good time for me to mention that I have a one-year rule."

"One-year rule for what?"

"Sex."

He frowns in a dramatically incredulous way. "What are you, Mother Theresa?"

I shrug and smile because even though I'm no nun, the one-year rule is legitimate.

"Are you seriously trying to tell me that your older biker

boyfriend waited for a year?"

"Yes, he did."

"Yeah, right."

"He did. He was a complete gentleman during his probationary period."

"Why? Was he a virgin?"

"No. He had lots of serious girlfriends, and a few not-so-serious flings before we started dating."

"Have you looked at yourself in the mirror and seen how you're built? There is no way that he resisted you for an entire year."

"Well, I'm not saying he wasn't satisfied in other ways, but he waited for the full meal deal."

"He's a saint. You should have held on to him."

Our teasing banter just took a one-eighty. He meant for that one to sting. I understand that he's disappointed, but I don't like that he isn't willing to work as hard as Aiden did. I watch the scenery go by out the window for a while. "So, you don't think I'm worth the wait?"

"I didn't say you weren't *worth* the wait; you're just too hot to *endure* the wait."

Oh. Well, okay, that's a different story.

"Sorry if it feels like I'm pushing you." He reaches over and holds my hand. "I just really like you."

It feels nice to hear him say that, but it doesn't change the fact that I'm not ready. "I don't want to rush into anything."

He rolls into the parking lot of a restaurant and turns off the car. "Okay, so you guys started dating when you were fifteen and a virgin. Correct?"

"Yes."

"You are now eighteen and no longer a virgin. Correct?"

"Yes."

"So, if I do the math and divide the one year he waited by three to account for your age now, that equals four months. Then we halve it because it's not your first time. That equals two months." He grins at me, proud of his negotiation skills. "We're not rushing anything. We're good to go."

"Clever. Even if I allow your calculations, are you sure you want to always be compared to Gylly knowing that he made it the full year and you couldn't do it?"

"His name is Jill?"

"Yeah. You should go tease him about it. I'll see you at your funeral."

He smiles in a goofy way. "I can't, I'm busy trying to convince you to sleep with me."

I shake my head. Not going to happen. "It doesn't matter what you say or how you crunch the numbers. Besides, I have rehearsal this afternoon." I kiss his cheek. "You're not getting any action today, so let's go eat."

His expression seems agreeable, but after he gets out of the car, he slams the door with more force than usual.

Chapter Thirteen

Tonight is opening night for the play. The dress rehearsal yesterday went well except for one set malfunction that almost took the head off a guy named Scott. There were a bunch of high school kids being our mock audience when the plywood building came crashing down and made a deafening echo through the auditorium. I think the kinks are ironed out now. They better be, because we go on in ten minutes.

I peek out from behind the curtain. Cooper is in the front row with Sam and my aunt and uncle. Blaine is fiddling with his camera. Elizabeth excitedly scans the room and waves at people she knows. Cara, Haley, and Reese sit about halfway back with their dates. Cara waves at me. In front of her is a row of people from the school in New York. If things go well tonight, they might remember my name when I audition for them. If things don't go well tonight, they will definitely remember my name. No pressure. It's only my lifelong dream riding on my performance. The collar of my costume is strangling me, so I undo the top button. Fortunately, I can't see my mom anywhere. I also can't see Leland. I never needed to search for Aiden. He used to come to every one of my opening nights, even before we were dating, and he always stood in the back where I could see him. I scan the back wall. Nobody is there.

"Places everyone!" the stage manager calls.

I look for Leland in the audience until one of the cast members moves me out of the way. I'm not in the first scene, so I stand offstage and watch the curtain go up. Butterflies flit in my stomach and it's the best kind of nervous there is.

On my cue, I run out onstage, and the rush of adrenaline turns me into Maria. The music beats through my body and, when I open my mouth, a voice that doesn't feel like it belongs to me comes belting out. We dance and all I see are the other people onstage with me moving in rhythm to the music as if we're being compelled. I channel my feelings for Gylly onto Tony. Our kiss is real because in my mind we really are in love.

The acts fly by and, before I know it, I'm leaning over Tony's body after he has been shot by a rival gang member. He dies in my arms and real tears pour down my cheek. My hand trembles as I point the gun at the gang members. The rage in my voice is raw as I yell at them for letting hatred come to this. I drop the gun, unable to bring myself to violence. The rivals assemble and carry Tony off together to show that the feud is over.

The auditorium erupts with applause, and it startles me because I'd forgotten they were there. Cooper jumps up and down and Sam whistles loudly through his fingers. Elizabeth is crying and claps wildly. I can't tell what Uncle Blaine is feeling because he has the video camera in front of his face. The girls clap and cheer. The New York people applaud courteously. I finally see Leland, and he is sitting on the aisle with his head down, texting.

That was the performance of my life and he's not even paying attention. My impulse is to leap off the stage and shove the phone down his throat but, lucky for him, the cast bows and the curtain closes. The audience continues clapping and whooping. Once the curtain opens again, we stand in a line to take a few more bows. When it's my turn for a solo bow, I walk up to the front of the stage.

That's when I see Gylly. He is standing against the wall near the door, smiling as if he couldn't be more proud of me. My heart hangs stuck between beats. I can't hear the audience anymore. It's as if he and I are the only two people in the auditorium and our bond cannot be broken. Overwhelmed by his unconditional love, I start to cry again. When he sees that I've noticed him, he gives me a thumbs up, then ducks out the door. It doesn't matter that he's gone, I can still feel his presence in my soul. It has always been there. It always will be. The fact that he has never let me down, not even now after I hurt him in the worst possible way, breaks my heart.

I can't breathe. I'm afraid nobody will ever be more devoted to me than Aiden is. Shit. I'm going to fall down. Fortunately, the guy who played Tony steps up next to me and holds my trembling hand so we can take a few bows together. He hugs me, and the crowd goes crazy as the curtain drops again. "You nailed that, Tienne," he whispers in my ear and spins me around.

"Oh my God. What a rush," I gasp.

"It was awesome," he agrees. He turns to hug more cast

members, and I'm swarmed by everyone, too.

Eventually, Cooper swims through the crowd backstage and lifts me up to swing me around. "That was your best performance ever."

"Thanks, Coop." Elizabeth walks up and hugs me. She holds me at arm's length and examines my face. "You completely transformed into a different person. It was mesmerizing. Really. Absolutely mesmerizing. Your parents would have been so proud of you up there tonight."

Sam leans in to kiss my cheek. "Tony Award worthy. Congratulations. Cara asked me to invite everyone back to our place for a cast party. She went ahead to order some food and get things ready."

"Thanks, but I don't want you guys to go to the trouble. We were planning to just order pizza here."

"Nope." He turns and yells to all the cast members, "After-party is being held at the Livingstone residence. See me for directions."

Everyone cheers.

Blaine hugs me and shows me the ending of the play on the screen of his camera. It's emotionally raw and powerful, especially the part when I thought about Aiden. "Wow," I say.

"Yeah. Wow." He hugs me again.

A man walks over and shakes my hand. "That was a very impressive performance."

"Thank you."

"My name in Neil Holmes. I'm from The American Academy of Performing Arts." He hands me a business card. "We're hosting auditions in this area next month if you're interested in attending one of our schools."

"I am. Very interested. Thank you."

"Congratulations. It takes a lot to impress me, Ms. Desrochers."

My legs are twitching to jump up and down. "Thank you." He walks away, so I let loose into a happy jig. Leland approaches carrying what must be at least three dozen roses, weaving through the crowd. He hands me the flowers, which are uncomfortably heavy, kisses my lips, and says, "You were amazing."

"Thanks. What was your favorite part?" I ask quietly.

He smiles uncomfortably and runs his finger along my cheek. "You."

"Which song was your favorite?"

"I liked them all, but probably, uh, the last one was my favorite." He combs his hand through his hair, like he does when he's being country club smooth, like when we first met.

"You texted through the entire thing," I accuse.

"No, I didn't."

Texting is bad enough, lying about it takes it to another level of assholiness. "I saw you," I snap.

"I responded to one emergency text from work after you finished. I watched every second of the show. You were amazing. Let me take you for a romantic dinner to celebrate."

"I can't. There's a cast party."

"Isn't that just pizza?" He rubs my arm, trying to soothe my anger. "I want to take you somewhere special."

Is he serious right now? "The cast party is a big deal. We all worked really hard for this night and I want to celebrate with them."

He nods and slides his hands into his pockets as if he understands, but I can tell by his disappointed expression that he doesn't get it.

A few cast members rush over to hug me. Leland wanders away as I tell them about Neil Holmes. They're excited for me, and we dance around like hyper kids before heading down one level to the dressing rooms to change. My phone vibrates in the bottom of my bag. It's a text from Aiden: *You blew me away from the moment you stepped onstage.*

I stare at the words for at least five minutes, trying to fit all my feelings into place. Finally, I wash off all the makeup and change into a pair of yoga pants and a hoodie. Everyone else has finished changing and gone back up onstage, so I slide down the wall to sit on the floor with my phone in my hand. Eventually my thumb moves to type: *Thanks for coming. It meant a lot to me.*

The message sends and even though it's exactly how I feel, I regret telling him. No matter how unconditionally I can count on him, he can't give me the life that I want. The confirmation that I still love him like crazy doesn't change anything.

The screen lights up with his response: *I wouldn't have missed it for anything. Enjoy the cast party. You deserve it.*

The fact that he understands the importance of the cast party and Leland doesn't makes me incredibly sad.

Cara pulled together a nice impromptu after-party. There are enough platters of sushi and sub sandwiches spread out across the kitchen counter to feed the entire auditorium. She has also opened her parents' liquor cabinet. I circulate and start to take a collection of five bucks from everyone, but when she finds out, she makes me give the money back.

"Cara, you don't have to pay for everything."

"We're celebrating. What do you think credit cards are for?"

"I know you can't afford it," I whisper.

She smiles and whispers back, "I got a little side job in merchandising. Don't worry about it."

"I'm going to pay you back."

"No, you're not. Just go have fun." She rushes off to ask people what they want to drink.

I look around and sigh. There are a few people, including Sam and Cooper, outside in the hot tub. Everyone else is crowded into the kitchen and family room. As I pop a sushi roll into my mouth, Leland sneaks up, wraps his hand around mine, and pulls gently. I quickly grab another roll before letting him drag me outside. We walk past the hot tub and head toward a private part of the yard near the back fence. The only light is the wavy blue glow from the underwater lights of the pool. I sit down on an old tire swing.

Leland shoves his hands in his pockets. "My parents are hosting a dinner party next Saturday night. A few people my mom knows who work in the theater business on Broadway are going to be there. I thought you might want to meet them."

That would be an unreal opportunity, but I'm still mad at him for not being Aiden. I know it's stupid since I don't want him to be like Aiden. God, I don't even want Aiden to be like Aiden. I just want Leland to understand me like Aiden does, to love me like he does. I don't say anything because he's never going to be able to do that.

"Are you going to ignore me forever or just the rest of

the night?"

"I don't know. I haven't decided yet."

"Okay. Well, I know you're not mad at me because you would have slashed my tires or set me on fire by now if you were angry."

I push my toe off the dirt and make the tire spin. He comes in and out of view with each rotation. When the momentum slows down I spin in the opposite direction and watch the rope unravel. He clutches the rope to make it stop swinging before he leans down to kiss me. I turn my head to avoid him and scoot around his body to stand behind him. He's still resting his weight on the rope, staring at the ground, looking dejected.

He closes his eyes in frustration. "What's the problem, Tienne?"

"Nothing. I should get back to the party."

He sighs and runs his hands through his hair as if he's exhausted and unsure whether I'm worth the hassle. "All right." He kisses my cheek. "I'm going to head home. Have fun."

I nod, not wanting to prolong an argument that I know full well isn't really about texting during the performance. After he leaves, I walk over to sit next to Sam and Cooper who are the only people still in the hot tub. Sam has his arm stretched along the edge behind Cooper's shoulders and they look lovey-dovey. "Hey super star. Are you having fun?" Cooper asks.

I should be having fun. I would be having the time of my life if I could figure out how to stop loving Aiden and start loving Leland. I sigh and tug at the cuff of my hoodie.

"What's wrong? Are you fighting with Leland?"

"Not fighting. I'm just disappointed that he was late and more focused on his text messages than the play."

"He must feel bad about it," Sam says. "I heard him on the phone postponing his business trip to Asia so he can attend all the other performances."

Oh. That's sweet, but doesn't change how I feel. "It still bothers me. He knows how important opening night was to me."

Sam laughs. "No offense, Tienne, but he works for a multibillion-dollar company on multimillion-dollar contracts. You should probably be happy that he even showed up."

Even though that's true, it feels like he slapped me. "Gee, Sam. Tell me how you really feel."

"Sorry for being blunt, but who cares if he was late and texting? You're overreacting. He likes you a lot and you're being kind of hard on him."

"How do you know how he feels about me?"

"I was in the locker room at the club, and his friends were bugging him because he hasn't sealed the deal with you yet. He told them that it was different with you, and he told them to shut up." Sam shrugs. "I don't know what that means in the straight world, but to me, it seems like he might like you."

That doesn't make me feel any better, and I don't know why. What I do know is that I don't want to think about it anymore tonight. I sigh again and then look at Cooper. "Do you want to catch a ride home with me later?"

Cooper slouches deeper into the water as if he's considering dipping under the surface to avoid having to answer the question. He glances at Sam and Sam smiles before answering for Cooper, "I invited Cooper to stay over."

"Ah."

Cooper checks my expression nervously. I don't know why since he knows I approve. He must just be embarrassed because it's his first time.

"If it's okay with you, I'll drive him home tomorrow," Sam says.

"It's all right with me if it's all right with Cooper."

Cooper blushes.

"Keep it safe, boys." I lean over the edge and kiss Cooper's cheek. "I love you, Lucky Boy."

I'm not in the mood to enjoy the cast party, but if I leave I know I won't go home. I read Aiden's text again. Then head inside to try to have fun.

Chapter Fourteen

Leland has attended every performance since opening night. He sits in the front row and gives me roses after each show. When the curtain goes down on our Saturday matinee, he waits backstage with another bouquet. I join him and he kisses me on the cheek as he hands me the flowers.

"It's really cool how you literally turn into Maria when you're onstage. You're the only one who doesn't seem like you're acting."

"Thank you." I press the petals of the roses to my nose and smile. I have to admit that I like getting flowers. And I like it even more that he didn't give up. "Are your parents still having the dinner party tonight?"

"Yes. Would you like to be my date?"

I pretend that I'm mulling it over. "If I go, it will be strictly to network with influential people."

"I'm pretty influential. Does that mean you and I get to do a little networking?"

"Not likely." I shove his shoulder playfully and he laughs.

He wraps his arms around my waist and sits on the edge of a table to make us closer to the same height. "Did you make Jill work this hard?"

"His name is Gylly, and yes, I did. He's known me since I was born and I made him prove for fifteen years that he was date-worthy before I gave in."

"Jesus. I'll be thirty-five by then."

"Everyone has to prospect, but I might fast-patch you if you can hold your mud."

"Everybody has to what?"

"Sorry. I forgot that you're not a One Percenter."

His expression is strange, and I'm not sure if he's confused by what I said, or if he has something else on his mind. He rubs his temple for a second, then looks at me hesitantly. "My mom is going to be way harder on you than you've been on me. You're probably not going to like her."

"I can handle myself."

He smiles and runs his hand along my neck. "I know you can. That's one of the many things I like about you." He leans in and kisses me in a way that takes my breath away.

Cooper picks out my outfit for the Crofton dinner party—a charcoal-colored pencil skirt, white blouse, and light blue formfitting cardigan that matches my eyes. It's a bit geek for my taste, but he insists that it will make a good impression. Elizabeth rushes in as Cooper is pinning my hair into loose tendrils. She looks excited. I watch in the mirror as she sits on the edge of my bed.

"Okay. Cecile Crofton is a little elitist and, although you are perfect just the way you are and she would be insane not to love you, you might want some ammo. She is very dedicated to her charity work. Ask her about the food bank or the youth-at-risk projects."

Cooper looks at me in the mirror and makes a face because he and I both spent years going to the youth-at-risk programs at our community center. "She'll definitely like the fact that her son is dating a charity case," I say and apply lip gloss.

Elizabeth either doesn't notice or doesn't care that Cooper and I are laughing. "She owns horses, which they keep at their farmhouse and stables. They have a cottage at Lake Tobin. She's a major donor for the performing arts program at her old university, and she used to dance on Broadway. Bryant Crofton owns an international construction business."

"You know a lot about the members. Does that mean the entire club also knows that your sister is a junkie who married an outlaw biker who did time for murder and then got smoked with a taste of his own medicine?"

"Tienne. Don't talk about your parents in such a negative way."

"Why not? It's true."

"I know. It just sounds so bad when you blurt it out. You'll terrify the Croftons if you talk like that."

"They've probably already asked around," I mumble.

She stands and hugs me. "You look beautiful. Just be yourself and they'll love you."

The doorbell rings and Elizabeth bolts out to answer it. Cooper sprays a tiny puff of perfume about three feet away from me, because one of his pet peeves is women who wear too much scent. He slides the chair out for me and offers his elbow to escort me downstairs. Leland stands in the foyer wearing a chocolate-brown suit and light blue shirt that matches my sweater so well you'd think he planned it. He looks insanely nervous and wipes his palms on his trousers before he shakes Blaine's hand. He smiles when he sees me, but his lip is actually trembling a little bit.

I slide up and kiss him. "Please don't be nervous. I've got this."

He smiles and squeezes my hand without his usual confidence. It's weird to see him rattled.

Elizabeth shouts, "Have fun!" as we walk down the path and waves as we drive away. Leland breathes out a short loud burst of air as if he's preparing to go into the ring for ten rounds.

"Seriously, calm down."

He presses his lips together and nods. "Okay. I'm good now."

I roll my eyes because he is so obviously not calmer. Gylly's dad is the international president of an outlaw motorcycle club. If I'm not nervous around him, I doubt I'll be nervous around two well-mannered socialites. Leland, on the other hand, looks like he's going to pass out. Maybe he's having second thoughts about bringing trash home.

He parks in his parents' driveway. I've only ever been to his apartment, so I take a good look at the family house. It's really big, but kind of cookie-cutter boring, like something you would see in a home and garden magazine. He walks around to my side to open the passenger door. I squeeze his hand and remind him that I can handle it. He nods again and leads me toward the front door. It swings open as we step up onto the veranda, and both of his parents appear in the doorway, smiling at us. His dad is tall and thin. He's wearing khaki pants and a pink checked shirt. His mom is wearing a beige dress with a pearl necklace and beige pumps. Her hair is dark and wavy like Leland's. They look like the middle-aged models in a department store catalog.

"Mom. Dad. I'd like to introduce you to Tienne Desrochers. Tienne, this is my mom, Cecile, and my dad, Bryant."

His mom steps toward me and air kisses my cheek. His dad shakes my hand with authority. I smile at Leland and make one of Elizabeth's happy chipmunk faces to encourage him to relax. His shoulders drop a little bit and he rests his hand on my lower back to lead me into the formal living room. Cassidy just asked me to order the same two-hundred-dollar-a-yard Steelcut Trio couch fabric for a client. It feels luxurious to the touch, but I would have a panic attack every time someone went near it with a glass of wine if it were in my house. Mrs. Crofton introduces me as Leland's girlfriend to the other guests. It sounds strange, but the way the people smile at me when they hear it makes me feel good.

After mingling for a while, Leland hands me a glass of wine. He downs his own in two gulps and refills it. After most of the guests step out onto the veranda, his mom walks over to where we're standing near the fireplace and lays her hand on Leland's arm. "Slow down, dear."

He doesn't appear to appreciate her telling him what to do and, in an act of defiance, he takes a very slow sip.

"You have a lovely home," I say and flash a Cara-type smile as if I didn't notice their exchange.

"Thank you, Tienne. Perhaps Leland will give you a tour after dinner."

"I enjoyed talking with your friend Catherine. She attended the school in New York that I would like to go to."

She smiles. "Oh, Leland said you were an interior designer. I didn't realize you were involved in the arts."

Leland gets tense and says, "She played Maria in the production of *West Side Story*. She wants to attend the Academy. I told you that."

"Of course. I remember now. Have you auditioned for the school yet?"

"I'm planning on it. The next round of auditions will be next month."

"Oh, that's wonderful. I'm glad you're planning to pursue something that you're passionate about. Leland was always such a good student, but he wasn't motivated to pursue post-secondary studies. He just didn't apply himself."

Mr. Crofton wanders over and stands next to her. He notices the way Leland is glaring at his mom with contempt but, instead of saying anything, he tips his glass back to take a swig of booze.

"I would love to hear about the time you spent on Broadway," I say to break the tension.

Her eyes sparkle a little and she chuckles slightly. "Oh, it lasted less than a year and it was a very long time ago. I barely remember it." Her hand rests on my arm momentarily. "Interior design is probably a better choice long-term, but good for you for following your dreams."

Leland's hand tightens around mine as if he knows that her comment made my blood pressure go up.

"What does your father do?" Mr. Crofton asks, and the ice cubes in his highball clink together as he finishes off the drink.

"My father passed away a few months ago."

Leland shoots a vicious look at his dad as if they had perhaps agreed not to talk about that topic, but his dad broke the promise. "Oh, that's terrible," his mom gasps. "I'm so sorry to hear that."

"What did he do for a living?" his father presses.

"He was in charge of manufacturing and distribution for an international organization."

"Which organization?"

I might as well be honest. It's not like he's going to have a clue what an outlaw motorcycle club is. "It was an OMC. Have you heard of those?"

His eyebrows draw together as if he is debating whether he should lie and say that he has heard of it to avoid looking uninformed, or fess up that he has no clue. "No. I can't say that I have."

Leland coughs as if he's trying to hide a snicker. The wine has relaxed him, hopefully not too much.

Mr. Crofton notices Leland's reaction, but stays focused on me. "How did your dad die, if you don't mind me asking?"

"It was actually a tragic workplace accident. The police are still investigating and charges may be laid. My brother and I moved in with my aunt and uncle after his death."

"Where is your mother?" Mrs. Crofton asks.

"My mother suffers from a debilitating disease, so my aunt and uncle have been kind enough to let us live with them while she seeks treatment." Using a throat breathing trick I learned from my junior high drama teacher, I make my eyes water. Imagining Aiden hurt in a motorcycle accident was the tragic thought that I always used for stage cries. It still works. They stop asking questions.

His mom's expression softens. "Oh, sweetheart, we didn't mean to upset you. I'm sure dinner is ready." She moves to invite Mr. Crofton and the other guests into the dining room. Leland offers his hand and we follow everyone to the table.

They have a maid who is actually dressed in a gray uniform dress. I feel uncomfortable letting her serve me without tipping in return. Leland holds my knee under the table and every time his mom says something critical about him, his grip tightens. Her compliments are backhanded insults and I can see why it irritates him. His dad just seems like he wishes he were somewhere else. I make small talk with the other guests for a while, then I ask Mr. Crofton some questions about his company. He's brief with his answers and the conversation doesn't go anywhere. I give up trying to be formal and instead ask him what I know gets the majority of the male species talking, "So, Mr. Crofton, are you a football fan?"

He nods. "I follow the Packers."

I groan and make a you-gotta-be-kidding-me face.

"Why? Who's your team?"

"The Steelers are pretty much members of my family, so don't even try to badmouth them."

"Well, then I guess I can't say anything about them at all, because the only thing that can be said is bad."

"Oh, no you didn't. Them's fighting words."

Mr. Crofton, Leland, and the two other men at the table laugh. Mrs. Crofton looks uncomfortable like a kid who doesn't fit in with the cool kids.

"Watch it, Dad. She's tiny but she's feisty."

"She's going to have to be tough if she's going to go around cheering for the Steelers over the Packers."

"Twenty bucks on the Steelers to win the Super Bowl next year," I challenge him.

"Ah, come on. That's a gimmie. I tell you what, if the Steelers make the playoffs, I'll pay your tuition at the performing arts school of your choice."

"What?" He must realize it costs over thirty thousand dollars a year for three years. Is he for real? People don't seriously say pretentious shit like that, do they? He doesn't even know me. I look at Leland and, from his expression, his dad really did just offer that bet. "Thank you," I manage to say, "but they probably will make the playoffs, so no."

"Take the bet." He winks in a patronizing way.

"I'm not a charity case, Mr. Crofton. When the Steelers make the playoffs you can sponsor a scholarship for a student at James Owens High School."

He pauses for a second, then nods approvingly as if I passed his test. "Deal." He smiles and picks up a fork to break off a piece of the pie the maid placed in front of him.

We finish our dessert and the guests talk about an interesting variety of things ranging from politics to sports cars for about another hour. I still can't get over the fact that his dad offered to pay my tuition. What would he have done if I accepted? It is the most outrageous thing that has ever happened to me, and I've witnessed some outrageous shit in my life.

Leland leans over his shoulder and says to the maid, "Thanks, Vera." He stands and looks at his mom. "Excuse us. I'm going to give Tienne that tour now."

"Okay."

"Thank you, Mrs. Crofton. It was lovely." I stand as he pulls my chair out for me. "Nice meeting you all."

"Break a leg at your audition, Tienne," Mrs. Crofton's friend Catherine says. "I'm looking forward to seeing you on the stage."

"Thank you." Wow. She sounded genuine. I can't believe I've spent my entire life connected to gang members and lowlifes when I could have been hanging out with sophisticated people who can open up doors to New York, or whatever else I might want to do.

Leland smiles in a sexy way and pulls my hand to drag me out of the dining room. He doesn't actually give me a tour, he just takes me straight up to his childhood bedroom and shuts the door. I'm about to wander around to check out his mementos when he abruptly pushes me against the wall and leans his body weight on me. "You were amazing tonight." His breath is warm on my skin and his hands move across my body. My sweater is already on the floor and the buttons on my blouse are undone before I know it. He unzips my skirt and it drops to the floor, then he pushes my blouse over my shoulders and lets it slide down my arms. It floats to the floor as well.

Okay, I'm liking his impulsiveness. It's hot. Maybe if we sleep together, it will take my feelings for him to the next level. "I thought you wanted to prove that you could wait," I whisper in his ear to tease him.

He moves my ring along the chain and drops it so it hangs down my back. Then he kisses my neck. "Do you still want to wait?" He leans down to kiss my collarbone and caresses my breast.

Half of me doesn't want to wait. The other half is worried that sleeping with him isn't going to change how I feel about anything. When I don't answer, he raises his head to search my face.

I close my eyes, trying to convince myself to go for it. He's so cute and so successful. It's a no-brainer. What am I waiting for?

He steps back, sensing I'm not into it. "What's wrong?"

I rest my forehead on his chest. "Your mom was telling everybody that I'm your girlfriend."

"I might have referred to you as that. Is that all right?"

I lift my head to make eye contact. "You probably should have asked me first."

"Would you like to be my girlfriend?"

"That depends. Is there anything about you that I should know before we move to the next step?"

He exhales heavily with a seriousness that actually scares me a little. "There is something I need to tell you."

"Okay."

"I want to be honest because I know how important it is to you, but you're not going to like what I have to say."

"Okay," I say more hesitantly.

"Get dressed. I can't tell you here."

Shit. What could it be? If he already knows for a fact that I'm not going to like it, it must be bad. Maybe I don't want to know.

Chapter Fifteen

Leland and I leave the Croftons' house and drive to a nearby park. He turns the engine off, exhales, and focuses on his hands that are balled into fists and pressing into his thighs. "This is hard. I don't know where to start."

"Whatever it is, I would rather know."

"When I was in my senior year, I got my girlfriend pregnant. We were both wasted one night at a party and didn't use protection. She told me she had a miscarriage, but I thought maybe it was an abortion. Then she moved away a few months later and we lost touch for a long time. The whole thing really screwed me up for a while. That's when I started smoking weed."

I don't know what to say, so I just sit and let it sink in. After a while, I turn in the seat so I can face him. "What was your girlfriend's name?"

"Ruby."

"You said you lost touch for a long time. Does that mean

you talk to her now?"

He presses his lips together as if he doesn't want to say, but doesn't want to lie either. "Yes, but we're just friends now."

I reach my arm over and hold his hand. "Thanks for telling me."

He smiles in relief and his muscles relax. "That's it?"

"What did you expect me to say?"

"I don't know. I thought you would freak out."

"It happened a long time ago, and you told me about it. There's nothing to freak out about."

His sinks deeper into the seat and rests his head back. "That was way easier than I thought it would be."

I lean over and kiss him. "You get rewarded when you're honest."

"Nice." He holds my face and pulls me closer. We make out for a while, but his car is not designed for anything too ambitious. "So, does this mean you're going to let me call you my girlfriend?"

"Yes."

"And you're going to call me your boyfriend?"

I laugh. "I didn't say that. Don't get carried away."

He laughs too. "Do you want to stay over tonight?"

I hold my breath as I decide what I want to say. Finally, I exhale and answer, "Yeah, okay."

His expression reminds me of the look on a marathon runner's face as they cross the finish line after a grueling race. He starts the car and pulls back out onto the street.

I'm not quite ready for what I just agreed to, so to stall, I ask, "Do you mind if we stop at a coffee shop first?"

"No problem."

He parks at the coffee shop near his apartment. Inside,

he orders a double espresso. I order a green tea. As we're waiting for the drinks, the window glass vibrates with a sound I know like my own breathing. Motorcycles pull up in front of the shop. I close my eyes and pray that they are middle-age men out for a ride on their Honda Gold Wings, but there's no mistaking the rumble of a Harley.

I open my eyes and try to send telepathic messages to the barista so she'll hurry up. My mind tricks aren't working—she's going slower. The bell on the door rings and I hear two pairs of boots on the wood floor. Shit.

The barista places my tea on the counter and turns to pull Leland's espresso. I consider running. I swear my back is on fire from familiar stares.

"Is that T Bear?" It's Mickey's voice. Shit. Shit. Shit. "What's with those clothes? Is she playing a sexy secretary in that play?"

Leland and the barista are chatting and laughing about something. Their mouths move, but on mute. The only sound I hear is the thuds of motorcycle boots moving toward me. "Leland," I say. He looks at me and his usual smile disappears at my expression.

"What's wrong?" he asks, concerned. "Are you feeling sick?"

"Go to the car now and, no matter what happens, don't unlock the door." He frowns at the strange request. "Please. Just do it. Quickly."

He glances over my shoulder and his posture stiffens. "No. I'm not leaving you here by yourself," he says in a hush-ed voice.

"They won't hurt me, but they will mess you up."

"I'm not afraid of them."

"You should be. Please go to the car. Trust me."

He inhales and seems torn before he eventually turns and pushes out the exit nearest to us. The metal buckles of their jackets and their wallet chains clunk against the counter where I'm standing. They're on either side of me and the leather creaks as they bend their elbows to lean on the counter. I recognize Aiden's cologne and close my eyes.

"What's up, T Bear?" Mickey asks from behind me.

Still refusing to look at them, I mumble, "Just getting some tea. What's up with you?"

"Hey!" he shouts over to the girl behind the order counter. "We'll have two café lattes."

Her lip curls a little, but she rings in the order. "That will be nine sixty-four."

Mickey turns his back on her to send the message that guys who wear patches on their backs don't pay for shit. There are other people waiting in line and the girl at the counter looks confused whether to wait for him to pay or start the next transaction. She finally shrugs and helps the next person in line. Mickey points at the barista who has just placed Leland's drink on the counter. "You better get that order. Don't make me ask twice."

She studies his stocky build, scruffy beard, and neck tattoos for a second before she quickly starts to make their drinks. I still haven't looked at Aiden. He is standing so close to me that I can feel his breath on my neck. "What are you guys doing in this neighborhood?" I ask while focusing on my shoes.

"This neighborhood is full of pretty rich girls looking to piss off Daddy by dating a thug," Mickey answers.

"Okay, have fun trolling. I gotta go." I grab Leland's drink and turn toward Mickey so I won't have to look at Aiden. Mickey steps to block my way.

"Aren't you going to say hi to Gylly?"

"Hi Gylly." I step sideways, but Mickey blocks me again. I roll my eyes in exasperation. "What do you want?"

"Aren't you going to introduce us to the country club dick?"

"No. Leave him alone."

Aiden moves to stand next to me. He runs his finger along my necklace and pulls it up until he's holding my engagement ring between his fingers. He leans in and whispers in my ear, "Does he let you wear this when he fucks you?"

I turn to glare at him. Oh my God, he's gorgeous. I shouldn't have looked. I knew seeing me with Leland would be a trigger for him. This is more than anger. He's seething. My throat closes and I have to swallow to say, "Mickey, could you give us a minute?"

"Gylly's going to tell me everything you say anyway."

I shoot Mickey an evil stare and say, "Despite how much you may want to be a part of this relationship, you're not."

"Neither is Gylly." He laughs his high-pitched giggle. People assume he's nicknamed Mickey because he drinks a lot, but it's because he sounds like the cartoon character when he laughs. Aiden punches him in the ribs really hard. It had to hurt because Aiden is wearing chunky rings on all his fingers. Mickey doesn't flinch, but he does make an involuntary gasp. "Too soon to joke? All right, I'll give you two lovebirds a little privacy." He grabs the two coffees then walks up to a woman who is sitting by herself at a table. He takes the date square that she has already bitten into and stuffs it in his mouth. "Whatcha reading?" he spits crumbs as he asks her.

She stares at him, too stunned to answer.

He tips the book forward. "*Attracting Love Into Your Life*." He snorts. "Don't waste your time on love, honey. If you want to go for a ride, I'll be outside." He looks back at us with a sleazy grin and laughs his Mickey giggle. "Afterward I'll take you for a ride on my bike too."

She clutches the book against her chest as if it will defend her. Mickey giggles again then walks out the front door.

"He better not go near Leland or I'll have him arrested."

Aiden ignores me and goes to the register to hand the girl twenty bucks. "For the drinks, and can you get that lady another dessert, please? Keep the change." He turns back toward me and creases form between his eyebrows before he asks, "So, he doesn't care that you wear the ring?"

"First of all, I don't get fucked because I'm not a whore. Second, the details of how I may or may not make love to someone fall under the category of none of your business."

The anger disappears from the surface of his expression and reveals the pain underneath that I already knew was there. "I miss you, Ti."

Shit. I can't keep pretending to be angry if he doesn't. I stare down at the cups I'm holding and whisper, "I miss you, too. Every single time my heart beats." I turn to walk away and he grabs my elbow.

"Then why are you doing this?"

I jut my chin in Mickey's direction. "Do you really need to ask? Let go of my arm before someone calls the cops."

His hand drops away from me, and I push out the door.

Mickey is leaning his butt against the hood of Leland's car. "You're having an affair with a pussy. He won't even roll down the window."

"He's just being a good prospect. I told him to stay in

the car and he's following orders." I open the passenger door and pass the drinks in to Leland. He seems concerned that Mickey hasn't left, and I don't want him to say or do anything, so I assure him, "Everything's fine."

Mickey moves and rests his arms on the window frame of my open door. "That's a great idea. I'm going to make chicks prospect to be my old lady."

I tap my palm against his cheek. "The only problem with that is nobody wants to be your old lady bad enough to prospect for it."

"Woman, please," he scoffs. "I've got assets."

"Yeah? Like what?"

"I'm hung like a motherfucking horse." He karate chops his leg down near his knee to indicate his alleged endowment.

I laugh. "So, that time I accidentally walked into the bathroom when you were stepping out of the shower, you were just really cold or something?"

"Ha-ha. You know you liked what you saw."

"Hardly," I tease.

The sound of his giggle brings back fun memories. I've missed him. His stupid jokes, his atrocious cooking, the portrait sketches he was always working on, and our secret discussions about the TV show *So You Think You Can Dance*. He never missed an episode, but he could never in a million years admit that to anyone in the club. Most of all, I miss his willingness to jump in front of a truck for anyone connected to the Noir et Bleu, including me. He was a good friend.

"Tienne," Leland says. "We should get going."

"Okay."

"Hey." Mickey lifts the bottom hem of his shirt and wipes my upper lip with it. "Your nose is bleeding."

I jerk my head back. "Gross. Your shirt is probably filthy."

"No, it's not. I just took it out of the dryer."

"Well, now it has blood on it."

"It's okay. It looks better that way."

I shake my head. "You sound like my dad."

"Why is your nose bleeding? Does this piece-of-shit country club prick hit you?"

"No." I glance through the coffee shop window. Aiden is sitting at a table looking pissed. I know he's waiting until we leave so he won't be tempted to confront Leland. "I gotta go, Mickey."

He looks at Aiden, too, and lowers his voice. "He's dying on the inside. You know that, right?"

"Take care of him for me." I slide into the car, and Mickey closes the door, then grabs the drinks off the hood and walks over to his bike.

Leland reaches over and places his hand on mine. "Are you okay?"

"Sure."

"Your hand is shaking."

I glance at Gylly. He looks angry and sad, as if he's imagining what Leland and I will be doing later. The only way I could feel guiltier is if I had literally stabbed a knife in his back and walked away. "Actually, I'm not feeling that well and my nose is bleeding. I should probably get some rest. Do you mind just taking me home?"

Leland eyes Mickey and then Aiden. I know he wants to do something to assert himself as my boyfriend, but that would be idiotic. Fortunately, he has the maturity to let the fact that I'm with him speak for itself. He starts the engine and drives me home.

Chapter Sixteen

It's been a week since we ran into Aiden and Mickey at the coffee shop and I'm still not exactly over it. I'm trying to forget about it. Leland and I are at a corporate party for his dad's company tonight. It's at a posh hotel downtown, the kind of place that my dad would have been asked to leave, but I actually feel like I fit in. When I'm with Leland, everyone assumes my family is like his family and treat me as if I belong.

"This steak is so tender I barely need to chew." I look at Leland and ask, "How's the lobster?"

"Pretty good." He hands me another glass of champagne. "Are you having an okay time?"

I smile, hesitant to admit it. "Yes. I like being your girlfriend."

He leans over and kisses my neck. His mom walks by our table and seems less than impressed, so I push Leland away. After dessert, I work the room with him. The older

ladies gush about how adorable we are together. The young-
er girls, although they seem envious, respect me. Being with
Leland is definitely a status thing in this crowd. I'm hoping
Mrs. Crofton notices that everyone else is being nice to me.

"Leland." A heavy, balding man in a tuxedo slaps him on
the back. "Who's this pretty little lady?"

"Tienne, this is Mark Fleming. He's Crofton Construction's marketing manager."

Mark smiles and glances down at my chest. "Nice to
meet you."

"Excuse me for a minute," Leland says. "I need to use
the men's room. I'll be right back."

Mark toasts his glass and watches Leland walk away,
then hones in on me. "You should definitely come down to
my place in Cabo next month. You look like you would be
fun to party with."

"Do I?" What an asshole. "Did you miss the part about
me being with Leland?"

He chuckles with contempt. "Little boss-boy doesn't
have a place in Cabo." His gaze wanders creepily over my
body. "And he won't keep a girl like you around for long."

So much for fitting in. A heat builds in my body that is
equally fueled by embarrassment and rage. I shake my head
and eye all the other people in the room. Out of every woman here, this piece of shit decides that I'm the easiest one. I
was obviously kidding myself when I thought I was starting
to blend, or that they were staring out of envy. "You want to
know something interesting, Mark?"

He lifts his eyebrows eagerly and checks out my cleavage
again.

"I was talking to your wife, Alice, earlier and it came up

that I'm the same age as your daughter." I wrinkle my nose in an overly cutesy way. "Isn't that a coincidence?"

He backs off a step and sips his drink. At least his eyes are above my collarbone. "You don't look that young."

"Maybe not, but you do look exactly like all my friends' pervert dads."

Leland returns. Mark glances at him, not even trying to hide his disdain, then turns and walks over to the bar.

"Hey, are you okay?" Leland ask me.

"Can we go?"

He looks over in Mark's direction, confused, then back at me. "Yeah, sure."

When Leland is placing my coat over my shoulders, his mom smiles, then walks away. Does that mean I did okay or she's just glad to see me leave?

Once we are in the car Leland says, "You did a great job tonight. But what happened with Mark?"

No point trying to pretend it didn't happen. It's going to keep happening. He might as well know why I wanted to leave and why I don't want to go to anything like that ever again. "He asked me to go to Cabo with him. He said I looked like a girl who likes to party, and that you wouldn't keep a girl like me around for long."

The tendons in his neck tighten. "He's fired."

"No. That's not my point. I don't care that he's sleazy. I care that he could tell that I don't belong there. Obviously who I really am is not good enough and, even when I'm acting, people can see through it to the truth."

"Tienne, he's just a creep." His foot presses heavily on the accelerator and his knuckles turn white on the steering wheel. "I'm sure he says things like that to girls whose dads own oil companies and airlines too."

"He thought I was cheap and easy."

"No he didn't. He targeted you because he's still bitter that my dad promoted me over him. He hoped you were easy so he could get back at me." We stop at a red light. He reaches over and lifts my chin with his finger until I'm facing him. "You are definitely not easy."

I smile because that's an understatement in his case, but it doesn't make me feel better. "Why *would* you keep a girl like me around?"

"Because you're beautiful and smart and so cool. The fact that you are also insanely sexy is just the icing on the cake. I'd like to keep you around for as long as possible, and I don't want you to be anything other than who you are."

That causes a flutter in my stomach. I have to admit he does have a charming way of saying the right things to make me feel better about myself. And when I feel confident, I really want to be a part of his world. "So, you're saying you like me?" I remove my shoes as the light turns green.

"Yeah." His hand rests on my knee.

"What do you like the most?"

His laugh is sexy as his palm slides up my thigh. "Probably the fact that you could kick my ass if you wanted to."

"Would you really fire him?"

"Yeah."

"Because you're the boss?"

"Yeah." He grins, then shoots me a sideways glance. "Do you like that?"

"Yeah, it's sexy."

He chuckles. "So, can we take this relationship to the next level yet?"

Um. Yes? I think so? I want to. I'm terrified to.

He senses the shift in my mood and gives me some space. We drive the rest of the way to Elizabeth and Blaine's in silence. He parks next to the curb and turns the engine off. I wring my hands for a long time before making eye contact with him. "Can you promise that you won't ever lie to me?"

After a hesitation he says, "Tienne, I promise."

"And promise that you will be there for me when it really matters."

"I will." His phone rings and he moves abruptly to get to it. It's in his jacket, which is in the back seat. "Sorry." He pulls it out of his inside breast pocket and turns it off. Then he reaches in the back pocket of his pants. He produces a different phone and turns it off too. I watch him as he puts the phone back in his pocket. He turns to face me and reaches his arm over to try to hold my hand, but I cross my arms. He glances at my face then rubs his palms on his thighs. "Sorry. I forgot to turn them off."

"You have two phones?"

"Yeah, for work." He avoids making eye contact with me and runs his hand through his hair. My head is telling me I'm paranoid. My gut is telling me that I know exactly what's going on.

I didn't spend eighteen years in an outlaw family and not learn a thing or two about liars and criminals. Maybe I don't know which fork to use at a fancy dinner, but I know this, and my decision is easy. "We're over," I say and reach for the door handle. "Don't call me."

"What? Why?" He grabs my wrist to prevent me from getting out of the car.

"You know why."

"Because I forgot to turn my phone off?"

How dare he act all innocent? "I'm not stupid. I know what kind of person needs two phones for work."

"Lots of people have work phones."

"I've seen you take Crofton Construction work calls on the phone I call you on. What type of work do you do from the other phone?"

His eyes remain locked on mine, but he doesn't say anything. He knows he's busted.

"How long have you been dealing?" I demand.

He releases my wrist and rubs his temples as if he has a headache. "I did it for a few years. I only sold to my friends, and the guy who grows it is someone I went to school with, but I quit."

Really? You think I'm stupid? "Why do you still have two phones if you quit?"

"I don't. There have been a few things that I needed to take care of to leave it completely in the past."

Exactly. It never goes away. You can try to walk away from it, but it follows you wherever you go. "Do you still use?"

"No."

He sounds genuine, but it doesn't really make a difference. My dad never used either, and it still killed him. "Why would you sell drugs? It's not like you need the money."

Beads of sweat have formed at his temples and his knee is bouncing. "It wasn't for the money. I was basically just the middleman who brought supply and demand together."

"Yeah, that's what my dad did for a living, too. He got a bullet in the head for being the middleman." I open the door and get out.

"Tienne."

"Do I have a big fucking sign on my back that says if you're a douchebag who does illegal things for a living I'll fall for you? I don't want that shit in my life anymore." I slam the door and run up the path. He catches up to me as I reach the porch. I yank my arm out of his grasp. "I was really hoping I would meet a nice guy who wasn't messed up in illegal stuff. I wanted a fresh start to live a life that was different from the one I was already living. I don't want to judge you, because obviously I've also done things in my past that I'm not very proud of. I just don't want to repeat the same old patterns and end up back where I started. I want to be proud of who I am for once. Having a druggie boyfriend is not something I would be proud of. Plus, you *lied* about it."

"I quit, Tienne. You're not the only one who has a U-Haul of shit that needs to be left in the past. I want to be proud of myself again, too."

He means it. I can tell by the conviction in his voice. I just don't know if I want to be a part of it. I sigh and blink back tears.

He steps forward and hugs me. "There was nothing to lie about because there was nothing to tell you. I quit. I swear to God."

I don't know what to do. Maybe I'm overreacting. It's only pot. Right? He quit. He has given me the benefit of the doubt and overlooked all my flaws. It would only be fair if I did the same in return. I guess in some ways the fact that he's made mistakes puts us on a more level field. Eventually, I sink in to the hug and his arms tighten around me.

"I quit," he whispers as he cups my chin and lifts my face so I'll look at him. We stand that way for a long time and he can obviously tell that I'm softening because he moves in to touch his lips to mine. Cooper walks up the sidewalk and slows, looking wary and protective at the same time. "Is everything okay?"

Leland steps back and squeezes my hand. "*Are* we okay?"

Cooper glances back and forth between us before positioning himself next to me in solidarity, even though he doesn't know what the issue is.

"You swear you quit?" I ask Leland.

"I swear." He holds my gaze as he says it.

It would be completely hypocritical of me to not give him the chance to leave his old life in the past and start fresh. I'm not perfect, he's not perfect, and we both want to leave our shit behind us. That's something he and I have in common, the one thing that Aiden and I never did. "All right. We're good as long as you're telling the truth. If I find out you're lying, I'm gone."

Relieved, he kisses me on the cheek, then walks back toward the car.

Cooper steps up onto the stair next to me and drapes his arm over my shoulder as we watch Leland leave. "What was that all about?"

"Hopefully nothing."

Before I go inside, I look both ways down the street, and realize I'm searching for a motorcycle that isn't there.

Chapter Seventeen

Leland had to go out of town for his postponed business trip, so tonight I'm having a girls' night with Cara, Reese, and Haley. The plan is to go out for dinner and bowling with some friends of the college guy Reese is dating. I dress in jeans and a cute low-cut empire waist blouse and pull my hair back in a high ponytail. I look young, but I don't care.

When I walk past Cooper's room, I notice that he's curled up on his bed in the dark. I push the door more open and tiptoe in to touch his forehead with the back of my hand. He stirs and looks up at me. "Are you sick, Lucky Boy?"

"No."

I sit on the edge of his mattress and rub his back. "What's wrong?"

"Sam and I had a stupid fight."

"Over what?"

"We went to a party last night and there was a guy who was being nice to me. Sam started acting like a dick. I told him he had nothing to worry about, but he got all insecure and jealous. I didn't want to be around the drama, so I left, and he hasn't called me since."

"Have you called him?"

"No. He's the one who needs to apologize."

"Aw. Your first lovers' spat. It's so cute."

"Yeah, adorable," he moans, then rolls onto his back and stares at the ceiling. "Is this how you felt every time you fought with Gylly?"

"Yeah, and we fought a lot. Does Sam have anything to worry about?"

Cooper glances at me, then closes his eyes as if maybe there is a valid reason for Sam's jealousy. "No. I mean, I don't know. I'm sixteen. I want to be able to meet people and talk to them at least."

"Do you want your relationship with Sam to end?"

"No."

"Okay, here's what you do—text him to tell him you miss him and then wait. He will either text you back or come over. If he doesn't do anything, he's not worth getting upset over."

"Okay, thanks."

I brush back his hair and offer, "Do you want me to stay home?"

"No. I'm fine."

"Leland left his car here when I drove him to the airport. If you decide to go by Sam's I'm sure he won't mind if you borrow it. The keys are on the kitchen counter." I kiss his cheek and stand to leave.

"Hey, Ti. How do you know if you're in love?" He sits up and watches me intently, waiting for me to enlighten him.

"If you have to ask then you aren't."

"What does it feel like?"

I'm not the best person to sell him on the benefits of love, since loving someone as much as I love Aiden and having it not work out is not a pain I would wish on anyone, especially not Cooper. "When you love someone it feels like their blood runs through your veins, their breath fills your lungs, their heart makes yours beat, and without them everything stops."

"Fuck. That sounds tragic."

Tell me about it. "It is." I bend to kiss him again, this time on the forehead. "But it's worth it. Call if you need me," I say before I leave.

As I walk out to the Mercedes, I open the picture of Aiden that's on my phone. The way he is smiling at me in the photo is love and, yes, it is tragic.

By the time I arrive at Cara's house, she has already made a jug of margaritas for us, but she's drinking club soda and cranberry since she's going to drive. She hands me a strong margarita and asks, "How are things going with Leland?"

I chug the drink. "Um, good."

"Have you slept together yet?"

"We, um—" I hold my glass out and Reese tops me up. "We're taking it slow in that department."

"Why? Aren't you into him?"

Wow. I didn't realize girls' night was code for put Tienne on the spot. "I am. He's cute and he's good for me. I just don't want to rush into anything."

"He must really like you if he has hung around this long without getting any action," Haley says.

Cara leans her elbows on the counter next to me. "He

won't wait forever."

Reese laughs in a you-got-that-right way. "You don't need to wait to be in love—you know that, right?"

That's good, since I can't imagine myself loving anyone other than Aiden. It would be pretty shitty if love was a non-negotiable prerequisite and I never got to have sex again. "I'm not waiting for, uh, that. I don't know. Who knows what love is anyway?"

"Do you see yourself with him in the long-term?" Cara asks.

I spin my glass around on the table and watch the slushy drink swirl up until it nearly spills over the rim. "He's a good catch, right?"

They all nod and focus on me, waiting for an answer to Cara's question.

I shrug, then down the rest of the margarita. The hot seat has become unbearably uncomfortable and, if the liquor kicks in, the topic of Leland is going to take a sharp detour and become about Aiden. We need a change of scenery, quick, before my resolve to keep my mouth shut falters. "Let's go."

When we arrive at the restaurant, the college guys we're meeting are already sitting at a booth. Reese slides in next to a guy who is built lean like a soccer player. He has straight blond hair and a slightly crooked nose that makes him look sexy. Haley sits beside a bulkier, body builder-type guy who has skin that reminds me of milk chocolate. Cara and I sit beside each other next to two other guys. One is handsome like a model, and his arrogant attitude confirms he knows it. The other guy is a little bit chubby with a farm boy wholesomeness and his cheeks turn rosy when we are introduced.

His name is Paul and I like him instantly.

My phone buzzes with a text. It's from Leland: *I miss you. Are you having fun with the girls?*

"Boyfriend?" Paul asks me.

"Sort of." I put my phone away. "How about you? Do you have a girlfriend?"

"Yeah, she's back in my hometown."

"What's her name?"

"Jill."

"No shit?" I chuckle. "My boyfriend's name is Gylly," I say without even thinking. Shit. Cara is listening to Reese tell a story, but I can tell from her quick, confused glance that she heard me. I don't even bother to fix the mistake. If she asks, I'll tell her that I'm drunk. I *am* drunk, which is why I said it. I better not talk or text for the rest of the night. The drinks Paul ordered arrive and I pound mine back before the waitress clues in that she should ask me for some ID.

After we eat, we stumble across the street to a bowling alley. Bowling drunk is a gong show. It's fun, but the family in the lane next to us might be wishing we weren't here. My ball lands in their gutter, so I apologize, then sit down and lean on Cara. "I should go for it with Leland, right?"

"Yes. You would be crazy not to."

When it's my turn, I stagger up to the ball machine. The ball slips out of my hands and hits the floor with a loud thud. It rolls backward and ends up in our pile of shoes. "Oops."

"Okay, she's cut off," Reese yells. She wraps her arm around my waist to escort me and prop me on a chair to help me change back into my fancy shoes.

I don't remember the ride home at all, and I only vaguely remember Haley and Reese helping me to the front steps. One of them rings the bell and I rest my forehead on the wall as we wait for the door to open. Uncle Blaine shows up wearing only boxer shorts and looks pretty good for an old dude. He doesn't seem particularly impressed with me, though. Haley apologizes and passes me over to lean on his shoulder.

"Thanks for bringing her home," he tells them, then closes the door.

"Sorry, Uncle Blaine," I say as the foyer spins around us. "I had too many margaritas."

"I see that." He helps me climb the stairs and leads me down the hall to my room. "How about you sleep it off and we'll talk about it in the morning."

"Is Cooper home?"

"I think he's at Sam's."

"Oh, good. Love sucks, but it's worth it. Don't you think?"

"Yeah, it's worth it." He gently places me on my bed and pulls a blanket over my shoulder. "You should go to sleep now."

"Okay. Thanks for being my uncle."

He bends over and kisses my forehead. "Thanks for being my niece."

A horrible screech wakes me like an ax slamming into my skull. The sound comes again, and it takes me a second before I realize that it's Elizabeth screaming. It is the most awful sound I've ever heard. Terror floods me. I jump out of bed, but the room spins and I fall onto my hands and knees. Elizabeth screams again and then starts wailing as if she is being brutally murdered. Still on my knees, I crawl to the door and fumble to turn the knob.

The door swings open. Blaine stands in the hall, his face completely void of color, and his eyes are dark with a pain that I've seen only twice before in my lifetime—once when my dad told me that Aiden's mom had been killed in an accident, and then again when my mom told me that my dad had been murdered. Blaine drops onto his knees beside me and pulls me tight. Each time Elizabeth screams, it feels as if I'm being electrocuted. The dread seeps into my pores and makes my skin turn cold. Uncle Blaine holds my head into his chest and rocks me. I don't even know what's wrong, but I know it's bad, so I start bawling. More electricity shoots across the surface of my skin as I consider the only two possibilities that would make Elizabeth scream like that.

I can't breathe. No. No. No.

"I'm sorry, Tienne," Blaine whispers.

"Is it my mom or Cooper? Just tell me."

"It's Cooper."

"Is he okay?"

"No, sweetie." He chokes on his own emotion and continues to say what I don't want to hear. What I can't hear. He squeezes me tightly. Then everything goes black.

My sheets are soaked with my tears, but I don't have the energy or motivation to move my face. I can hear people coming and going downstairs. My mom slept next to me for a while, but she's not here now. I'm all alone, and it's dark.

The sun angles into my window and the fog in my brain lifts just enough for the agony to inch back in. A wave of nausea lurches through me and I leap up, barely making it to the bathroom in time to puke into the toilet. After another round of retching, I crawl back into bed and drop my cheek back down on the wet sheets. This must be how people feel right before they decide to kill themselves. I never understood before how excruciating hopelessness can be. My phone is ringing, but I don't even look to see who's calling.

The next time I wake, I hear voices outside my bedroom. Blaine whispers, "His body was found at the bottom of a high-rise under construction. The police are concerned that it may be linked to Bert's death, like some sort of turf war payback or something."

My mom responds, but she speaks so softly that I can't make out the words.

A few minutes later, the door opens. Mom kisses me on the forehead and places a glass of water on the bedside table. My eyes are open, but I don't look at her, I don't blink. I just stare at the clothes in my open closet. The mattress shifts as she slides into bed next to me then wraps her arm over my waist.

"What happened to him?" I ask.

She strokes my hair and sighs. "They don't know if he fell or—"

"He didn't jump."

"It might have been retaliation. They don't know."

Who would do that to a kid? I know for a fact that children are off-limits according to the Noir et Bleu creed. Anyone who would kill a sixteen-year-old as innocent as Cooper in retaliation for a drug deal gone bad either disregarded the outlaw laws or isn't a One Percenter. If there really is someone that monstrous in the world, I look forward to the justice that they have coming.

Mom must be able to tell that I'm getting worked up because she whispers, "They're going to take care of it. Don't worry."

"He wanted you to know that he was gay," I say quietly. "He wanted to know that you accepted him for who he really was." I roll over so I can see her face.

"He told me."

I search her haggard face for her reaction. "He did?"

She nods and reaches up to tuck my hair behind my ear. "He told me after we went to see the matinee of your play. You were really good, by the way."

"Oh, I didn't—"

"It's okay, baby. I know why you didn't want me there. I'm not proud of what happened last time. Cooper and I went out for dinner afterward and we ran into Sam. He introduced him as his boyfriend."

"Were you shocked?"

"No, I already suspected that he might be gay."

"Were you disappointed?"

"No. I loved him just the way he was. He was so special." She runs her hand down my arm then holds my hand. "I love you just the way you are, too." Her eyes fill with tears, which is surprising. It has been a very long time since we've talked. It's been even longer since she was sober when we talked. The fact that she's not high right now, even though I'm sure she desperately wants to be, is the most motherly thing that she has done since I was five years old. It makes me feel safe, and I wish she could always be like this. I close my eyes and fall asleep clutching her hand, still feeling the warmth of what she said inside my chest.

It's dark again when I wake up. Mom's gone. Elizabeth and Blaine are outside my door whispering. "Maybe we should invite him to come in. She might respond to him."

"I don't know if it's a good idea," Elizabeth says. "She was trying to stay away from him and she's so vulnerable right now."

"I know, but…" Blaine hesitates before he says, "I feel bad making him sit out there on his bike all night again."

"Let's wait until Leland comes home."

"What's taking him so long to get back?" Blaine sounds frustrated, maybe even angry that Leland is MIA.

"I don't know. I told him what happened and he said he would get on the next available flight."

After they go downstairs, I turn on my lamp and slide out of bed. It takes all my energy, but I crawl to the window and kneel with my cheek resting on the windowsill. Aiden is sitting on his bike in front of the house. He looks up at my window and lifts his hand in a solemn wave that I know doesn't even begin to convey how devastated he feels for me right now. He reaches into his jacket and types on his phone.

My phone buzzes: *Do you want company?*

It breaks my heart, but I can't handle anything right now. Instead of answering, I crawl back, turn off my light, and slip under the covers.

It's raining outside—the drops pelt off the roof. Elizabeth sits on the edge of my bed and brushes my hair. "You have to eat something."

I roll onto my stomach and hug the blankets. She leaves and comes back with a bowl of soup. She places it on my desk, then steps into the hall to open the linen closet. She forces me to drag my ass out of the bed so she can put fresh sheets on it. I sit slumped at my desk staring at the soup until she is finished, then I climb back in and bury my face in the pillow.

"The funeral is the day after tomorrow at one o'clock," she says softly and sits back down on the edge of my mattress. "If you want to say something at the service let me know. It's fine if you don't feel up to it." She rubs my back.

"I want to say something," I mumble into the pillow.

"Okay. The police want to speak to you when you're ready. They're working really hard to figure out what happened."

I don't say anything and I don't move, but rage rips through my body.

"Leland was held up in Hong Kong because there is some sort of storm. All the flights have been grounded. He asked me to tell you that he's incredibly sorry and he'll be home as soon as he can. Cassidy is taking care of every-thing at work for both of us, so don't worry about that. Cara has called a lot, so let me know when you're ready to have visitors."

"Mmm," I groan so she'll know I heard her and hopefully leave me alone.

She leaves and my nose starts to bleed. The stain grows across the fresh sheets.

The sky is dark again. Blaine takes the untouched bowl of soup away after checking on me. He left a folded hand towel next to my pillow, I guess in case my nose starts bleeding again. After the door clicks shut, I turn on my lamp, slide off the bed, and crawl to the window. Aiden is sitting on his bike, but he's reading, so he doesn't notice me. I reach over and grab my phone off the bedside table.

"Chang's. What you want?"

"Hey Chang, it's Tienne."

"Ah. Hi, Ten Ten. Regular?"

"It's for Gylly."

"15 and 36. Chicken and rice. Black bean sauce and broccoli. Those his favorite."

"Can you ask Eddy to deliver those and a coffee or a Red Bull to 1349 West Pendlebury? Gylly's sort of on a stakeout, so he's on his bike in front of that address."

"Okey dokey. You want something?"

"No thanks. I want to pay for it with my credit card, though."

"Hold on. Okay, shoot."

I give him my number and tell him to add a tip for Eddy and then hang up. Aiden notices me sitting at the window and waves. I blow on the window and trace a heart with my finger. He texts to ask if I want company. I don't respond.

Eddy shows up about twenty minutes later and Aiden texts again to thank me. I turn off my light and crawl back into bed.

It's sunny when I wake up. I roll over and check if Cooper brought me a cup of tea yet. My bedside table is empty. It takes a second before I remember why the tea isn't there. It doesn't make me sad. It makes me really mad. I get out of bed and shower. My hair is still wet when I sit down to write a eulogy. Anger bubbles up in my blood, so I pull out my Noir et Bleu tank top. I tuck my dad's switchblade into the back pocket of my cut-off jean shorts then paint my fingernails and toenails black and blue alternating. I line my eyes with heavy black eyeliner and coat on a couple layers of red lipstick. I tuck the eulogy into my front pocket, and the last thing I do is open my jewelry box to find the silver bracelet that Cooper gave me for my sixteenth birthday.

"All right, let's take care of business," I say to myself and leave my room.

Chapter Eighteen

Both sides of my family and their friends file down the aisle of the church in solemn silence. To my left, dark suits, expensive shoes, and conservative dresses. To my right, ripped denim, leather vests, and skanky skirts. Twenty uniformed cops watch from along the back wall with their arms folded across their chests.

My push-up bra is creating way too much cleavage for a real church, but the Noir et Bleu Motorcycle Club tank top is a necessary show of respect. If God is somewhere up there in the rafters, He's probably disappointed with my trashy funeral attire. There's no sign of Him. Maybe He's too scared to be here.

One of my dad's old helmets rests on a chair next to me at the altar. Uncle Ronnie set it there to remind everyone who my father was. As if anyone could forget. My mom is sprawled across the pew in the front row to my right. Her blond hair matted, her makeup smeared, she leans on Uncle

Terry's leg as if she's the one who's dead. It's pathetic. The judgmental whispers from the left side of the church make a tingly feeling creep up my throat. I swallow hard and close my eyes. Too bad that doesn't make the mortification disappear.

The eulogy clenched in my hand is soggy from sweat. I place the curled paper on my lap and wipe my palms on my cut-off jean shorts. Shit. It's too hot in here. If they don't get this over with soon I'm going to pass out and end up a worse mess than my mom.

Leland walks in. Now I can't breathe. The sun silhouettes his face, but the tailored suit and his perfect posture confirm it's him. To avoid eye contact between us, I focus on Auntie Elizabeth sitting in the front pew to my left, as far away from my mom as possible. She's crying into Uncle Blaine's linen handkerchief. He smiles at me and mouths, *Are you doing okay?*

I force myself to nod, even though I'm not doing okay. I stare up at the ceiling to prevent tears from escaping.

The minister sneaks out of a side door and slides onto a wooden bench behind me. My hands shake, partly because his arrival means the service will start soon, and partly because if he sits there during my speech, my ass in my short shorts will be in his direct view the entire time.

Sam sits in the third row sobbing. His parents and sister are several rows behind him, but nobody comforts him. I catch Auntie Elizabeth's attention and point at Sam. She leans back and waves him forward to join them.

The door at the back opens and the Gyllenhalls enter.

Aiden stares at me as he walks down the aisle. My entire body trembles and I can't swallow. The black jeans, motorcycle boots, and white dress shirt under a leather vest are his version of dress clothes, and he's even more striking than I remember. His sleeve cuffs are rolled up and his collar button is undone, which gives me a glimpse of a new tattoo on his neck.

He steps aside to let his dad and uncle file into the reserved pew directly behind my mom. Then he continues toward me. The church appears to spin around him as he walks. The faces and stained glass windows circle in a blur of color as if we're inside a kaleidoscope. He takes the two steps up onto the red-carpeted altar, reaches out, and squeezes my hand tightly. His skin on mine makes the spinning stop. My eyes close as he leans down. "Sorry, Ti," he whispers. His right palm slides to my neck and his lips graze my cheek.

The tears I've been fighting win the battle and drip over my eyelashes.

Before he can turn to go back and sit with his family, I reach for his hand. "Stay, Gylly."

He nods. The only other chair beside the altar is the one my dad's helmet is on, so he leans his back against the wall. Leland is still near the door of the church next to a cop. His eyebrows angle together and he glares at Aiden with contempt. He better not let Aiden see it. Better yet, he should wipe it off his face regardless. What the hell did he expect? He hasn't been here for me. I don't give a shit that there was bad weather, or that he works for a multi-billion dollar company on important international deals. I needed him here. Aiden would have quit his job, stolen a plane, and flew himself through a cyclone to get to my side. Leland let me down, and I don't think I'll be able to forgive him for that.

When the minister stands, one of the cops shuts the double

doors with a loud bang. Uncle Blaine speaks first and talks about things that make my mind wander back to when I was a kid. His voice drones, and more people speak after him, I think. I'm wearing flip-flops, so during the prayers and sermon I stare at my toes. My black nail polish looks ridiculously inappropriate. It doesn't matter. Cooper would have understood that I needed to feel like myself in order to get through this.

"Tienne," the minister's soft voice interrupts my thoughts. With a gesture, he invites me to take my place at the podium. My fingertips dig into the plastic seat of the chair. Maybe if I don't let go, none of this will be happening. Not that freezing time would help, since the worst part has already happened. My heart races and the room suddenly gets stuffier. I absolutely don't want to say good-bye, but I will regret it if I don't take this opportunity to tell everyone what a special person Cooper was. I refuse to cry. Not now. After a stuttered attempt at a breath, I pry my fingers off the chair and stand. My head is light and my mouth feels crammed full of cotton balls, but I force myself to step forward.

Instead of looking at anyone in the congregation, I stare at the wood of the podium and unroll my speech. The minister bends the microphone lower for me. The first thing I see when I look up is the row of cops at the back. They don't invite themselves to all Noir et Bleu funerals, but when it is a suspicious death linked this closely to Randy's family, they do. I can almost feel them tense up, waiting for me to say something that will either be incriminating or incite violence. I push my hair back over my shoulders to show off the motorcycle club support patch. *Breathe.*

Everyone is silently waiting for me, which makes the thuds of my mom sliding off the pew and my uncles moving to prop her back up even more obvious. The silver bracelet Cooper gave me for my birthday slides up my forearm. To ward off tears I bite my lip until I taste blood. I glance at my dad's empty chair then begin reading the eulogy I wrote.

"On Cooper's first day of kindergarten, my dad was in prison and my mom was, well, she was like that." I point at the platinum blond puddle of skin and bones in the front row. People to my left gasp.

"The laundry hadn't been done in weeks, so I had to dress Cooper in a pair of my jeans and roll them up at the bottom. The pockets were embroidered with sparkly butter-flies, but he didn't complain. He didn't ever complain." The tears are winning again, so I pause for a second to look up at the ceiling. "I packed a granola bar that I stole from a friend's house into a brown liquor store bag for Cooper's lunch, and we walked to school holding hands.

"The other kindergarten parents were staring at us as I dropped him off at his classroom door. Cooper's lip quiv-ered, but he didn't cry because my dad always told him that crying was for sissies. While he wasn't looking, I snuck away and ran down the hall to my own classroom, hoping he wouldn't follow me. It was torture to think about how sad he might be that I abandoned him with a bunch of strangers. As the morning passed, my guilt faded because I hadn't heard him crying or anything. But just before recess, my grade two teacher said, 'Tienne, your brother can not stay here.' I looked over my shoulder. Cooper was sitting cross-legged on the floor behind my desk eating the granola bar. He was being as quiet as a mouse."

Auntie Elizabeth smiles wistfully, maybe at the mem-ory of how quiet and gentle Cooper was. Aiden winks to encourage me to keep going, so I wipe my palms on my shorts and remind myself again to breathe.

"I pulled Cooper's hand and dragged him to the back of my classroom. He held out the other half of the granola bar to share with me and asked, 'Please can I stay in grade two with you, Ti?' I said, 'No. Dad's going to whup your butt when he gets home if you don't go back to kindergarten.' Cooper shook his head and whispered, 'I don't care. I want to be with you.' The kids in my class laughed at me and the teacher stood with her hands on her hips, waiting. I made promises. I bribed him. I threatened to take his favorite things away. Nothing worked. Finally, I had to say, 'Cooper, if you don't go back to your classroom, I won't love you anymore.' His big blue eyes filled with tears and his mouth dropped open. His shoulders drooped as he shuffled his little butterfly butt back down the hall toward the kindergarten room. I let him down and I never felt a worse feeling until—"

I pause and press my hands into my eye sockets to force back the tears. *Breathe.*

"I never felt a worse feeling until the morning Uncle Blaine came to my bedroom door and told me that Cooper was dead."

I pause again and clench the podium. Uncle Ronnie's broad shoulders shake because he's crying behind his black wrap-around sunglasses. Other people are sniffling too. *Breathe.*

"Cooper's nickname was Lucky Boy because his heart stopped when he was first born and the doctor was surprised that he survived. Maybe if he hadn't used up all his luck that day, or maybe if I had done a better job taking care of him and keeping him safe—"

My voice cracks, so I stop. Leland's staring right at me,

but his expression is difficult to read. Aiden focuses on his boots to hide the fact that he's choked up. I try to forget the casket with my brother's body in it, the chair that has my dad's helmet on it, and the line of cops. I inhale and stand taller.

"My dad deserved what happened to him, but Cooper was the sweetest person on the planet. He never did a hurtful thing to anyone in his life. He didn't deserve to die."

Sam sobs and hides his face in his hands. I scan the sea of black leather and scruffy hair. Every Noir et Bleu member from my dad's chapter is here. The other one hundred guys are from other chapters all over North America. They didn't know Cooper personally, but my dad was their brother, which makes Cooper and me family. The assurance that they all have my back is exactly what I need right now. My blood rushes through my body and I can taste something metallic on my tongue as I prepare myself for what I'm about to say.

"The person responsible for taking Cooper away from me should know that I bleed black and blue." My hands clench into fists as I swallow back rage. I lift my chin and say, "My name is Tienne 'T Bear' Desrochers. My father was Albert 'Big Bert' Desrochers." I pause and scan each face in the church. "And I am my father's daughter." I roll up the eulogy, then lean into the microphone. "If I were you I would start sleeping with one eye open."

The cops' heads swivel, examining the crowd. The country club side of the church looks nervous and confused. The motorcycle club side looks jacked. I move and stand next to the casket. My uncles, Aiden, his dad, and his uncle—the same six men who carried my father's casket—join me. My mom can't stand, let alone walk, so I follow the casket by myself. Auntie Elizabeth, Uncle Blaine, and Sam step into line behind me.

As I pass Leland at the back of the church, he steps forward to wrap his arm around me, but I whisper, "Don't," and keep walking.

The one side of the parking lot is entirely full of chrome Harley handlebars sparkling in the sunlight. There are about twenty more cops standing in the shade beneath the trees around the perimeter of the property. They're videotaping and taking pictures of everyone. My uncles and the Gyllenhalls slide the casket into the back of the hearse and close the door. It's like déjà vu from six months ago, only this time I want revenge.

I stand by Aiden's bike to avoid well-meaning hugs from anyone. He shakes a few people's hands and then heads over to me. "You did good." He slides his sunglasses and helmet on before he steps over the seat, straddling his long legs on either side. "Put your helmet on, babe."

I reach into the side bag and find my helmet exactly where I left it four months ago. I step over the seat and let my body slowly slide down his back. He reaches his hand behind and runs it along my thigh the way he used to. My dad would have yelled at me for wearing flip-flops on the bike, but whatever. Aiden starts the engine and revs it, which sends vibrations through my body. The rest of the bikers also start their engines and the rumbling is incredibly loud. I almost forgot what it felt like to hear them all at the same time. The sound bounces around inside my ribcage, as familiar as my own heartbeat.

My uncles pull black bandanas up over their noses and wait for the hearse to roll out. Auntie Elizabeth's country club friends hold their purses clutched tightly to their chests, looking terrified. Leland steps right up to Aiden's bike, which he may not realize takes a lot of balls. He exchanges a look with Aiden before he reaches to give me something. He presses a folded piece of paper into my palm and kisses me on the cheek. If he tries to say anything, I don't hear him as Aiden revs the engine and the bike lurches forward, leaving Leland behind.

We pull out behind the hearse, and about one hundred bikers, led by his dad, follow us in a thunderous procession. The wind blows through my hair and the adrenaline rushes through my blood. Once I figure out who killed Cooper, there will be retribution.

Chapter Nineteen

Something licks my face. I open one eye only to have it shut by a big tongue slopping over my eyelid. It tickles. Zeke jumps up on the bed and sprawls his one hundred pounds on top of me. He pants and it looks like he's grinning. Probably because he thinks it's funny that he's got me pinned.

"Hi Zekey, boy. Oh, yes. Hello. Did you miss me? I haven't seen you in a long time. Did you miss me? Yeah. You're a good boy." I pat him under his ears where he likes it. "You're so cute. Oh, big kisses. I missed you too. I missed you so much." He buries his gigantic head in my chest and nuzzles his wiggling body against mine.

"Zeke! Leave her alone. You're bigger than she is," Aiden says. He's seated at his desk and it looks like he was studying from a thick textbook. "Sorry. He's just excited to see you."

"It's okay." I hug Zeke and watch Aiden. He looks sexy in his jeans, black T-shirt, and red bandana tied across his forehead to keep his hair from falling in his eyes.

Not much has changed in his bedroom since I was last in it. His bookshelf is a little fuller. The old sheet that covered his window has been replaced with wood blinds. The closet door isn't hanging off one hinge anymore, and the hole he punched in the drywall is patched, but not painted. The tiny snow globe of kissing penguins that I gave him for Christmas when I was twelve still sits on the shelf with all his sports trophies.

"Were you studying?" I ask.

"Yeah."

"Studying what?"

"Biology and psychology. I have a couple exams on Monday."

"You're going to the university?"

He nods and snaps to get Zeke to lie down. I'm confused. "What do biology and psychology have to do with the Noir et Bleu?"

There is a pause that feels like he's being cautious with his answer before he says, "Nothing."

"I thought your dad wanted you to take business courses at the community college so you could take over the international operations."

"He thinks I am taking business courses."

I frown and sit up, wondering if I heard that right. "But you're not?"

He shakes his head and his stare is so intense it makes my skin tingle.

I don't know what that means, or what anything means right now. I don't even know how I got here. "Uh, I seem to be in your room and I'm only wearing one of your T-shirts. You want to fill me in on what exactly happened last night?"

He smiles in a kind of cocky way. "Don't you remember?"

"I remember going to the cemetery. Uncle Ronnie poured a shot of whiskey on Dad's grave and then on Cooper's." I close my eyes trying to recall the rest. "I think I might have had a few swigs from the bottle."

"Yeah. A few." He leans back and stretches out his legs.

I clutch his pillow to my chest and drop my head to smell it. Part of me wants to know if he's had other girls in his room in the past four months, and part of me doesn't want to know. It would only be fair if he had, but the pillowcase only smells like laundry detergent. The picture of us when we took a road trip to California is still in a frame on the desk. "Did we, uh, you know?"

"Would you be upset if we did?"

"Gylly, I have a boyfriend."

His smile fades away and he abruptly stands.

"What happened last night?" I ask.

"Nothing. Get dressed and I'll take you home." He throws my shorts and tank top on the bed, then disappears into the bathroom across the hall. Zeke stretches out on the wood floor with a loud sigh. I get dressed and sit on the bed to wait for Aiden to come back. A minute later, the bathroom door opens and his footsteps approach. He doesn't step back into the room though; he just holds my old toothbrush out for me. It's still in its pink plastic travel case.

I take the toothbrush and cross the hall into the bathroom. Looking in the mirror, I think about all the other times I've stood in his bathroom and brushed my teeth. I can't tell if it makes me feel happy or sad. After I wash my face and comb my hair, I head back to his room. He's propped against the doorframe. I scoot past him into the room and step into my flip-flops.

"Don't forget your phone."

My phone, keys, and my dad's switchblade are on the bedside table next to the note Leland gave me at the funeral. "Did you read that?"

"No. Let's go."

I lean over to pick up my things, then stop and stare at the wall. Something feels unfinished. When I glance at Aiden, I can tell that he doesn't really want me to leave, no matter what he says, so he must feel it, too. "Gylly, can we talk?"

"Go ahead." He sounds like he's mad, but underneath is a sadness that says he's really upset. My heart feels like it's getting a cramp. I pull him into the room. He acts reluctant, so I tug his hand and guide him to sit on the bed with me. He looks down at our intertwined hands and, after a while, he runs his thumb across my skin the way he used to. I sit cross-legged and face him, but I don't speak. I watch his expression and let my skin remember what it feels like to be touched by him.

"I didn't cheat on you. I would never cheat on you," he finally says.

The guilt of hurting him slams against the wall of emotion that I was already barely strong enough to hold up. If I try to speak, I'll break down. I can't do this right now. "I changed my mind. I don't want to talk about this." I stand and storm toward the door, but Aiden lunges in front of me. Zeke scrambles to his feet to get out of the way as I try to sidestep Aiden.

"Ti, please don't go." He steps forward and wraps his arms around me. "You've known me your entire life. We both know this isn't about Leah."

Don't make me say it. I push his arms off and step backward to lean against the wall. "How can it not be about her? I caught you half-naked with her."

"What's this really about?"

"It's about you fucking your ex-girlfriend right after you gave me an engagement ring."

"I didn't sleep with Leah. She dropped by crying because the guy she was dating beat her up. I cleaned up her cuts and gave her some ice for her shoulder. Then I told Mickey to take care of the guy. That's all that happened. Deep down inside you *know* that I would never cheat on you. What's this really about?"

I slide my back down the wall and sit on the floor beside Zeke. He lifts his head and flops it onto my lap. Aiden sits on the edge of the bed with his elbows resting on his knees. The fact that he sees right through me is exactly why I love him. Right now I wish he were clueless so I could avoid the truth.

"Why did you shut me out, Ti?" His voice cracks a little.

Tears pool up along the rims of my eyes. If I blink, they're going to drip over onto my cheek. I stare at the floor for as long as I can. Eventually, the blink comes and so do the tears.

"Ti, talk to me. I've been waiting four months for you to tell me what happened. What did I do wrong?"

I bury my face in my hands. Zeke barks as if he's trying to let Aiden know that I'm upset. "I'm sorry, Gylly." When I look up, he's staring at me. There's a deep crease between his eyebrows as if he wishes he knew how to make everything better. My heart twists with the shame of treating him like shit. Zeke whimpers and licks my leg.

"Is it because you wanted to go out with that country

club poser?"

"No."

Aiden's forearms tense as he cracks his knuckles. His head snaps up, and he glares at me accusingly. "You didn't waste any time moving on with that lying piece of shit." Immediately, he winces, maybe because he can't handle the image of me being with another guy, or maybe because he wishes he hadn't used such a harsh tone.

Didn't waste any time? Lying piece of shit? I gently place Zeke's head on the floor and stand up. "What exactly are you implying?"

"Let's just say I know everything about that rich prick, and he's really lucky I didn't mess him up."

I prop my hands on my hips and cock my head to the side. "No, *you're* really lucky that you didn't mess him up. You don't own me. How do you know everything about him? Were you following me?"

"No."

"Who was?"

"It doesn't matter." He stands and takes a step toward the door before I dig my fingertips into his biceps to stop him.

"I don't appreciate being stalked."

He presses his finger to his lips to get me to be quiet, and then leans over to shut the door. "It wasn't to stalk you. Forget it. Forget I said anything."

"If it wasn't so you could keep tabs on me, why did you have me followed?"

He glances down at me for only a brief moment, then turns away to avoid the question. The muscle in his jaw twitches, and he moves as if he's going to leave, so I dig my fingers in even harder. He could easily go if he wanted to, but he doesn't. "Ti, I love you. I have always loved you and I wish I could tell you everything, but I can't. There are a lot of things you don't know."

"If it's about me, I have a right to know."

"It's complicated."

"Uncomplicate it."

"My dad thinks you might be in danger," he whispers.

I blink. Like getting pushed off a building type of danger? My mind spins at the implications of that. "Why? Is it related to my dad?"

There is a knock at Aiden's door, so he leans over to open it a crack and I hear Randy say, "Breakfast's ready. Is T Bear still with you?"

"Yeah. We'll be right out."

"Tell her I made all her favorites."

"Thanks, Dad." He closes the door, turns to face me, and lowers his voice, "Can we talk about this later when my dad's not around?"

I bite my bottom lip as I contemplate whether to let it go for now or insist that he tell me. He wraps his hands around my upper arms and pushes me up against the wall. His thumb grazes my bottom lip to free it from the grips of my teeth. "You know it drives me crazy when you do that."

I swallow hard, cursing my mouth for having a sly mind of its own. "What kind of danger does your dad think I'm in?"

His palms slide down to my wrists and then back up the sides of my body. "The kind that I can protect you from, so you don't need to worry."

I angle my head and his breath tickles my exposed neck.

It feels like it used to—safe and right. I want to tear his shirt off. I want him to lift me up and walk me over to the bed. I want to remember how good it feels to be that close to him. My skin shivers thinking about it and my breathing deepens. Out of habit I run my hand up his abs and over the muscles in his chest and then grab his neck. That's when I notice his new IIWII tattoo in more detail. I know it stands for "It is what it is" because Uncle Len has the same one. It looks cool, but it brings me back to reality. They are gang members and they are the reason I'm not safe in the first place.

"I have a boyfriend. Did you forget?" I push my palms into his chest.

He shoves me back against the wall and leans in to speak into my ear, "You have a fiancé. Did you forget?"

I punch him in the stomach and he steps back. "The engagement kind of became null and void when you banged someone else."

"If you believe that," he challenges, "why do you still wear the ring on your necklace?"

I reach down and hold my hand over my chest where the ring is resting on the curve of my cleavage. "It's complicated."

"Uncomplicate it."

I inhale and lock eyes with him. Once I peel away every layer that confuses my life, or doesn't matter, or can't be changed, there is only one constant, one unwavering common denominator. It's simple. "I still love you."

Chapter Twenty

Aiden smiles with relief when I say that I still love him. He tries to reach for my waist to hug me, but I know I'm going to end up kissing him if I let him, so I slap his hands away and fling his bedroom door open. He and Zeke follow me down the hall toward the kitchen. When I sneak a glance over my shoulder, he's still grinning. God, I've missed him so much—the way he makes me laugh, calls me on my bullshit, and would literally die for me. I have complete faith that he would be here for me, always. It really is simple. I love him, I have always loved him, and I can't imagine not loving him. The question is, do I want that?

When he sees that he's got me contemplating things, he slaps my ass.

"Hey." I scoot away from him and jog the rest of the way into the kitchen. His dad is standing in front of the stove flipping French toast on a griddle. I know better than to come out and ask why he thinks I'm in danger, since he doesn't talk business at the house. There is a bowl of fruit salad on the table and scrambled eggs with salsa and avocado sizzling in a frying pan. It smells delicious. Out of habit, I open the fridge to see if there is any orange juice. Not only is there orange juice, it's organic. There are also apples, organic milk, cheese, and a rainbow of vegetables. "Wow, did you guys go on some sort of health kick since I was here last?"

A snort-like laugh comes from the living room. A guy who is at least six-six and three hundred pounds is asleep on the couch. His back faces me, and he's fully clothed with his collection of patches on display. Another guy is laid out spread eagle on the floor as if he passed out and hasn't moved since he fell. He's only wearing jeans and his cut with his bare torso exposed. The club tattoo on his forearm has six skulls above it. My dad's club tattoo had four skulls above it. It also had the letters ANNA above the skulls.

The only person conscious in the living room is a rough looking woman who can't be much older than Aiden. She has bleach-blond hair, two beach balls for a chest, and tattoos on her knuckles. She looks at home in Randy's armchair, which means she's his latest girlfriend, or fuck buddy. He doesn't date women seriously and hasn't since Aiden's mom died, but given the fact that this one looks as if she could easily beat Randy in an arm wrestle, she might be able to bully herself into the position of Old Lady, at least for a while.

She smiles in a way that makes me feel unwelcome and says, "I wondered why Gylly was all eager to go grocery shopping yesterday." Her voice is scratchy like she's been smoking six packs a day and screaming for the past ten years straight. "I ain't gonna complain if he wants to stock the fridge to impress some skinny chick."

I return a fuck-you smile to make it clear that, despite my four month absence, I was here first. She shrugs in concession and lights a cigarette. That was easy. Randy's definitely not going to keep her around.

I grab the carton of orange juice and bend over to whisper in Aiden's ear as I pour him a glass, "What made you think I would be here for breakfast?"

He lifts his eyebrows in a sexy way, but doesn't say anything. He doesn't need to. That's the whole point. He knew without a doubt that I would end up here and I hadn't even admitted it to myself. I forgot how comforting it feels for him to know my thoughts and feel my feelings.

Randy hacks for a second, then drinks from a bottle of beer to soothe his throat. "T Bear, that's Connie." He waves the spatula in the woman's direction.

She has the nerve to look me up and down, blowing smoke out of the side of her mouth, before she goes back to flipping through a magazine. Randy saw her do it and I can tell that he's not impressed. His jeans are unbuttoned at the waist and he's shirtless. The tattoo of Aiden's mom's name, Isabella, is scripted in an arc across his chest from armpit to armpit. She was killed in a motorcycle accident that was Randy's fault and he doesn't ever talk about her. It happened when Aiden was seven, so I only vaguely remember her. The scar that runs from the inner corner of Randy's eye, across his cheek, and down to just below his ear looks like it's faded a bit. He got that scar in a different motorcycle accident that happened six months before my dad was killed. It was his tenth accident, so Aiden convinced him to start wearing his glasses when he's riding. His goatee is a little longer since I stopped hanging out here but, other than that, everything looks the same.

Eventually, he smiles at me as if he's missed me and turns back toward the stove. He coughs and asks, "How's the head, T Bear? You were hitting Grandpa's sauce pretty hard."

"Not bad. I don't remember anything, though."

"Ah, that's the beauty of Grandpa's sauce." The toaster pops and he reaches for the two slices of bread. "It's nice to have you around again." He pauses after opening the peanut butter jar and rubs tension out of his neck, as if what he's going to say next is difficult. "I just wish it wasn't because of Cooper's funeral."

Oh my God. I've only seen Randy upset twice in my entire life — once when Aiden was in surgery after he crashed his bike, and once when the dog they had before Zeke died of cancer. Randy doesn't show emotion like a normal person, but I know him well enough to recognize it when I see it. If Randy can't even keep it together, how will I ever be able to?

"I need air," I say, gasping as I rush to the back door.

Aiden lunges to catch up and leads me out the screen door onto the back porch where we sit on the top step. He hugs me and runs his hand over my hair. "Is there anything I can do?"

"No." I start bawling. Not unless you can bring Cooper back.

"Maybe if you talk about Cooper you'll feel better."

"I can't talk about him. I don't want it to be real. Nothing can make me feel better."

Aiden tightens his arm around my shoulder and rocks me. He rubs his thumb over the back of my hand and it feels comforting.

I pull my hand away. I don't want to be comforted. "Please, don't be nice to me, Gylly." He frowns, as if I slapped him, and I soften my words. "I mean, thank you for everything, but I can't do this right now."

He nods with the understanding and patience that he has always shown me, and it just makes me feel worse for pushing him away. He rests his elbows on his knees as he stares at the maple tree in the back yard. After a while, he sighs and asks, "Do you remember when we used to climb that tree? It was way smaller then."

"Yeah." I angle my head back to look up at how tall the tree has grown. The first time I ever climbed it, I was about six years old and he said I wouldn't be able to do it, so I proved him wrong. The last time I ever climbed it, I was twelve years old and accidently witnessed him kiss a girl on his back porch. I was completely devastated and refused to talk to him for at least a month. He never found out why. "Do you remember when Cooper and I ran away from home and we sat up there all night?"

He nods as the memory flickers in his expression.

It feels so familiar to be here and, in this exact moment, I can't remember why I ever left. I lean against his shoulder. We sit quietly and I listen to the sound of his breathing. "Gylly."

"Yeah."

"If you knew what happened to Cooper, you would tell me, right?" He sits up a little straighter and the muscles in his arm tense under my cheek. He doesn't answer, so I lift my head to check his expression. "Would you tell me?"

His jaw looks like it was chiseled from stone and the

intensity in his eyes sends a shiver through my body. "If I knew what happened to Cooper I would take care of it."

I rest my head back on his shoulder and reach over to hold his hand. "Thank you."

"You don't need to thank me. I would do anything for you. You know that."

I turn my head and kiss his cheek. "I know, but you'd have to beat me to it."

He knows I'm serious, and my reckless declaration doesn't impress him, but he also looks fairly confident that I would never beat him to it. With the club working on it, I have to admit it's probably true they will get to the guy first. If the chance presents itself, though, I won't hesitate.

"How have you been?" I ask so he'll stop worrying about what kind of stupid trouble my impulsive anger might land me in.

He's quiet for a while. "Do you remember when I tried to break up that fight Mickey was in?"

"The one when you got stabbed?"

"Yeah. Do you remember how much pain I was in from the collapsed lung?"

I nod and cringe from the memory. The night he got stabbed, someone told me he was hurt and, when I got to him, he was writhing in horrific pain. He couldn't breathe and his face had turned blue. I was hysterical. Thinking about it gives me a crushing feeling in my chest.

"When I heard that you slept with that Crofton asshole after only knowing him for a couple weeks, it hurt more than getting stabbed. Only this time the pain hasn't gone away."

What is he talking about? Whoever was tailing me got it all wrong. "I didn't sleep with him."

He frowns and looks directly in my eyes accusingly. "Don't lie."

"It wasn't like that, Gylly."

"I don't believe you."

I shrug, too tired to fight. "You can believe whatever you want. I didn't sleep with him."

"Why not?"

I blink hard and pick at the paint of the porch step. "I knew you didn't cheat on me with Leah."

He exhales, and the relief releases tension from his muscles. "Why did you take off, then?"

How am I supposed to tell him I left because I don't believe he can give me what I want? I don't answer. I refuse to crush him like that.

"Was it the ring?"

The ring. The club. My entire messed up life. Where would I even begin? It takes a long time to work up the courage to say, "I got scared."

"You could have just talked to me about how you were feeling."

No. All that would have done was make it crystal clear that I was unhappy. Nothing else would have changed. He deserves an answer, I know, but it's cruel to twist the knife that I left impaled in his back.

"You didn't need to run away."

"Yeah, I did." I didn't want to have that conversation then and I don't want to have it now.

"Why?"

Because I could already feel the pull of this world sucking me down, enticing me to give up on my dreams, and luring me into a suffocating trap with people the real world despises. "Because I love you so much."

"You're not making any sense."

"I know." I stand and step down into the backyard. "Do you mind taking me home?"

"Stay for breakfast."

"I can't." I can't stay. I can't tell you the truth. I can't do any of this.

"If you don't want the ring, I'll take it back."

I clutch my fingers around it. "I don't want to give it back."

"What the hell, Ti? Just tell me what's going on in your head."

The tears pour down my face again. I have to bend over and prop my hands on my knees to hold myself up. "I can't deal with this right now, okay?"

"No, it's not okay." His voice deepens with frustration. "You say you still love me, you want to keep the ring, you claim that you haven't slept with anyone else, but you don't want to be with me. Just say it. Admit that you're ashamed of me."

I shake my head and close my eyes. I'm not ashamed of him. I'm ashamed of who I was. "Please, don't."

"Tell me why you left."

"No."

He stands and grabs my shoulders firmly, but still in complete control.

"Let go!"

"You can't keep avoiding this. I deserve an answer."

"Leave me alone, Gylly."

"No. Cut the bullshit. Tell me."

My jaw clenches in a last ditch attempt to prevent the

words that will slay him from spewing out, but it's too late. "Fine! You really want to know the truth? I don't want to end up like my fucking mom, okay? I don't want to marry some charming lowlife outlaw when I'm eighteen and watch my future get sucked down the drain. I actually want to know that my husband isn't going to end up facedown in a river somewhere with a bullet in his head. I actually want my kids to see their father once in a while, and it would be really cool if they could look up to him and maybe want to be like him one day instead of hating his fucking guts. I also don't want to take my children to visit their dad in prison or at a gravesite. Most importantly, I don't want my baby girl to have to feel the pain of losing her brother because he was a pawn in a stupid turf war that had nothing to do with him. I don't want that life."

His chest rises and falls with rapid, adrenaline-fueled breaths as the impact of what I've said sinks in. "I'm not your dad, Ti."

"Yeah? You look like him. You talk like him. You act like him."

"You know that's not true. I'm going to school. I don't do drugs. I don't even have a juvie record."

"So what? If it all leads to the same place, six feet under with your cut framed on the wall at the club, what does it matter?"

A Harley engine rumbles down the alley and a second later, Mickey pulls up to the chain link fence. "Gylly! Something's come up. We gotta go."

Aiden reaches for my hand and steps in closely to speak in my ear. "I have to do this."

"Of course you do," I snap.

"This conversation is not over."

I pull away from him. "Apparently it is."

His expression is pained, torn between me, fuming with my arms crossed, and Mickey, revving his bike. Finally he says, "This business is about Cooper. You know I wouldn't leave if it wasn't important. Please be here when I get back." He kisses my cheek, then rushes down the path and hops the fence. He doesn't look again before they take off, maybe because he's afraid that I'm already gone.

Chapter Twenty-One

When I step into the Gyllenhalls' kitchen through the screen door I see Randy, Connie, and the spread eagle guy eating their breakfasts in the living room. The giant who had been sleeping on the couch is now at the kitchen table. The denim jacket under his leather cut reeks of engine oil, gasoline, and exhaust grime. His skin is just as pungent with alcohol, tobacco, and sweat.

He shovels a heaping forkful of scrambled eggs in his mouth and eyes me, wondering why I'm frozen. "What?"

"You smell like my dad."

He laughs and makes a gesture to invite me to sit at the table with him. "Nasty?"

"Yeah. It reminds me of him."

"I knew your daddy," he says as he squirts half a bottle of ketchup on the hash browns. "I met him in prison and we rode together quite a few times after that."

"What's your name?"

"Wing Nut." I nod as I remember some of the stories that included a Wing Nut character. "Bert was a good guy," he says, as if it is indisputable.

I make a snorting sound and roll my eyes in wholehearted disagreement.

Wing Nut snaps his hand up as if he's going to backhand my mouth. It makes me flinch, but then he relaxes and returns to eating. "Don't sass your dead daddy."

They're even more alike than I thought. "He wasn't much of a dad."

"Listen here, I got eight kids spread all across North America and I ain't even met half of them. Your daddy called and checked in on you and your brother every damn night."

"Big deal. When he called, my mom spent the entire time screaming and swearing at him for not being home. They never got around to talking about Cooper and me, and she usually threw the phone against the wall before we had a chance to say hi to him."

"At least he tried." He sits back and pulls a pack of cigarettes out of his jean jacket. "I was with your daddy when he got the call that you'd got yourself into some trouble. He hopped on his bike and drove all night to get home if I remember right."

"Yeah, he came home and whupped my ass. That's real quality parenting." A deep resentment boils inside. I don't know if it's because Wing Nut reminds me so much of my dad, or if it's because I'm too exhausted to keep the bitterness buried anymore, but all the animosity I never felt safe enough to unleash on my dad starts to surface. "Is it chapter seven in the parenting handbook that states that a father should turn his fifteen-year-old daughter black and blue because she did something stupid to get his fucking attention?"

"You didn't need to fuck up to get his attention."

"No? Are you sure? I got straight As and that obviously didn't impress him. I was the lead in three plays and he didn't show up to watch any of them. I was chosen to attend a drama conference in New York and he didn't send the check to pay for it, so I didn't get to go." My laugh is loaded with hostility. "I got caught stealing once and he tore home as soon as he found out."

"He was proud of those other things. He told me you're a smartass and that you want to be an actress. Your mama must have videotaped your plays and emailed them to him. He had them saved on his phone."

Maybe he's telling the truth, but I shake my head. I don't care. It's too little, too late.

Wing Nut watches me for a while before saying, "My oldest daughter is fifteen and getting in some trouble. I wouldn't mind hearing what you were going through at her age. Maybe you can help me understand her better."

Is he fucking kidding me? "You need to spend time with her to understand her. It's simple."

Connie enters the kitchen with the stack of dirty dishes from the living room and places them in the sink that is already filled with soapy water. She spins around and props her hands on the counter as if she wants to hang out with us. Wing Nut growls, "Get outta here, woman. Can't you see we're talking?"

"Oh." Her cheeks blush and she quickly makes her way across the floor. "Sorry."

I didn't want her loitering any more than he did, but it

wasn't necessary to snap at her. "You don't have to be a dick," I mumble. "She didn't know."

He shrugs as if he doesn't care.

The resemblance to my dad is infuriating and I have an urge to shake him violently until he changes. "This is exactly what we've been talking about. If you treat women like that, your daughter will think that's how she's supposed to be treated by men. Is that what you want?"

"Hell no. I don't want her to be a dumb old lady. I'll whup her ass, too, if she starts doing illegal shit. Why did you do it?"

"Partly because I needed the money to buy groceries for my little brother and partly because even if I got caught, at least my dad would come home."

"Well, it worked. He was worried about you." He rubs his beard, which looks more like weeks of personal hygiene neglect rather than a legitimate styling choice. "He sent you plenty of money. Why didn't you have no groceries?"

"My mom's a junkie."

He nods as if he just remembered. Randy laughs loudly at something they are watching on TV in the other room, and the timing makes it sound as if he thinks my mom is a huge joke, which isn't inaccurate. I kind of want to cry, but I kind of want to scream too. The opposing forces trap me in an emotional void.

"Why didn't my dad want to be with us?" I ask, hoping that even though he's a total stranger, he'll know more about how my dad thought than I did.

"He did want to be with you."

I'd be more convinced if he claimed that my dad had never done a crime in his life. "No, he didn't want to be with us or he would have been. Why don't you want to be with your kids?"

He shifts in the chair uncomfortably. "It's not that I don't want to be with them. It's just that I can't not be out on the road. It would kill me for real if I was tied to one place."

"Seriously? You enjoy roaming around from one sleazy place to another, couch surfing and stinking like a bum?" Give me a break. "Don't even try to feed me a bullshit line about how you need to be free and not tied down, because we both know that the club has more laws telling you what to do than society does."

He stands and carries his plate to the sink. He rinses it first, then slides it into the bubbles. "I live for the road, and my brothers, and everything that comes with it. It's hard to explain to someone who ain't got it in them, but family life comes last on the list of priorities."

I ball my hands into fists and press them against the table. Their narrow-minded mentality is so maddening. "Stop having kids if you don't want to be a proper dad."

His eyes narrow, but his expression softens as he considers what I said. "You have no idea how hard it is to switch from being the guy who is holding a gun against some low-life's temple one minute and playing hide-and-seek with his kid the next. We have to be a certain person for this profession and it doesn't just turn off because we ask it to, or because our kid needs us for something—no matter how bad we might want it to."

"Then get a different profession." I stand, weary from a conversation that isn't going to go anywhere. It makes no difference to hear the excuses. Nothing is ever going to change.

He rests his ass against the countertop and crosses his

arms. "Your daddy loved you. He just didn't show it like average folks because he wasn't no average guy."

"Yeah, well, if you don't want your eight kids to be messed up, you better find them and start giving out hugs like an average guy."

After a few seconds of silence, he crosses the kitchen headed directly at me. I back up, worried he's going to hit me or something. Instead, he extends his arms out. I stare at him for a long pause, then step forward and press up against his chest for a hug. His heart beats slowly and it brings tears to my eyes because I won't ever be able to hear my dad's heart beat again.

"He was proud of you, T Bear."

I know, but that's not the problem. "I wasn't proud of him. No kid wants a murderer for a father."

"He did what he did for the right reasons."

"For the club?" I push away from him, furious at the absurd creed they dedicate themselves to. "You've got to be fucking kidding me. I don't care about all your brotherhood bullshit. There is no justification for taking another person's life."

"Sometimes there is."

"Yeah? Enlighten me."

He frowns at my question. "Didn't no one ever tell you what happened?"

"Yeah. Four guys crossed the club. My dad took care of it, and then he went to prison."

"There's more to it than that." Wing Nut rubs his leathery forehead, then runs his gnarled fingers through the coarse hair of his beard. "There were four hang-arounds who wanted to get approval to become strikers. Your daddy wouldn't give them his vote because they were inhaling more coke than they were selling. He figured they'd be hard to manage, and he was right. They broke a few rules and got run off. They blamed your daddy so, when he was out of town, they went over to your house and gang-raped your mama."

"What?" I gasp and reach for the table to steady myself. A horrible chill soaks into me as if I'm a sponge and I just got thrown into a bucket of wet evil. My heart pounds and the room spins. "What?" I repeat, barely audible.

"You and your brother were sleeping in the house when it happened. They were there all night. Your daddy hunted them down and took care of it. I would have done the same thing. That's how guys who aren't average show their love."

Stunned, I blink repeatedly. "Holy shit," I mutter. I kind of remember when it must have happened because my mom changed. I was five years old and Cooper was three. My mom started crying all the time and I thought it was because my dad was never around. He went to jail a year later and that's when she became a hard-core addict.

"Sorry to upset you when you're already dealing with the death of your brother, but you should know that your daddy had his reasons."

What about the reason Cooper was killed? Who could possibly have a reason for that? "Do you guys know what happened to Cooper?"

"No, not yet, but we'll take care of it. That's what your daddy would have wanted."

I nod and cry because it *is* what my dad would have wanted. He must be so disappointed with me right now.

Wing Nut seems uncomfortable with my tears. He clears his throat, squeezes my shoulder for a second, and says again,

"We'll take care of it." Then he leaves me alone in the kitchen.

No wonder my mom is such a mess. I should have known that it was because of something serious. How did I not know that? She used to be so gentle and sweet, exactly like Cooper. My dad always insisted that I take it easy on her when he was around to hear us bickering. It only made me hate him for taking her side. He should have told me.

I need to go see her.

I bolt out of the back door. With my flip-flops in my hand, I hop the chain link fence and hit a full sprint before I reach the end of the driveway.

Chapter Twenty-Two

I can see through the back porch screen door that my mom is in the kitchen. In her jean cut-offs and tank top, we look like twins, except for her weathered face and the dark circles under her eyes. She's holding a spatula and cigarette in one hand and steadying the handle of the frying pan with the other hand. It's quiet in the house. Usually she has the radio or the television on, so the silence seems almost creepy. When I come in, she looks over her shoulder at the creak of the springs on the screen door.

She seems about to cry and smile at the same time. "T Bear," she breathes out slowly.

The guilt of being so disrespectful to her for the majority of my life overwhelms me and I don't know where to start. I must be looking standoffish or cagey because she doesn't try to approach me for a hug. "Hi, Mom."

The cry wins the battle over her face. Tears fill her eyes and, as she takes a drag from her cigarette, her hand trembles so badly that she can barely get it to her lips. "How are you holding up?"

"Uh, not good."

She nods and bites at her thumbnail the same way I always do. "Are you hungry? Do you want something to eat?"

I glance at the black-edged fried eggs sizzling in the pan. "No thanks."

She turns off the stove and moves to sit at the kitchen table. I watch her push her hair away from her forehead and take another drag from her cigarette. She blows the smoke out the side of her mouth and stares at me as if she doesn't have a clue where to start, either.

I sit down at the table, picking at the grain of the wood.

"They're working on finding out what happened to Cooper," she says quietly. Her eyes look incredibly blue from the sunbeam that is angling through the window. For a second, I see Cooper's eyes, then she blinks and I see her again. She frowns and the evidence of too much hard living etches her complexion like a road map. She lights another cigarette.

"I know," I say. "That's not why I'm here."

She moves in her chair and scratches her neck, then forces a tight smile. She's acting skittish, as if she's worried that I'm staging an intervention and going to make my uncles haul her off to treatment. But I'm not. Not this time. "What's on your mind, T Bear?"

Um, okay. It's probably best to just spit it out. "I came by to tell you that I found out why Dad went to prison."

"You already knew that." She frowns as if she's trying to fully comprehend what I'm saying. Based on the flicker of recognition in her eyes, she knows exactly what I'm talking about.

"No. I knew he murdered people. I didn't know why."

The memory of it seems to hit her in the gut. She places her palms over her belly and leans back in her chair. Her tongue slowly rolls across the front of her teeth. "Who told you?"

"It doesn't matter. I just wanted to tell you that I'm sorry."

Her eyes clench as if she's trying to force the memory to stay locked away. "That was a long time ago, T Bear. It's better if we forget about it."

"Forget about it how? With lines of coke or syringes full of heroin?" Shit. Why did I say that? What is wrong with me? I wasn't going to go there.

She glares at me, but doesn't say anything.

"Sorry." I exhale. "I didn't come here to fight."

She shakes her head. "I don't want to fight either."

"I'm sorry about Cooper, too. I'm sorry I didn't keep him safe." I burst out crying—the out-of-control-wailing kind of sobbing. My forehead drops to the kitchen table and the tears pool on the wood.

Her arms wrap around my shoulders and she rocks me gently. "Shh. Shh. It wasn't your fault. It was my fault. Don't ever blame yourself, T Bear. Shh. Shh. I brought you and your brother into this life and left you to fend for yourselves. It's my fault. Shh. Don't cry. Shh. I love you, baby, and I know I've been a shitty mother. I'm sorry." She pulls my head tightly into her chest and continues to rock me. Her heartbeat reminds me of when I was little and used to crawl into bed with her. She used to hug me until I fell asleep in her arms.

"I miss him so much," I sob.

"I know. Shh."

"I don't want to live without him."

"Don't talk like that, T Bear. He wouldn't want to hear you saying that and you know it."

"It's just not fair. Why did it have to be him?"

"I don't know." She kisses my hair. "I don't know."

My tears drip down onto her leg and leave little trails of moisture across her skin as they roll off her thigh. I wish I could turn back time. I would turn it back to before I was five years old so we could be happy again. Not that it would have probably made a difference if my dad was still Noir et Bleu. Something bad would have eventually happened and we'd be right back here again. The only thing that would have changed everything is if he hadn't been a member and, if I turned time back that far, Cooper and I would have never been born. I'm not sure which is worse.

Mom clutches me tightly. "You did a real good job raising him. He was such a good boy and we both know it wasn't because of anything your dad or I did."

"He was just a good boy. It had nothing to do with me, either." I sniffle and rub my eyes. Although being that close to my mom is something I've missed, too much of it feels overwhelming. I push away and exhale. "Is it all right if I hang out in his room for a while?"

"Of course." She sits back and lets me go.

I walk down the hall and stand at the closed door for a long time. We lived here our entire lives and every single thing that ever happened to us had something to do with this house. At my waist level is a line of stickers that Cooper stuck on when he was about eight years old. They are shiny cars, but he arranged them in the shape of a heart. He said the heart would make Mom and Dad love each other and not fight anymore. I run my finger over the surface of each of the stickers and imagine his tiny finger pressing them on.

Eventually, I work up the courage to turn the doorknob and slowly push the door open. The room is neat, the way he always kept it. It still smells like him. The shelf above his bed displays his collection of model cars. Resting against the pillow on his perfectly made bed is the teddy with a blue bowtie that he used to carry with him everywhere. On the desk is the framed ticket stub from the time my dad took him to a baseball game when he was ten. An overwhelming sadness presses down on me like a thick wool blanket, hot and suffocating. I slide my back down the wall, hug my legs into my chest, and rest my forehead on my knees.

Mom slides down next to me. I hadn't realized she'd followed me. "It's going to take some time, T Bear. You can come by any time you need to. You're always welcome here."

I nod, but I don't lift my head off my knees. I don't want to come here. It had already been too painful to come here and remember all the shitty times. Now, I will also remember the good times. The realization that Cooper and I will never make another memory, good or bad, shatters me.

We sit together silently. She's twitching for a hit of something, but she stays until there's a knock on the front door. She kisses the top of my head again and goes to answer it. It's a man's voice, but I can't make out what he's saying. They talk quietly for a while, but then my mom yells, "Fuck you, motherfucker. I just lost my son. Have some God damn respect, you insensitive piece of shit."

What now? I stand and walk through the living room to see who is on the front steps. It's the guy who owns the house. We call him Nesbitt. He's a nerdy dweeb who wears high-waisted pants and golf shirts buttoned right to the top. He bought the house from my mom after my dad died and then she used all the money on drugs. My uncles had tried to transfer the house over to my name because they knew she would blaze through the money, but she figured out what they were up to before they could get it done. She sold it and arranged to stay on as a renter. She's an addict, but she's not stupid.

"You're short and three days late already, Anna."

"Are you fucking deaf? My kid just died. I'll get the rest to you when I get it to you. Don't harass me."

I stand behind her in support. Despite the fact that I'm ashamed of having a junkie for a mom, she is family and I don't appreciate the fact that's he's being an asshole.

Nesbitt glances at me and his face softens, maybe because it's obvious that I've been crying. He peers over his glasses at my mom. "Did your kid really die?"

"Yeah. What have I been fucking telling you?" She starts crying and lights another cigarette.

"Sorry, Anna. I thought you were bullshitting me."

"What kind of sick fuck bullshits about their kid dying?"

"Yeah, I don't know. Sorry." His face turns even pinker. He glances at me again and runs his finger between his neck and the collar of his shirt as if it's suddenly strangling him. "Sorry. I'll come by again at the end of the week."

"How much is she short?" I ask.

"Two hundred."

"I'll get it to you by tomorrow." I've got plenty of money saved. Even though I'd cut myself off from her, I still put aside most of my paycheck into an emergency fund. Maybe because I never got into the habit of spending money on myself. Or, maybe because I knew one day she would need me to bail her out, and I knew I would do it.

He nods apologetically. "No rush. Sorry to hear about your loss." He turns and hustles down the stairs.

"Fuckin' weasel," my mom mutters as she slams the door.

"You're the one who sold the house to him and snorted the money up your nose. Deal with it." And, apparently, I'm still bitter. I guess I need to work on the forgiveness part.

She huffs, but she doesn't say anything because she knows it's true.

I can't handle any more of her right now. I'm emotionally spent. My nose and eyes are raw and my skin stings from all the tears. "I gotta go." I swing the door open. The screen slams behind me and I can feel her watching me walk away. Before I even get to the end of the path, my phone vibrates in my pocket. As I take it out, Leland's note falls to the sidewalk.

I read the text from Gylly as I bend over to pick up the note: *Where are you, babe?*

I read the note from Leland next.

Tienne,

I'm sorry I wasn't there when you needed me the most. I'm here now.

Love, Leland.

I debate who I should call. I'm not up to dealing with any more drama, so I decide to go with the easiest option. I dial my phone and wander down the street as it rings.

"Hey, where are you?" Uncle Blaine asks.

"I went by my mom's. Do you mind picking me up here?"

"I'll be right there."

"Thanks."

I sit on the curb a few houses down from my own, staring at Gylly's text in one hand and Leland's note in the other. I finally decide to text Gylly. I'll call Leland when I get back to Elizabeth and Blaine's. He'll probably want to come over to talk, and I'm definitely going to need a shower and maybe a nap before I feel up to that.

I write to Gylly: *I'm with Blaine. I'm fine.*

He writes right back. *Don't lie. Stay at your mom's. I'm on my way.*

What the hell? I stand and look down the street both ways. There is not a motorcycle in sight and the only person around is a woman pulling some weeds in her front garden. There are a few cars parked along the side of the road, so I wander down the sidewalk casually looking into each of them. The fourth one down is a black sedan and there is a guy I don't recognize sitting in it. I walk around the front of the car and onto the street to stand next to the driver's side door. He's not wearing a cut, but he looks tough and is probably a prospect. They send prospects out to do shit jobs like babysitting. He doesn't look up at me, so I tap the window and yell through the glass, "Roll down the window."

He ignores me.

"Hey. I want to ask you a question."

He pulls out a cigarette and lights it to avoid looking at me.

"Why does Digger have you following me?"

He exhales the smoke toward the ceiling and smiles a little.

I hit the window with my fist and yell, "Roll down the window, you bitch-assed prospect."

His eyes slowly roll to glare at me and his jaw tightens. He twists his head to crack his neck then stares out the windshield again.

I slam the window and yell, "I told you to roll down the window, asshole!" He doesn't look at me, but he snarls a little. "Why does Randy have you following me, shit for brains?"

He growls through the glass, "You better settle down, little girl, or you'll end up like your brother."

Okay, he just pissed me off. I kick off my flip-flops and stomp on the driver's door. The first two kicks don't do any damage, but on the third try my heel makes good contact and leaves a dent. "What's your problem, Nancy? Why are you hiding in a cage? Are you afraid of a teeny little girl or something? You're applying for the wrong line of business if you're a pussy. Open the fucking window and tell me why they sent a girl with less credibility than I have to babysit me!" I kick another dent in the door, taking out every single one of my frustrations.

He slams his forearm against the window so I see the club tattoo. Shit. He has three skulls. I'm dead. I thought he was a prospect. He's going to kill me for talking to him like that.

I turn and run. The car door opens and his boots pound against the pavement behind me. Oh my God, why did I do that? I should have noticed that he was a member. Having an anger management problem and taking it out on random tweakers is one thing—taking it out on a full patch member is a death sentence. He's gaining on me, but he's breathing heavy like a smoker. Maybe if I sprint long enough, he'll run out of gas. Uncle Blaine passes me in his BMW SUV going the opposite direction. His face contorts as he recognizes me and then sees that I'm being chased by an outlaw. I keep running because if Blaine tries to intervene he'll probably get stabbed or shot or stomped—better me than him.

I cut across a few lawns and turn the corner. Aiden and Mickey ride past and turn around when they see me. Randy won't let the guy kill me—I don't think. When I'm about three houses away from the Gyllenhalls', I scream, "Digger! Wing Nut! Help!"

Randy and Wing Nut and the other guy who was passed out on the floor earlier all tear out of the house onto the front lawn. Connie steps out onto the porch, too, and Zeke is barking like crazy. The bikes jump the curb behind me as two hundred pounds of sweaty muscle tackles me. My knees and elbows ram into the driveway. My cheek hits the grass hard. The impact with the ground isn't nearly as bad as the pile driving from the guy's body a fraction of a second later. His weight crushes the air out of me. I gasp for what little oxygen I can and scream hysterically.

The guy rolls me over and straddles my waist. I flail my arms and legs and scratch at every bit of his skin that I can. His eyes turn almost black with rage and his mouth is locked into a ravenous snarl like a wolf. I reach for the switchblade in my back pocket, but his weight keeps me from rolling. He cocks his arm back as if he's going to punch me in the face.

Aiden flies through the air, knocking the guy off me. He gets in a few really good punches before his dad and Wing Nut pull them apart. Mickey hauls Aiden to his feet and pushes him toward the house. The guy scrambles to his feet to go after Aiden, so Wing Nut throws a chicken wing and slams his elbow into the guy's nose. He drops cold on the driveway.

"What the fuck?" I scream. "That's what you assholes call protection? I would rather take my chances with the bad guys." I struggle to my feet and wince from the pain in my ribs. Zeke stands protectively between me and the twitching body on the driveway, barking ferociously. "That moronic cretin could have killed me!" I shout.

Connie leans against the porch post smiling. Uncle Blaine stands frozen with his door open like he jumped out to help, but then didn't know what to do. He looks very strange standing there in his white golf pants and light green V-neck sweater.

I point at Randy. "Keep your fucking goons away from me and my family. They obviously can't do their jobs worth shit anyway or Cooper wouldn't be dead."

Aiden winces as if the sight of me upset and hurt causes him actual physical pain. He struggles to break free from Mickey's grasp, unsuccessfully.

"Zeke, shut it," Randy growls. Zeke stops barking and moves to sit next to Randy's foot. Randy stares down at the goon who is still twitching on the ground. He scratches his head and frowns, probably trying to figure out why my body-guard just chased me down and tried to beat my ass when he was supposed to be protecting me. It takes him a second, but then he chuckles and cocks his head to look at me. "What did you say to him, T Bear?"

I roll my eyes, smooth my hair, and brush the blood and dirt off my knees. "I called him a bitch-assed prospect," I admit.

They all laugh, except for Aiden.

"It's not funny, you degenerates. Thanks for reminding

me why I left this fucked up life behind me."

The fact that my voice is shaky just makes them laugh more. They thrive on the adrenaline of dangerous situations and I'm sick of it.

Aiden shoves Mickey off him and shouts, "Shut the fuck up. All of you." It's like it just hit him how messed up everything is if you observe it from the outside looking in. He points at his dad with a tension in his arms and neck that etches the definition of his muscles. "It's not funny."

Randy's face transitions into something serious, but not out of respect for my feelings. Aiden hasn't challenged his dad's authority since we were very young because, whenever he did, his dad reasserted his power with a fury that made sure no one ever questioned it again.

They are locked in a stare-down. It is the most defiant I've seen anybody be toward Randy since Uncle Len had it out with him years ago. Uncle Len won that power struggle because Randy needed him. Maybe that's what's going through Randy's head right now because he breaks the stare first and turns to go back to the house. Before he steps through the doorway he shoots Aiden a glare that makes it clear that he's letting Aiden off the hook, just this one time.

Aiden rushes toward me. "Ti. I'm sorry."

I pull away. "Sorry isn't enough. I need a different life than this."

I run to Blaine's truck, hop in the passenger side, and slouch down in the seat. Blaine gets in without saying anything and, since the engine is still running, he shifts it into drive and we roll past the chaos. The intensity in Aiden's eyes as he watches me go hurts more than being pounded into the ground by an outlaw.

Chapter Twenty-Three

Auntie Elizabeth made tuna casserole because she knows it's one of my favorites, but I can only force down two bites. Uncle Blaine obviously told her about what happened at Gylly's house, but neither one of them tries to talk to me about it. We glance at Cooper's empty chair and then stare down at our plates. Eventually, Elizabeth breaks into tears and runs out of the dining room. Blaine nods as if he already knows that I'm going to excuse myself as well.

I load Elizabeth's and my dishes into the dishwasher, then drag myself up the back stairs. The shower runs cold before I muster the strength to turn off the water and step out. My knees start bleeding again, so I stick fresh bandages on before dressing in sweat pants and one of Cooper's T-shirts. I plan to curl up in my bed and never get up again, but even though I can barely keep my eyes open, I can't fall asleep. The expression on Aiden's face after he stood his ground with his dad haunts me. If Cooper saw it, he would know what love looked like.

At midnight, I grab my phone from the bedside table to call Leland. He answers on the second ring. "Hey. How are you doing?"

"Not good," I say. "I can't sleep, and I miss Cooper."

"I'm so sorry I haven't been there for you. Do you want to talk about it?"

"Can you come over?"

"Uh." He pauses and I picture him running his hand through his hair. "I would, but I'm not home."

"Oh. Your note said you would be here."

"I know. I'm sorry, but something came up, and I had to go out of town again. I'll hopefully be home soon. I promise I'll take time off to spend with you then."

My throat makes a noise, but no words come out. How could he leave again? Who abandons a person they care about while they are going through the worst thing that has ever happened to them?

"Tienne, I'm sorry."

I close my eyes and hold the phone tightly to my ear. I am so sick of hearing *I'm sorry*. *Sorry* doesn't do shit. I finally say, "Bye," and hang up.

Be a decent human being. Do the right thing. Stop making fucking excuses. How hard is that? Maybe it's too much to ask. Or, maybe I asked the wrong person. I stare at my phone for a little while, then text Aiden: *I miss Cooper. I need some company.*

He answers right back: *On my way.*

Even though, deep down, I knew that's what he would say, the reminder that he is, and always has been, here for me makes me smile. I get out of bed to open the window and turn on the lamp because he won't come to the front door. I crawl back under the covers and hug my pillow. Fifteen minutes later, his bike stops in front of the house. It's silent for a few seconds. Then I hear him climb the outside of the porch to the sloping roof beneath my window. He steps in and smiles before closing the sash behind him. He hangs his leather jacket on the back of my desk chair, then kicks off his boots and lies down next to me. After I reach over to turn off the lamp, he wraps his arms around me. He feels like my shelter from the storm.

"Thanks, Gylly," I whisper.

He kisses my cheek and hugs me tighter. "I'm sorry about today. I promise to give you the life you want." I roll to face him. His expression leaves no doubt in my mind. "Is that all right with you?" He tilts my chin up and waits for my answer.

I didn't think it was possible to love him more than I already did. I nod, choking back happy tears. He pulls me tight to his chest.

Feeling safe is the last thing I remember before I fall asleep.

In the morning, I wake up to the sound of water running in my shower. Aiden isn't next to me. The sheets are still warm where he slept, though. Ten minutes later, he gently opens the door to the bathroom and tiptoes into my room toward his boots. His hair is wet and he smells good.

"Hey," I say softly, glad last night wasn't only a dream.

"Sorry. I was trying not to wake you."

"It's okay." I push my lip out in a subtle pout that he falls for every time. "Do you have to go?"

He thinks for a second, then shakes his head. "No. It's not that important. I can stay if you want me to."

It's obvious that he's trying to downplay something. I glance at the clock. It's eight twenty-six. "Do you have class?"

"Yeah, but I can miss it." He shrugs it off, to convince me it's no big deal.

"Sorry, I shouldn't have done the pouty thing. I don't want you to miss school."

"If you get to miss work, I should get to miss school. I'll stay."

"Wait a minute." I jump out of bed and grab his boots, then snatch his jacket off the back of the chair. "I just remembered that you said you have exams today. I'm not letting you miss an exam. You'll fail the course."

"I can take it again next term."

"Nope." I push his chest. "You're going." I step toward my dresser and pull a sweater and jeans out of the drawers. "Give me a second. I'll come with you. How's that sound?"

He smiles as he ties his boots. "Sounds like a good plan."

"Give me two seconds."

After freshening up, I step back into my bedroom and take out enough money from the My Little Pony tin on my shelf to pay my mom's rent. Aiden looks happy. I'm sure I look happy, too. I don't even try to ask him to sneak back out the window because guys like Gylly might sneak into places, but they always walk out the front door when they leave. I'm going to have a ton of explaining to do to Elizabeth and Blaine, but whatever.

He watches me dress and his expression changes. "So,

about that boyfriend of yours…"

I pause midway through pulling up my jeans. The words sting, and I react defensively from the guilt that's been eating away at me. "What about him?" I yank up my jeans.

He draws back at my tone, and his expression darkens. "I was just going to tell you he left town." He stands and reaches for the doorknob. "He sounds like a real keeper. I have to go."

No. I position myself between him and the door. "Can we please not fall back into our old ways of dealing with things? I don't want to push you away anymore. I don't want to fight every time I'm too scared to tell you how I really feel. And I don't want to avoid shit just because it's hard to deal with." I exhale and dig deep for the courage to stop hiding behind my hostility. "I snapped at you because I feel horrible for hurting you. I'm ashamed that I treated you like you weren't good enough, when you are." My posture deflates and I slump against the wall. "You're more than good enough. I don't deserve you. I'm so sorry."

Feeling exposed without my guard up, I cover my face with my hands. He gently pulls my wrists so he can see me. Eventually I open my eyes. His expression seems amused, like he's mocking me. I shove his chest, right back to hostility in one second flat.

"What?" he laughs.

"You're making fun of me."

"No, I'm not." He stretches his arms around me and bends his knees so we are face to face. "You have absolutely nothing to be ashamed of. My whole life I knew I wasn't good enough for you. Everything I've ever done was to make you notice me, love me, be proud of me. I'm the one who doesn't deserve you, and I like being reminded of that because it makes me want to keep working on being a better person. I wasn't mocking you, I was smiling because I can't believe how lucky I am to have someone as amazing as you in my life."

I throw my arms around his neck and squeeze tight enough to strangle him. "Thank you for saying that. I love you." I release my hold and tug his hand. "But we need to get going so you don't miss your exam."

"I don't want to go." His hands rest on my hips. "I kind of like this whole sharing our feelings thing."

I smile and open the door to shove him into the hall.

We see Elizabeth as soon as we step out of my room. She's carrying a basket full of laundry and nearly walks right into him. "Oh. Sorry. Whoa, um, well. Hello. Good morning." She shoots a laser beam glare at me. "I didn't know we had a guest."

"Elizabeth, this is Aiden."

"Oh." She presses her lips together and nods. I can tell she wants to ask a million questions, but instead she shoots me another scowl and says tersely, "Nice to meet you, Aiden."

"Nice to meet you, Mrs. Montgomery."

She appears flustered as she walks away. After she disappears into the master bedroom and shuts the door, I glance apologetically at Aiden. He shrugs, undeterred, before we head downstairs.

Right. Undeterred. Maybe it doesn't matter whether Elizabeth accepts him with open arms, tolerates him, or rejects him. Who am I kidding? It does matter. I want her and Blaine to adore him and be excited for me. They never will be, though, unless maybe by some miracle he figures out how to keep his promise. Since I don't see how Randy will ever let him walk away from the club, I probably shouldn't get my hopes up.

Blaine is at the front door carrying his briefcase in one hand and a coffee travel mug in the other. I rush Aiden down the stairs and squeeze behind Blaine. "Hi. You remember Aiden. Okay. Have a good day. Bu-bye." Once we're out the door, I grab Aiden's hand and make him hurry down the front path toward his bike, which is parked on the street right in front of the house. I'm not quite strong enough for undeterred yet.

We both put on our helmets and I glance over at Blaine as we ride off. He's pissed. Aiden still seems completely relaxed. I wonder if it's because he couldn't care less what they think, or if he's confident he can win them over one day.

Aiden doesn't ride like an outlaw when I'm on the back of the bike, which means that he actually obeys traffic lights, stop signs, and speed limits. If I'm not on the bike, he rides like the rest of them. They're suicidal maniacs and it's terrifying to watch them. They travel at ridiculous speeds and other cars have to swerve out of the way.

Because of Aiden's grandpa speeds, we're running a bit late. He parks the bike on the sidewalk right in front of the building where his exam is. "Good luck kiss?" he asks with a mischievous grin, after we've both unassed.

I step forward, slide my hand along the side of his jaw, and let my lips hover close to his. I run my other hand under his jacket and feel the heat coming off his body. In some ways, it feels as if we were never apart. In other ways, it feels as if we are meeting for the first time. I look down to try to hide the excitement and attraction that is exploding inside me. "Good luck," I whisper and glance up at him.

He bites his lip in a sexy way that makes my cheeks feel like they are sunburned. I've changed my mind. I wish he would skip his exam. It must be obvious to him what I would rather be doing with him because, instead of kissing me, he winks, then jogs toward the auditorium door just as the instructor is pulling the doorstop up to close it. He always did like to leave me wanting more.

An hour and forty minutes has passed and nobody has come out of the auditorium, so it must not be an easy exam. The lounge in the lobby is filled with students. It's weird. Even though Aiden got good grades all through school, I never pictured him as someone who would fit in with the studious crowd. I wonder what else I was wrong about.

Aiden left his book bag with me and, since I'm bored, I pull out his phone to see if the password is still the same. It is, so I play games for a while, then eventually break down and snoop through the photos he has saved. The first thirty or so pictures are of me, or him and me together. The last picture is one of Cooper and me that was taken right before my dad was killed. Cooper's arm is draped over my shoulder and mine is around his waist.

I already can't remember what it's like to touch Cooper. It makes me feel like he was only a dream. Shit. I wipe the tears from my cheek and rub my nose on the sleeve of my sweater. Staring at the picture, I try to remember everything about him. If I close my eyes, I can almost remember the warmth of his body next to mine. Then I open my eyes and the air feels cold and empty again.

"Hey." Aiden sneaks up and tickles my waist.

I turn off his phone and hand it to him. "Hi."

"Were you snooping?"

"Yes." I move over on the vinyl couch to make room for him to sit beside me.

"Find anything juicy?"

"Nope. How was the exam?"

"Hard, but I think I did okay. Were you crying?" He tucks my hair behind my ears and shifts to look directly in my eyes.

I wipe my cheeks and breathe. "I saw the picture you have on your phone of Cooper and me, and it reminded me that he's gone."

"Oh, sorry." He reaches his hand over to hold mine. "I can't even imagine what you're going through. Do you want to talk about it?"

"Sometimes I have moments when I miss him so badly I wish I were dead so I wouldn't have to feel the pain, and sometimes I have moments when I forget that he's not just in his room or out with a friend." Sobs convulse through my body despite my attempt to control them.

Aiden wraps his arms around me, and I can tell that he knows how much it sucks. Cooper was like a brother to him, too. He doesn't say anything; he just holds me. By the time my tears subside enough to see, there is nobody left in the lounge and the last stragglers in the auditorium stumble out looking disheveled and dazed. Aiden moves his hand to rub my arm.

I stare at his blue eyes—they are beautiful. Over the years that I've known him, he's changed. He has stubble and he walks with a bit of a limp from when he dumped his bike. He has a bunch of tattoos and a couple of battle scars from fights, but his eyes are the same as they have always been. I memorized every one of his expressions by heart, and the way his eyes are looking at me right now is the same way he looked at me the first time he told me he loved me.

I sigh and say, "Maybe we should go get something to eat since we have to be back in time for your exam at two o'clock."

He chuckles. "I should have changed the password." He holds my hand as we walk to the cafeteria. We both order breakfast burritos and orange juice. I also get a slice of banana bread. As he eats, I try to get a read on his mood. He still seems pretty relaxed. Maybe a good time to press him for information.

"Are you going to tell me why your dad has been keeping tabs on me?"

The way he shakes his head makes it seem like he wants to tell me, but wants to protect me at the same time. "He'll tell you when he can."

"Or, I can bug you until you tell me." I tickle his ribs.

"Not going to happen." He tickles me back until I give in. "Talk to my dad."

"Fine. I will." I dial Randy's number. He doesn't answer and he doesn't have voicemail, so I can't leave a message. "Is he avoiding me?" I ask.

Aiden raises his left eyebrow to point out what a stupid question that was. We both know I'll have a better chance of tickling it out of Aiden than getting Randy to share club business with me.

It is a harsh reminder that Randy doesn't do anything he

doesn't want to, which will include letting Aiden leave and build a life with me. Part of me wants to know if Aiden has a plan for how he is going to deal with his dad, but part of me won't be able to handle the disappointment of hearing him say he hasn't figured it out yet. Avoiding the conversation isn't going to make the problem solve itself, though.

"So?" I finally ask. It's only one word, but it's loaded with a truckload of questions. I want to know what it means that my feelings for him have not only not gone away, they've become stronger. I want to know if the outlaw life can ever go away. I wonder if it's stupid to hope that maybe we could make a different life together than what our parents had. I wonder if this is how my mom felt when she was trying to choose between Dad and Chet.

"So," he repeats slowly. I can tell that he knows my "so" was a loaded question, but he changes the subject. "I should probably go over my notes before my next exam. You can come with me to hang out at the library, or I can drop you off somewhere. What do you want to do?"

It seems like what I say next is important to him because he watches me cautiously as he waits for my answer. "I would rather be with you."

He grins and stands to pull out my chair for me.

"Aiden. Do you have a plan?"

He whispers, "Yes. Don't worry about that right now."

Don't worry about it? My entire future depends on it. "I need to know what it is because I can't commit to this if I'm going to end up losing you to the club."

"Do you trust me?"

"Of course. It's just that some things are impossible to change."

"There is only one more thing I have to do to make it happen. I promise."

I study him carefully as we walk and get back on the bike to ride across campus to the library. He leads me to a private study corner away from other students, sits at the table, and pulls out a stack of papers covered in his neat printing.

"Wow. Do you have to know all that for one test?"

"Yes."

"Hmm." I trail my fingertip across the spines of the books on the shelf. "You must be clever." He watches intently as I saunter past him. When I reach the end of the stack, I turn and lean up against it. He rubs his chin, then looks down and tries to focus on his notes. Only a second later he glances back at me. I subtly lick my bottom lip and run my fingers through my hair. He chuckles and shifts in his seat. Arching my back slightly, I turn and walk slowly past him again. "Why aren't you studying?" I slide my hair over one shoulder and turn so my back is facing him.

"You're distracting me."

"Really?" I bend over to look at the books on the bottom shelf.

"Careful. If you keep acting flirty like that, I might take you behind the stacks and make you forget all about that loaded boyfriend of yours for a few seconds."

"Ah, a few seconds. You can say that again."

"Hey, we both know I can rock you all night long."

"Mmm hmm." I straighten up and read more titles. "I don't see why you keep insulting his net worth since I can guarantee that your dad makes more money than his dad."

"My dad doesn't flaunt it like a pretentious prick."

I look over my shoulder. "He can't flaunt it because he

didn't earn it in a legitimate way."

He chuckles. "What do you consider legitimate? You might want to do a background check on that boyfriend of yours."

"Stop calling him my boyfriend. I don't want him to be my boyfriend anymore." I frown and sit on the table. "Back at your house, why did you say he was a liar?"

"Ask him."

"I'm asking you."

He shakes his head and focuses on his notes. My phone vibrates in my pocket. It's Leland. Speak of the devil. I would rather avoid the call, but I don't want our relationship lingering on, either.

"I should probably take this, excuse me."

Aiden's jaw tightens and he blinks slowly before looking back down. I can't tell if he's jealous or glad that my opportunity to break up with Leland is literally in my hand.

I answer the phone as I walk through the stacks and quietly say, "Hold on one second." I rush toward the door and step outside. "Hi. Sorry, I was in a library."

"How are you doing?"

"Not good." If he were here, he would know that.

"Yeah," he says, preoccupied.

Something is up with him, more than just not being able to be here for me. He doesn't sound like himself at all. "Is everything okay?"

"I'm busy with problems at work. I might have to stay away even longer than I thought. I'll let you know when I know. I'm sorry, Tienne. I know I'm letting you down because I'm not there for you."

"Yeah, well, whatever you're doing must be pretty important."

He sighs. "I'll get there as soon as I can."

"Don't bother. This isn't going to work out."

"Tienne, please, give me a chance to talk to you when I get back."

"Bye," I say with zero enthusiasm. I don't wait for him to say anything else before I hang up and glance over my shoulder. Aiden is watching me through the window. He knows what else is going on with Leland. I can tell by the concern in his expression.

Chapter Twenty-Four

Aiden met me outside the library and took me to his dorm room. Apparently, he moved onto campus right after we broke up because he knew he wouldn't get any studying done at his dad's house. It blows my mind that he's working on his undergrad degree.

It's four o'clock and he's not back from his exam yet. I fell asleep after he left, and now I'm just lying in bed taking in the décor. It's plain — a bed, a desk, and a bookshelf. There is a framed picture of me on his bedside table, and his one pillow smells like him only.

Sliding out from under the covers, I layer one of his sweatshirts over my sweater. His laptop is on, so I sit on the desk chair, pulling my knees into my chest, to snoop. Most of his emails are boring and about school related things, but there is one from the police department that catches my attention. I glance at the clock and then open the email. I assume that it's going to be a citation or order to appear or something. His key slides into the lock before I have a chance to read all the information. I slam the laptop shut and leap back into bed.

He swings the door open and smiles. "Good. I was hoping you'd still be in bed when I got back."

"Oh? Why's that?" I roll onto my side, bend my elbow, and rest my head on my palm.

He drops his bag and kneels on the mattress to take off his jacket. His mouth angles suggestively as he slides down beside me. "I was hoping you'd still be in bed because—" He gazes down my entire body and gently touches my chin as if he's going to kiss me, then he rolls over so his back is toward me. "I'm exhausted and I need a nap." He pulls the covers over his shoulder. "Night, T Bear."

"Hey. I'm not tired anymore." I tickle his ribs and he rolls onto his back, laughing.

"Well, what do you suggest we do if you're not tired?"

"Hmm." I sit up on my knees and look down at him. "How did your exam go?"

"It probably would have gone better if I wasn't visualizing you in my bed the entire time. I was a bit distracted."

"Maybe I should go home. I noticed on the calendar in your phone that you have an English exam tomorrow at eleven. You should probably study, and I don't want to be a distraction."

He shakes his head, pretending to be annoyed. "I forgot what a snoop you are."

"Speaking of snooping, did you get a speeding ticket recently?"

"Not that I know of."

"Were you called for jury duty?"

"No. Why?"

"I was just wondering. I saw an email from the police department."

"Oh. That was nothing. An unpaid parking ticket."

I slide my knees closer and grab the hem of his shirt to pull it up and off over his head. My palm slides over his TDAGF tattoo. "So, you're not wanted on some sort of warrant?"

He smiles and reaches up to cradle my face in his hands. "Ti. I will give you the normal life you want. Will you please give me a second chance to prove that to you?"

My eyes fill up with tears, excited that normal is what he wants, too, but worried it's not possible no matter how much we both want it. "I'm so proud of you for going to school. If I get accepted to the Academy in New York, I'll be moving away. I don't want you to quit school."

He shakes his head to indicate that it doesn't matter. "I'll transfer."

"You would move to New York to be with me?"

"I would move to New York just to be near you. I would move anywhere in the world to be with you, if you would let me."

I've dreamed about leaving everything behind for a long time. In that dream Aiden always leaped up and went with me. I honestly never thought that the dream could come true. The tears trickle over my eyelids and slide down my cheek. "What about the club?"

"Don't worry about it. If you want me to go with you, I will."

I'm too overwhelmed to speak, so I nod and wrap my arms around his neck tightly. He abruptly flips me onto my back and his upper body hovers over mine. His hand moves

down my side and over my hip. He pulls my hair back to ex-
pose my neck and kisses from my collarbone up to my ear. I
turn my head so our mouths meet. I wiggle out of my jeans
and he pulls the sweatshirt and my sweater off over my head.
His jeans drop and his belt thuds against the wood floor. My
bra is already hanging from the chair and he's gently kissing
my ribs. His left hand takes mine, interlacing our fingers. His
right hand slides my underwear down my legs and he runs
his thumb along the TDAGF tattoo on my bikini line. "I love
that you have that there," he whispers before kissing his way
up from my tattoo, along my abs, and over my breasts to the
ridge of my collarbone. When he reaches my lips, he pauses
and opens his eyes to gaze into mine. "I love you so much,
Ti. If you don't want this forever, tell me now, because I can't
survive you leaving me again." His face is locked in the same
expression of undying love that I saw yesterday.

My fingers clutch clumps of his hair and I pull his face
closer before whispering, "You're the one I want. Forever."

He smiles, elated and reassured, then his hand slides up
the inside of my thigh. I gasp and drop my head back. "Oh
my God." My back arches and I breathe out before clutching
the bedspread and wrapping my legs around his hips. The
tension in his muscles makes me tremble, and I gasp again
as he hoists me closer and makes love to me with a renewed
passion that sends bursts of euphoria through me.

We were meant for each other—there is no doubt about
that.

We lay in bed snuggling for a long time, staring at each other.

Both our phones are ringing, but we don't get up.

I trace my finger across the lines of his super-chiseled muscles. "You kind of let yourself go after we broke up."

He rolls onto his back with his hands resting behind his head. "We didn't break up. You took off and had an affair. I had to go to the gym twice a day just to make sure I didn't snap that prick's neck."

"Well, anger management workouts seem to be good for the physique. You look extra sexy."

He pulls me in to his chest and kisses the top of my head. His fingers unclasp my necklace, then remove the ring from the chain. He lifts my left hand from where it is resting on his chest and slides the ring onto my finger. I smile and turn my head to kiss him.

"You don't have to wear it if you don't want to. I just wanted to see it on you."

"I want to wear it."

"I didn't mean to rush you or pressure you when I gave it to you."

"I know. I should have talked to you about why I was scared. I'm sorry."

He smiles, then hugs me. "It's okay. I'm just glad you're here now." We lay quietly for a while before he asks, "Did Crofton tell you that he knocked up a girl?"

Really? He wants to talk about Leland right now? "Yes."

Aiden seems surprised. "Have you met the kid?"

"What?"

"His son. Have you met him?"

I sit up. "What? He doesn't have a son. He said that she miscarried or had an abortion."

Aiden laughs scornfully.

I blink as if that will help the information sink in. "He has a kid?" That doesn't make any sense. Why would he have hidden that from me?

"A son named Braden."

"Oh my God." What else did Leland lie about? I am such an idiot.

"Do you know about the drugs?" Aiden asks.

"Yes."

His eyebrows climb in surprise. "And you were okay with it?"

"No, but it wasn't that big of a deal. He was just selling pot to some people at the country club. He stopped when I asked him to."

Aiden makes a snort of contempt. "Sounds like he kept more secrets from you than I thought."

Jesus. The lies just keep piling up. "You don't think he quit?"

"No, I don't think he quit, and it wasn't just weed for socialites."

This is too much reality to take in at once. I lean over the edge of the bed to grab my clothes and slip into the bathroom. I take my time in the shower, thinking. I can't believe Leland has a son he didn't tell me about. And it was more than weed. God, I'm so stupid. How could I have been that blind? What if I'm still living in a naïve la-la land convincing myself of what I want to believe to be true?

When I eventually open the bathroom door, Aiden's standing in the middle of the room. He's put on his jeans, but he's bare-chested and has tied a bandana across his forehead.

"We have to go," he says with a tone he only uses when he's working. "My dad called. He wants me to take you down to the clubhouse. Get dressed."

I stare at him, completely shocked, as he pulls on a black T-shirt. "I don't want to go to the clubhouse."

"We have no choice."

I lean against the doorframe and squeeze my eyes shut. We are right back where we started. He couldn't last one day. "How could I have been so gullible to believe that you would actually be able to stay away from club business? God, I'm an idiot. I'm not going there and, if you do, then what just happened here didn't happen."

Aiden gives me a level look. "It's about Cooper."

The mention of Cooper's name stops everything else that is spinning in my brain. I want to know what they've learned about his death, but I don't need to go to the club-house to get it. I think of most of those guys as family—a demented family, but family nonetheless—unfortunately, they're different when they're working. I don't want to be around that. I refuse to go there when there's an alternative.

"Phone your dad back," I say, "and tell him to meet us at the house."

Aiden shakes his head. "He wouldn't have asked us to go to the clubhouse if it wasn't important."

"Fuck that. I'm not stepping foot in that cesspool."

Frustrated, Aiden gives in and dials his dad. "She doesn't want to meet at the clubhouse... Yeah... Fucking, you tell her." He hands me the phone.

"Hello," I say.

Randy coughs and growls, "Get your ass down here, T Bear."

"No thanks. If you want to talk to me we can meet at your house or a damn Waffle Palace."

"How are the brakes working on your aunt's new car?"

I want to swear at him and call him a bunch of names, but I know better. "I hope that's not a threat, Randy, because I'm pretty sure your taxes are not in order."

"See you in thirty minutes. Don't be late." He hangs up.

I throw Aiden's phone across the room. It bounces off the wall and, fortunately, lands on the bed. So much for managing my anger. "Sorry." I lunge over and check that I didn't break it. "He threatened to tamper with Elizabeth's car if I don't go to the clubhouse."

Although he knows his dad is capable of something like that, Aiden doesn't seem concerned. He hands me my jacket. "He just wants to tell you what they've found out about Cooper's death and then we can leave."

"Fine. I'll go, but only because I care about what happened to Cooper. He can't bully me to do things by threatening the people I care about. He's such an asshole sometimes."

"Yeah, well, it is what it is." He takes off his eight different big chunky rings with skulls, Celtic symbols, and the one with the letters TCB, which stands for taking care of business. He drops all but one of the rings on his desk. He tucks the shamrock ring that I gave him to ward off evil into his pocket.

"Why are you taking off your rings?"

"Don't worry about it." He hides a switchblade in his boot and puts his cut on, then walks over and holds my face. "Once we figure out what happened to Cooper, we'll leave all this behind us. Deal?"

I'm really not comfortable with any of this, but I do trust that he knows what he's doing, so I nod and kiss him.

As we're walking to where his bike is parked, I call my

mom's landlord, partly because I said I would get him the money today, and partly because I'm worried I'll never see the money again if I take it into the clubhouse with me.

"Nesbitt. It's Tienne. Meet me at my mom's in ten minutes if you want the rest of the rent."

"I'm busy. I'll meet you there at eight."

"It has to be now. Unless you want her to snort it, inject it, or smoke it, you better be there."

"Or I could just evict her."

I laugh. "Yeah, you try that and I'll tell my uncles to shove your tiny car up your ass. See you in ten minutes. Don't be late." I hang up.

Aiden laughs at me as he passes me my helmet. "You're as bad as my dad."

"Shut up."

He kisses me and we take off. He's riding like an outlaw now. I dig my fingers into the leather of his cut and close my eyes when we blow through intersections with red lights. It's terrifying and completely exhilarating.

Chapter Twenty-Five

When Aiden and I pull up in front of my mom's house, she's standing on the porch smoking. Her landlord is already there, sitting in his Smart car. I don't get off the bike, so he has to get out and walk over to me. He takes the money and scurries off. Mom walks down the path toward us. "Thanks, T Bear. I'll pay you back."

I pretend like she means it. "Don't worry about it."

She takes a drag from the cigarette, trying to work up the nerve to say something more. "I'm going away for a while."

"Where?"

She drops the cigarette on the sidewalk and twists her foot to stamp it out. "A treatment center."

"Really?" She has had intentions to do it before, but it never got past the contemplation stage. I'm not sure what to think of it.

She nods, and her mood seems different this time—not like someone who is desperate to make amends for something, but like someone who is just really tired of being this way.

I don't want to get my hopes up but, if she's serious, I don't want to discourage her, either. "That's great, Mom." I reach over and hug her around the neck. "When do you leave?"

"Ronnie's going to take me out there tomorrow."

"How long do you have to stay?"

She shrugs, nervous. "A couple months probably. Your uncles are going to take care of the rent here."

She notices my ring and catches my hand to get a better look. She smiles approvingly, but doesn't say anything. "Aiden and I have to go meet Digger right now," I tell her, "but I'll come over tomorrow morning to say good-bye."

"Sounds good. I love you, T Bear."

"I love you too, Mom." Aiden reaches back and runs his hand along my thigh, probably because he thinks it's nice to hear me being kind to my mom. "We really have to go. Digger's waiting." She nods and Aiden revs the bike. I wave as we take off.

There are about twenty other bikes lined up in front of the clubhouse. Aiden parks closest to the front gate as if he's expecting that we'll have to make a quick exit. I've never actually been inside, but my mom used to send Cooper and me down to the gate to get our dad to come home. She knew that even the gorillas who work the door couldn't turn away two cute, hungry kids when they came knocking for their daddy.

The perimeter is monitored with several obvious security cameras and a bunch of hidden ones. The front gate is made of eight-foot metal bars that have been painted in alternating club colors. The garage door has a large and particularly vicious looking lion head club logo painted on it. At night, it's lit up and looks like it's rising out of the flames of hell. The fence is sheet metal so people can't get near or even see the house from the street. There is a smaller solid steel gate that leads to the front yard. It has one of those small lookout windows that the doorman can talk to visitors through, and, if necessary, I guess he could get a good shot through it.

Aiden knocks twice, waits, and knocks one more time.

The lookout hatch opens. "Hey, Gylly. Come on in." The gate opens and we walk into the front yard. The guy who answered the door is Flow. I used to babysit his daughter. "Hey, T Bear," he says. I have to stand on my tiptoes just to reach my arms around his gigantic waist. He smells like beer. When he hugs me back, it makes me groan because my ribs shift. "Sorry to hear about Cooper."

"Thanks, Flow. How's Penny?"

"Good. She's in the eighth grade now."

"Don't forget to tell her that you love her or she'll end up dating thugs."

He laughs. "Go on up to the house. Chaz is expecting you."

The path to the door is illuminated with garden lights, and the yard looks professionally landscaped with a cascading waterfall and a rock garden. Ironically, it's almost tranquil. Aiden knocks on the front door. Instead of holding my hand, he clutches my elbow, prepared to chuck me out of the way if he needs to.

Chaz opens the door wearing a shoulder holster with two guns. His goatee is braided and he's wearing dark glasses even though it's dark out. He nods at Aiden, then bends over to give me a hug. "Hey, T Bear. Sorry about Cooper." His gun digs into my ribs, which makes me flinch. His whiskers scratch like sandpaper on my cheek.

"Thanks, Chaz. How's your back?"

"Good. I tried that acupuncture shit you suggested and it's pretty much better."

"I told you not to be a pussy about the needles."

"The needles still creep me out." He closes and bolts the door behind us and then leads us into what looks like a waiting area at a Hard Rock Café. There are leather benches lining the perimeter of the small alcove. Club paraphernalia is hung in framed glass cases on the blue walls. The collection consists of things like rockers and other patches that were likely stolen from rival clubs, photos of famous people with members at rallies, and the cuts of dead members all on display. The encased cut above my head has a brass plate on the frame with the name "Southpaw" engraved on it. My dad's cut is in the case next to it. I recognize it without even reading the nameplate because there is a purple stain on his bottom rocker from the time when Cooper hugged him with a Popsicle in his hand. I thought he would get in trouble for staining the patch, but my dad said the dirtier the better. He also said that it would remind him of us wherever he went.

"Phones." Chaz holds out his dry, sausage-fingered hands. He checks our pockets, pats us both down for weapons, and takes Gylly's switchblade out of his boot. "Wait here. Someone will come out to get you," he says as he lights a cigarette.

Aiden sits down, and the muscles in his arms and neck are as tense as iron cables. He avoids making eye contact with me. A guy I don't recognize shows up and doesn't say anything. He jerks his chin toward a hallway and walks away. I glance at Aiden before we follow the guy. He's not that tall, but his shoulders are so wide he barely fits width-wise in the hall. More memorabilia lines the walls. The floors are sticky and the windows are all blacked out. It smells as if everything in the building has been marinated in alcohol and smoke.

Females aren't really allowed in the club unless a member invites them and Randy approves. Even then it's usually only if they have been hired for services. I tap my thumbnail against my teeth as we get farther away from Flow and Chaz. Individually, one-on-one, none of the guys who hung out with my dad is overly intimidating. All together, mixed with members I've never met before, they are volatile and scary.

Men's voices are loud at the end of the hall. Aiden's hand slides up and clutches my elbow again. The sounds are coming from what is essentially a big living room with a bar at one end and a bunch of overstuffed leather lounger chairs in front of a gigantic big screen TV. Music is playing, but not that loudly. The wall has another club logo painted on it and beneath it is a poker table. On the other end of the room there is a pool table. At least twelve guys are sitting around or playing pool. Uncle Len is stretched out in a lounger with the footrest up in front of the big screen TV, watching a UFC fight. He meets my eye and nods. A girl in a bikini dances on a mini-stage complete with a stripper pole. She looks wrecked, and she can barely stand, let alone dance.

Someone whistles, which is followed by catcalls. Aiden's hand tightens around my arm. We follow our guide deeper into the room and everyone else looks up. "Fresh pussy. Dibs," a skinny guy with long stringy hair and crooked teeth says, as he leans his pool cue against the table and walks toward me. The guy who is escorting us straight-arms the skinny guy right in the Adam's apple. The skinny guy clutches his throat. "What the fuck, man?" he chokes out between coughs.

"This is Gylly's girl and Big Bert's daughter. Have some fucking respect, motherfucker, or I'll fucking bury you." The skinny guy looks at me and waves apologetically with one hand while still holding his throat with the other. The wide guy, whose name I see now is Poncho from the patch on his chest, says, "Stay here, Gylly."

Aiden nods and releases my arm, but I can tell by the way he's clenching his jaw that he doesn't want to.

"No," I say. "Gylly comes with me or I'm not going." I flop down in an empty lounger and cross my legs. "Ew. Why is this chair sticky? Gross." I stand up and rub my hands on my jeans. "Tell Digger I'm not going anywhere without Gylly."

Uncle Len is smiling as if he's listening, but he's not looking at me. He's watching the fight on TV. Poncho pulls out his phone. He has a short conversation with someone about how I'm refusing to go in without Gylly. He nods a couple times and then puts his phone back in his cut, steps toward me, and clutches my hair with his meaty hands. Aiden tries to pull me free, but two guys grab his arms and hold him back. Poncho drags me kicking and screaming toward a door. Hair rips out of my scalp. I dig my fingernails into his flesh. He doesn't care, so I try repeatedly to knee him in the crotch.

"Hey!" Uncle Len yells. "Take it easy."

It's not clear whether he's talking to me or Poncho. Uncle Len is the Sergeant-at-Arms for the club, which means he enforces and maintains order among the members. He's responsible for internal discipline, so whether he meant to control Poncho or me doesn't make a difference—we both comply.

Poncho loosens his grip on my hair and I stop struggling as he pushes me out of the room. Mickey is standing guard down the hall outside what looks like a bedroom door.

"Mickey, tell this Neanderthal to let me go," I plead.

"Just keep your mouth shut and do what you're told, T Bear." Mickey sighs as if he wishes he didn't have to have anything to do with the situation.

He knocks and Randy grumbles, "Yeah."

Mickey opens the door and shoves me in. He stays out in the hall and closes the door behind me. There's a guy sitting on a chair in front of Randy's desk, but he stands and turns to look at me as I stumble in.

"Hey, Cisco," I say.

"Hey, Ti. Sorry about Cooper."

"Thanks."

"Excuse us," Randy says to Cisco. "Tell Cain I'll call him back." Cisco nods and exits out a different door than the one Mickey is guarding. Randy squints at something on a computer screen. Surveillance monitors line the wall behind his desk. They are aimed at Flow at the gate, Chaz at the front door, the stripper in the living room, and some empty rooms and hallways. Four monitors are turned off and only show a black screen. They must be the views of the pool table and bar and lounge because none of the working cameras are showing those areas.

"Why aren't you watching the assholes in the living room? I want to be able to see Aiden."

"The cameras are broken."

"Bullshit. I'm outta here." I turn to leave, but when I open the door Mickey shoves me back in and slams the door. "What the fuck, Digger? You can't keep me here against my will."

"Actually, I can do whatever I want. Sit down, watch your language, and stop being so goddamn ungrateful. We've been working on finding out what happened to Cooper."

"Thank you for that, but I don't see why I had to come to this toilet to hear what you have to say. We could have just talked at your house. I like you better when you're not acting like a P."

"Sit down."

"No. Don't tell me what to do."

He rolls his eyes, but I can tell he's exasperated, not angry. His gaze lands on the ring that Gylly gave me and his expression turns more serious. "Please, have a seat, T Bear." I sit down and cross my arms. He shakes his head and mumbles something about Gylly having his work cut out for him. "Do you make everything this difficult?"

"I told you I didn't want to come here. You're the one who's making it difficult."

"I only talk business in this office and at church, so get over it." He sits back in his chair and stretches his arms behind his head. "We try to make it pretty nice here. Eighty percent of the guys have known you since you were in diapers. I don't see why you don't like it."

"I don't like what it stands for. I don't like what goes on here. Most importantly, I don't like that my dad liked it here better than he liked it at home, and that's why he's dead now." My hand touches something sticky again. I examine my palms and wrinkle my nose. "I also don't like that it's filthy and it stinks in here." He chuckles, but I glare at him with stone cold seriousness. "This place is going to kill you one day, too. You know that, right?"

"Don't worry about me, T Bear." He leans forward and rests his elbows on the desk. "The reason I asked you here is to tell you what we know so far. The bitches who hit your dad are taken care of."

"What does that mean? You killed them?"

"I didn't do shit." He reaches into his cut and pulls out a pack of cigarettes, then lights one. "Let's just say that two of them are dead and the other two are behind bars. The cops were conveniently tipped off after a different hit and they got pulled over riding dirty."

"What did my dad do to them?"

"You don't need to know all the details. Things got fucked, he tried to unfuck them and there was a miscommunication."

"What does this have to do with Cooper?"

"We're still making all the connections." His tone has exactly the same calm confidence that he uses when he's at home. It seems eerie now, given the severity of what we are talking about it. It must mean that he deals with as serious, or worse, things all the time.

"I don't understand why they would go after Cooper if they already got my dad."

"It's not about your dad anymore. It's about you."

"Me? What?" I shake my head to give myself a second to process the shock. "Why?"

"It looks like that Crofton kid works for the gang that popped your dad."

"What?" I'm so confused right now. Leland has a kid. He deals more than weed. He works for a gang that murdered my father. And all this is connected to my brother's death. That can't be true. I don't want that to be true. "Leland doesn't work for a gang. He works for his dad."

"He's been using his dad's company to move shit internationally for an Asian gang."

My heart hammers as the horrible truth sinks in. I can't

believe I didn't see it, but I still don't understand how all the pieces fit together. "Cooper had nothing to do with Leland. It doesn't make any sense that he would be killed because of Leland's *alleged* connections."

"It's only one possibility. I don't know if it was a hit, an accident, or — " He scratches his head and glances at me. "Or suicide."

"Cooper wouldn't have killed himself."

He shrugs and takes a drag from his cigarette as if he's uncomfortable suggesting it, but believes that it's a feasible theory.

God, this is painful. I really wish I didn't need to be here talking to the president of an international outlaw motorcycle club about the death of my innocent little brother. I inhale and squeeze the armrest, searching for the strength to continue as the redness drains from my knuckles. "If you've had guys tailing us, I don't understand why Cooper is dead and nobody knows why."

"He wasn't being tailed when it happened."

"Why not?"

"He went to his" — Randy makes air quotations with his fingers — "'friend's' house, and every other time that meant they were staying in for the night, so the tail left. No offense, but it's hard to get my guys to stick around while two guys are fucking." He shudders like the image that he conjured makes him sick.

"Grow up."

"Anyway. Cooper must have gone out after he was at that Sam kid's house. Maybe they had a fight. Maybe he was depressed. I don't know."

Fuck you, Randy. You didn't know him like I did. "Cooper wouldn't have killed himself."

"They found his body at the base of a fourteen story building under construction. You have to consider it as a possibility."

"Maybe one of your homophobic goons pushed him off the building because he was gay. Have you considered *that* as a possibility?"

"All my guys, including the guy who was tailing him, were here for a patch ceremony that night. Besides, most of the guys have known that Cooper was gay for a long time. They don't really care, or at least they don't show that they care, because your dad and uncles always supported him."

"They knew?"

"Sure." He glances over his shoulder at the surveillance monitors. He turns back toward me, but avoids looking directly in my eyes. "If you want to know exactly what happened to Cooper, I suggest that we ask Sam again what he was doing that night. I'll send one of my guys to—"

"No," I interrupt. "Don't send anyone to talk to Sam. I'll do it myself."

"Fine, but I don't want you to go anywhere near that Crofton cocksucker. Make sure Aiden is with you at all times until I get it sorted out."

"Yeah, whatev— Hey. What the hell?" I stand up and stare at the monitor that shows the stripper on it. She's sprawled out on the floor because Aiden just flew across the screen and crashed into her. I run to the door. Mickey is in the hall leaning with his back against the wall and his arms crossed. He obviously wasn't expecting me to come running out and I'm able to scoot past him before he reacts. I sprint down the hall, but he catches me by the waist before I get halfway to the second door.

"Let go of me!" I screech. "They're beating Aiden up."

"He can handle it."

"Let go of me!" I scream and struggle as if I'm having an epileptic fit. "He can't handle twelve against one. You're supposed to be his friend." I punch him in the face and he winces a little.

He holds me by the shoulders and pushes me against the wall. "Settle down. He knew this would happen when he applied to be a pig."

"What? I didn't know he wanted to be a cop."

"He doesn't want to be a cop."

"Then why did he apply?" I ask, confused and still just as terrified for Aiden.

"The club doesn't allow members who have applied to be either a cop or a prison guard."

I study Mickey's expression and suddenly understand. "He's trying to get kicked out?"

"Yeah."

"Why didn't he just quit?"

"It doesn't work that way. I pulled door duty so I wouldn't have to be involved."

"Not doing anything to help him is just as bad." I can't believe that Aiden's idea of a plan consists of getting his head kicked in. I start flailing again. "Please, let go of me."

"No. It's better if you stay here until they're done."

"Digger!" I scream. "Make them stop. He's your son!"

His dad doesn't say anything, and he doesn't come out of the office.

Mickey leans his body weight on me and traps me up against the wall. "This is your fault, Ti. He did it for you and these are the consequences."

"Let go of me, or I'll tell Aiden what you did on New Year's."

He steps back, but doesn't let go of my arms. The color drains from his face. He lowers his voice, "Don't do that, Ti. I was super high and I didn't mean it."

"I think you need to let go of my arm because, if I remember correctly, a member doesn't take very kindly to another member trying to move in on his woman without permission."

"I only tried to kiss you, and Gylly wasn't a member then."

I hiss a threat in his ear. "But Mack was a member when you fucked his wife in Gylly's bed without asking Mack first. They'll probably take a cheese grater and scrape that club tattoo right off your arm for a violation like that. Let go of me and then help me get Aiden out of here or your secret will be club gossip."

He steps back and lets go of my arms. I run down the hall and push open the door that leads into the living room. Aiden curls up on the floor as three guys kick his torso. The rest of the members, including Uncle Len and Aiden's Uncle Vern, do nothing but watch with amused expressions. The girl is up dancing again as if it's nothing worth even noticing. I grab a pool cue off the wall rack and swing it like a baseball bat at the guy who just toe-punted Aiden in the kidney. It slams against his ear and shatters into a million splinters. The guy cringes like it hurt a little, but all it seems to do is enrage him.

"That was dumb, bitch," he growls and lunges toward me.

Uncle Len stands up to come to my rescue, but he doesn't need to because I stomp the guy's knee sideways to blow out his MCL the way my dad taught me. He drops like a tranquilized rhino. Aiden punches one of the other guys while he's distracted and that guy drops, too. The third guy smiles in surrender after noticing his two incapacitated buddies. Then he stretches his arm across Aiden's shoulders. "Good job, Gylly. You held your mud pretty good."

Aiden's face is completely cut up and already starting to swell. He smiles triumphantly and stumbles over to fall onto one of the loungers. Uncle Len nods at me to check that I'm okay, then sits back down to watch the TV. A guy named Oscar brings Aiden a drink and pats his shoulder. "Good job, Gylly. Should I get your girl a drink, too?"

They all laugh and go back to playing pool and watching the girl dance. Are they fucking insane? Who finds something like that humorous? This is how they entertain their feeble little minds? It's sick and juvenile. I want to vomit. Mickey and Cisco both stand near the door to the living room with proud grins. Aiden struggles to push himself out of the chair and limps over to them. They both hug him and pat his back with big swats as if he just graduated from college or something.

The guy who Aiden punched comes around and attempts to sit up. The guy I kicked is trying to get to his feet. He's in a lot of pain. If I did it right, he'll need knee surgery. He glares at me and mumbles, "She's definitely Big Bert's daughter."

Aiden grins and it makes me furious that he's not mad or disgusted that his brothers would do that to him. I throw a couple of empty beer bottles at him, then storm out. I hate everything about this place. When I reach the waiting room, I push Chaz off his stool. I pick it up and swing it to smash the glass encasing my dad's cut. I rip it off the wall, stomp on it, and scream, "I hate you! Why did you make all this fucked up bullshit my life? I hate you. I hate you. I fucking hate you. Bastard."

I dig my heel into the patch that has his name stitched on it, trying to rip it off, but stop short when I notice the tiny gold guardian angel pin that I gave him when I was ten to keep him safe. It is still pierced through the leather above the left chest pocket. I drop to my knees and touch the wings with my finger. I knew by that age that my dad was the bad guy because he'd already done time, but I was afraid that the good guys would kill him if he didn't have a guardian angel. I stole the pin from a gift shop and gave it to him before he left for one of his road trips. When I told him why I wanted him to have it he hugged me so tightly I couldn't breathe. He said he would never take it off, and clearly he never did.

I lift the vest off the floor and hug the leather in to my chest. It still smells like gasoline, oil, and road filth. I'm not sure whether to be sad that the guardian angel eventually failed him, or happy that it kept him alive for eight years longer than he deserved. Actually, I am sure how I feel. I'm heartbroken that he got what he deserved. I'm devastated that his guardian angel failed him and he's not here anymore. I miss him.

"I'm sorry I didn't keep Cooper safe, Daddy," I whisper into the collar. "I love you and I'll take care of everything. I promise."

After hugging the leather for another second, I stand up and neatly fold the cut so that only his name and the guardian angel pin are showing. I wipe the tears off my cheeks with my sleeve and look up to see Aiden and Uncle Len standing next to Chaz, all watching me.

This is why they don't let females into the clubhouse.

I grab my phone off the counter and demand with a completely steady voice that Chaz let me out. He quickly unbolts the door and I run to the gate and ask Flow to open it. He looks through the lookout window first, then opens the gate. I walk right past all the bikes. I feel like knocking them over, but I'm not that stupid. Not even Randy and Len together could help me if I trashed a bike.

I storm down the street, not sure where I'm going. I could catch the bus or call Uncle Blaine. Maybe I'll just keep walking until I manage to sort out my feelings. Aiden pulls the bike up beside me. He's still grinning like an idiot. "Hop on."

"You're not wearing your cut."

"I'm not a member anymore. They kept it."

I can't believe it really happened. I'm stunned that he actually went through with it. "And you did that for me?"

He nods with a look of fierce commitment that leaves no doubt in my mind that he would do anything for me. All right. I guess it's real. I don't know how I'm ever going to top that level of dedication, but I'm determined to do everything in my power to prove to him that his sacrifice was worth it. I straddle the seat and rest my cheek on his shoulder.

"How pissed is your dad?"

"Don't worry about it." He shrugs as if it doesn't matter, but I know that disappointing his dad is probably killing him.

"I can't believe he let them beat up his own son."

"None of that matters anymore." He reaches his arm back over his shoulder and grabs my neck, then pulls me forward to kiss him. "All that matters is that you are going to have the life you want—a safe life. I will still make sure justice is served for Cooper, but I don't have to do anything for them ever again. I won't do anything you don't want me to do."

"Promise."

"I promise."

"If you break that promise I will stab you."

He pats my leg. "You might need to get your anger management problem treated by a professional."

"Ya think?"

He laughs. "I can't believe you said you left me because you didn't want to turn out like your mom."

"Why? It's true."

"That never would have happened. You're nothing like your mom. You're a carbon fucking copy of your dad."

Yeah, based on my behavior earlier, I would have to agree. I stand on the pegs and lean over his shoulder to kiss his cheek. "Do you have a problem with that?"

"No." He starts the bike. "I love that."

"We need to go talk to Sam," I shout over the rumble of the engine.

Aiden nods like he already knows, and we take off.

Chapter Twenty-Six

Sam answers the door and looks incredibly relieved to see me. He eyes Aiden briefly, then waves us into the house and closes the door. "Cara's a wreck. You need to talk to her."

"Why? What's wrong?"

"She's convinced that Cooper's death is her fault and she's been inconsolable." He pulls my hand, and Aiden and I follow him up the stairs.

"Why in the world would she think it's her fault?"

"Just follow me."

He looks both ways down the hallway as if he's worried that their parents are lurking, then pushes us into her bedroom. Cara is on the window seat with her knees tucked up against her chest. She's staring at the glass absently and it's obvious she's been crying. She doesn't seem to notice us come in.

"Cara. Tienne is here," Sam says gently.

She turns her head and sobs when she sees me. "I'm sorry,

Tienne. I'll understand if you hate me and can never forgive me."

I cross the room and sit next to her on the window seat. "What are you talking about? You were with me the night Cooper died."

She gulps for air and blows her nose in a tissue. "After I dropped you guys off, I drove home and found Cooper sitting on the front steps."

Sam paces and says, "I didn't know he was here. He didn't call to say he was coming over and he must not have rung the bell."

Cara blows her nose again. "I offered to give him a ride home, but he had Leland's car and he said he didn't want to go home anyway. We sat on the steps talking about the fight that he had with Sam." She glances at her brother, who seems crushed that their fight led to something so horrible. "He also told me that some guys at school were giving him a hard time for being gay."

"Who?" Aiden asks.

Cara flinches as if she didn't know he was in the room. She sits up and runs her hands down her hair to smooth it. Then she frowns because his bruises and cuts make him look like he was hit by a truck. "The boyfriend named Gylly, I presume."

I nod. Aiden's mouth turns up at the corner, pleased to know that my friend has at least heard about him.

"I don't know who was harassing Cooper." Cara turns to face her brother. "Do you, Sam?"

Sam shakes his head. "No. All I ever saw were the normal everyday homophobic whispers and snickers. If someone was really bothering him, they did it when I wasn't around, and he didn't share it with me."

"But what does this have to do with you?" I ask Cara.

She inhales and rubs her temples before closing her eyes. "I'm not proud of what I'm about to tell you. I didn't tell the police because I was so afraid of what my parents would do if they found out." She buries her face in her hands. "If I could take it all back I would."

Aiden's eyebrows angle sharply in a tense frown. I swallow hard and brace myself for what she's going to say. "Just tell me, Cara. I would rather know."

She exhales heavily. "Leland came up to me at the club and asked if I would be interested in taking over his clients."

That's infuriating. I can't believe he stooped that low. When I see him, he is going to be so sorry he ever met me.

Cara wipes her eyes and continues, "He thought I would appreciate the extra money and, honestly, I did. You know my parents have been struggling financially and I need the money for college—I would have never even considered it otherwise. His clients are all people I know and it sounded super easy. He said some guy would drop the stuff off at my house with a list of names, I would deliver it to everyone at the club, and the guy would come by at the end of the week to pick up the money, minus my cut."

Sam paces and clutches his hair in frustration as if he can't believe she was naïve enough to get sucked in to it.

"I still don't understand what this has to do with the night Cooper died," I say.

Cara sits up straighter, bracing herself for what she is about to say. "Cooper was really stressed with taking care of your mom, fighting with Sam, coping with your dad's murder, and dealing with assholes at school. He hadn't been sleeping for weeks. I gave him some drugs to calm him down and help him sleep."

"No," I gasp. That's impossible. "Cooper wouldn't have taken drugs."

"It was supposed to be the same stuff a doctor would have given him. Just some generic anti-anxiety meds."

"Supposed to be?" Aiden asks. Thankfully he is thinking clearly enough to come up with useful questions, since I'm too stunned to get past the idea that Cooper would have taken anything, let alone something illegal.

Cara starts crying again. "I think I might have given him the wrong stuff. I had two different bags and if he took pills from the wrong one it would have made him high."

Sam rests his hand on her shoulder to comfort her. "Cooper and I used to climb a building at the construction site where his body was found. We went there when we wanted to be alone. It's quiet and you can see out over the city if you climb all the way to the top. It's quite dangerous and if he was high, he could have easily slipped and fell."

"I'm sorry, Tienne," Cara sputters out.

I hug her and look over her shoulder at Aiden. I can tell he thinks that's probably what happened. Part of me wants to believe it was a freak accident, but Cooper wouldn't have taken pills, especially if he didn't know what they were. "It's not your fault, Cara. I'm sure if he fell, it was just an accident."

"They'll find out if he had drugs in his system when the autopsy results come back," Sam says. "Should we tell the police that this might be what happened?"

"No," I say and stand up. "I don't see the point in getting Cara in trouble. Even if he took a pill that made him high and then fell, it was an accident. I don't think that's what happened, though."

"Why?"

"Because I know Cooper." I hug Sam and whisper in his ear, "He cared about you a lot. Thanks for making him happy." He starts to cry. I turn to Cara and say, "Stop dealing immediately."

She nods, wiping her face. "I already did."

"Whether it turns out that he had drugs in his system or not, it wasn't your fault. Thanks for being honest." I walk across the room and Aiden drapes his arm across my shoulder.

Neither one of them says anything before we leave because they're both crying.

"It's probably what happened," Aiden says as we step out their front door.

"Maybe." He heads for the bike, but I stop and pull out my phone. "I have to make a quick call. Give me a second." Aiden frowns, but gives me some space, and I dial Leland's number.

When he answers, he doesn't say anything, but I can hear him breathing.

"I just had a chat with Cara," I say with a bitterness that sounds harsh even for me. "It was nice of you to give her a job since she needs the money for college."

He matches my tone and fires back, "I stopped dealing. That's what you wanted."

"I didn't mean that you should get one of my friends to take over for you."

"Can we talk about this when I get back?" His tone has deflated as if he's too exhausted to fight.

"No. We're talking about this now. Why didn't you tell me about Braden?"

After a pause he exhales slowly. "I wanted to, but I couldn't. I get my trust fund when I turn twenty-five. If my parents find out about Braden before then, they'll disown me and cut me off."

"Why aren't you here right now? Tell me the truth."

"It's complicated, Tienne."

"Complicated as in you've got problems with your international drug trafficking business?"

He lowers his voice to a whisper, "Leaving my past behind hasn't been as easy as I thought it would be."

Even though I already knew that, something about how he said it makes all of the pieces fall together. The link that Randy has been searching for was right in front of my eyes the entire time. A new storm slams through my body. I crouch and cover my mouth with my trembling palm.

After several attempts, I suck in enough air to ask, "Do you know what happened to Cooper?"

He's silent for a while before his breath catches and his voice cracks. "I'm so sorry."

I stand and scream into the phone. "Fuck you, Leland! He was just an innocent kid. He didn't do anything to deserve that."

"You think I don't know that?" he shouts back. He's crying, which makes me tear up, too. "If I could trade places with him, I would. I know how much he meant to you and it's killing me that I can't make it better."

Aiden stands in front of me and, based on how tense he is, I assume he put the pieces together as well.

"Why Cooper?" I ask Leland.

"They made a mistake. I told them I quit and they didn't exactly accept my resignation. I was the target and some guy thought Cooper was me because he was driving my car. Cooper was just in the wrong car at the wrong time."

I turn away from Aiden so I won't be distracted by his protective rage. I walk down the sidewalk furious and fighting back nausea. "Why did you pursue me?"

"What?"

"Why me? Why did you ask me out?"

"Because I like you."

"Don't fucking lie to me. You work for the gang that murdered my father. It wasn't a coincidence, was it?"

He's silent for a while then he says, "I didn't know who you were when I met you."

"But once you did?"

"When they found out we were dating they asked me to get information about Noir et Bleu business. I told them I wouldn't do it."

I shake my head, though he can't see it, and tears roll down my cheeks.

"I didn't do it. I quit. I swear to God." He breathes out tension. "They came after me and got Cooper by accident. I'm so sorry."

"Who did it?" I shout.

"I'm going to deal with it."

I nearly laugh. What does he think he's going to do about it? Even if I thought he could or would, I don't trust him to do it. "Braden needs you. I'll take care of it myself. Tell me the name of the person responsible."

"You can't take care of it. He's super connected."

Now I do laugh out loud. "So am I. Did you forget?"

"You shouldn't mess with this guy."

Wow. That almost sounded convincing. If I didn't know

better, I might actually believe that he was concerned for my well-being. "He shouldn't have messed with me, and you shouldn't have either."

"He will kill you and me and everyone we care about."

"He won't be able to." I glance at Aiden, who is close enough to hear everything and appears ready to do whatever it takes if I say the word. "Tell me who did it or I'll call your parents and let them know about Braden."

He doesn't respond, but I can hear his breath quicken. I struck the chink in his armor. I know because the only thing that would have stopped my dad short is if anyone ever brought up his kids in relation to business.

"Tell me his fucking name."

"Johnny Lee."

I hang up and, in a bizarre, rage-filled calm, I walk over to the bike to put on my helmet. Aiden shoots me a warning glare and says, "Don't even think about it."

"What?" I avoid eye contact and channel the fury into coming up with a foolproof revenge plot.

"I can tell what you're planning by the expression on your face. You're not allowed to get involved."

"Don't tell me what to do." My voice sounds like it doesn't belong to me. It sounds like my dad.

"Ti, it's too dangerous. Let the police handle it."

"With what proof? If Leland gives them evidence, he'll be incriminating himself."

"So? It's the least he could do. Your brother is dead because of him."

"No, my brother's dead because of me. It wouldn't have happened if I wasn't stupid enough to get involved with a drug dealer."

"It wasn't your fault. You didn't know how deep he was in."

I raise my eyebrows, unconvinced, then straddle the bike so I don't have to look at the trepidation in his eyes.

"If you aren't going to go to the police, at least promise that you'll tell my dad the guy's name and let your uncles take care of it." When I don't respond, he reaches over and gently holds my chin to turn my face toward him. "I didn't leave all this shit behind to win you back. I left it to keep you safe. If you go running back into it, what was the point?"

I start bawling and cover my face with my hands. "But it's all my fault. I have to fix it."

Chapter Twenty-Seven

The knowledge that Cooper died because of my relationship with Leland kept me awake all night. The knowledge of what I now need to do about it is what motivated me to get out of bed this morning. Uncle Ronnie picked me up from Blaine and Elizabeth's house and we're driving my mom to the treatment center. Aiden wanted to come too, to make sure I don't do anything stupid like go after Johnny Lee by myself. I had to swear on Cooper's grave that I wouldn't do that in order to convince Aiden that he should stay and take his exam. I need to talk to Ronnie alone, anyway.

The treatment center looks like a country estate. All my uncles and a couple other Noir et Bleu guys pitched in to pay for it because they want Mom to have the best treatment possible, since it was her choice, and they want her to succeed this time. It looks like it's going to be a holiday, but I doubt it's going to feel like that for her.

She hugs me when we get out of the car, but she doesn't

say anything.

"I'll see you when you get out," I say encouragingly.

She nods and picks up her bag. Ronnie and I both lean against the hood of the car as she walks toward the front gate and presses a buzzer at the guard station. The gate opens and she glances back at us briefly before walking in. Once the gate closes completely, Ronnie stretches his massive arm across my shoulder and hugs me into his side. It's kind of touching since he doesn't know anything about parenting.

After giving me one more squeeze, he stands and walks around the front of the car to get back behind the wheel. I slide into the passenger seat and gaze at him.

"What?" he asks as he checks over his shoulder to back the car up.

Um, okay, this is my one chance to pitch the idea. It needs to be perfect. "I have a plan to get the guy who killed Cooper."

"Yeah, so do I."

"No. I don't want to do it your way."

"You're not going to do it my way or your way." The volume of his voice increases and booms within the confines of the car. "You're not going to be involved at all."

Yeah, well, like it or not, I'm not a weak little girl and I'm the only one who knows the name of the guy. "You can't stop me."

"The hell I can't."

"I'm going to get the guy whether you help me or not and, since I have vital information that you need, you might want to at least hear my plan."

He glances at me and frowns with a hint of concession. "Fine. What's your plan?"

"You have to swear that you'll let me do it."

"I ain't swearing shit. Tell me your idea. If it could work, we'll run it by Digger. If it can't work, we're doing it our way."

I tell him my plan and when I'm done, I study his face, waiting for a reaction.

Eventually, he smiles, impressed. "Damn, girl. That might just work."

I clap to celebrate the small victory. "I told you."

His belly bounces as he chuckles. "You're so much like your daddy, it's scary."

"No." I point at him in a sassy way. "My dad was stupid enough to get caught." I pull out my phone and call Randy. Unfortunately, he won't let me tell him my idea over the phone, which means Ronnie has to take me to the clubhouse again. I roll my eyes and hang up on Randy. I desperately wish I could do it without his help, but I can't, so I guess I'll have to suck it up and deal.

We drive for a while and Ronnie says, "I think your mom's going to be able to do it this time."

"I doubt it. Cooper and Dad both died within six months. If there is ever a good time to be numb to the world, it's now."

"Cooper's death is what made her decide to check herself in. She can't ever make up time with Cooper now, but she still has a chance with you. She doesn't want to miss out on being in your life anymore."

I sit quietly and watch the crop rows distort as we pass them. After a while I turn in my seat to face him. "I wish someone would have told me why Dad killed those guys so I would have understood why she became an addict."

His eyes shift to meet mine briefly before he focuses back on the road. "That's not the kind of shit a kid should know happened to their mom."

"I wouldn't have been so mean to her if I had known." I start to cry, but try to stifle it because Ronnie won't like it if I'm blubbering.

He reaches his right arm over and pats my shoulder roughly. "Don't cry. You can make up for that shit when she's clean. Don't worry about it."

Ronnie isn't the type to say something just to make me feel better. He tells it as he sees it and he has known a lot of drug addicts in his lifetime. If he actually believes she's going to be able to do it, maybe it would be all right for me to have a little faith. I nod and wipe my cheeks, feeling both hopeful about my mom and scared about sharing my plan with Randy.

An hour and a half later, I'm sitting in the chair in Randy's office. He must have ordered someone to clean it because it's not sticky anymore. Ronnie stands against the wall with his arms folded. Len and Terry stand behind me. They all listen to my plan. Randy scratches his neck when I finish, but doesn't respond.

I break the silence by saying, "You have to promise not to tell Aiden because, if he finds out, he'll try to stop me or get involved. I don't want him to get hurt, especially after everything he has done for me."

"Yeah," Randy says absently.

"Promise you won't tell him."

He coughs and drinks from a beer bottle. He exhales and looks at each of my uncles. "Are you all okay with it?" Ronnie nods his agreement and I turn in the chair to face

Terry and Len. They both nod in solidarity, too. "All right," says Randy. "Only you four know about it. Get 'er done."

I jump up and bound around the desk to give Randy a big hug. "Thanks, Digger."

"This makes you a One Percenter."

"Yeah right. I smell too good to be a One Percenter."

A growl rumbles in his throat and my instincts make me step away cautiously. "I wonder what Aiden would think of your plan." The tone of his voice is casual and conversational, but that's what makes it terrifying.

Panic surges through my veins as I consider the possibility that he will use this favor to bribe Aiden to come back. "I don't want him involved."

"I'm fully aware of that." He shoos me away.

"I'm serious, Randy. You'll never see either one of us again if you try to drag him back in."

"Just say thank you and get out."

I turn and check the expressions of all my uncles. Oh, man, this might have been a mistake. "Thank you," I mumble, then leave, my mind racing with second thoughts.

Chapter Twenty-Eight

Randy used his resources to find out where Johnny Lee lives. Then my uncles did surveillance on him for two weeks to learn his patterns. He's a mid-level gang member, unmarried, no kids. The wait is annoying and nerve-racking, but they want to take their time and do it right with no mistakes—especially since I'm going to be involved. I went back to work after a few days and rehearsed for hours on my audition every evening to distract myself. It's not really working, though. Concentrating on drapery colors, flooring samples, and script lines is impossible while the revenge plot plays repeatedly in my mind.

It's killing me to keep the secret from Aiden. I told him my uncles are taking care of everything, which is technically true. If there were a better way for them to get back at Johnny that didn't require my involvement, I would be all for it, but my way is the only one I would be able to live with in good conscience for the rest of my life. Every time Aiden gets suspicious or asks me why I'm so jittery, I kiss him to make him forget. He's been getting a lot of action lately. He's finished his school term now and is working the night shift at a group home, which is where he is tonight.

Elizabeth walks into the kitchen and sits at the barstool watching me as I get the ingredients ready for dinner.

"I'm making tacos if you and Blaine want to join me."

She spins the salt and pepper shakers around on the counter a few times. "How are you doing?"

"Fine."

"No, I mean how are you *really* doing?"

I can't tell her that I'm a mess of nerves, so I dodge it and say, "I don't want to talk about it." I wash some lettuce and break it up in a colander.

"When is your audition?"

This is good. I can handle superficial conversation. "Next Friday."

"Are you feeling ready?"

"Yeah, I think it's going to go well."

"How are things at the office?"

It's actually been a shit show since she's been away, but I don't want her to feel like she needs to worry. "Cassidy will be relieved when you're ready to come back, but she's handling everything, so there's no rush."

"What's Leland been up to?"

Shit. That is way far from superficial conversation. "No idea."

"What happened between you two?"

"It's complicated."

She nods as if she understands, but her expression makes it clear that she doesn't. "He called the house today and said you haven't been returning his calls. He said he has something important to talk to you about."

I don't respond because she'll definitely hear the anger in my voice if I do.

She sighs, then changes the subject. "Have you heard from your mom?"

"No. She's not supposed to talk to family or friends until she's been there for a while in case it sets her back or something." That's a first. Who would have believed that the topic of my mom would ever be a welcome relief?

Her head keeps bobbing with the same uncertain understanding until she gets up and walks out. Blaine wanders in and opens the fridge.

I wish I could do more to comfort and reassure Elizabeth, but I can't afford to mess anything up.

"Do you want tacos?" I ask Uncle Blaine.

"Sure, but I should probably check on Liz first. She's really struggling with Cooper's death. She thinks he jumped and she's blaming herself for not seeing the warning signs beforehand."

Shit. I don't want her to suffer. Maybe I could tell them enough that she will at least not feel responsible. "He didn't jump."

"Well, we just don't know yet. Maybe we'll never know for sure," he says as he twists the cap off a beer.

"He didn't jump," I repeat with absolute authority.

His eyebrows angle together. "You know what happened?"

"It's being taken care of," I say and slice the tomatoes.

Blaine moves to stand next to me. "Shouldn't we let the police handle it?"

"Don't worry about it. Just tell Elizabeth that it wasn't

her fault."

He nods slowly, then reaches for the stool as if he needs to sit before he falls down. "Please tell me you're not going to be involved in any way."

I force a smile and slide a plate across the counter for him. "Cheddar or mozzarella?"

Long after Elizabeth and Blaine have gone to bed, I'm in my room memorizing lines when my phone rings. I don't recognize the number on the screen, so I assume it's Aiden calling from his work. It's not. It's Leland. I take a steeling breath and slide down onto the floor. "What do you want?"

"I'm sorry about Cooper. I'm sorry that I had to lie to you. And I'm sorry that I wasn't there for you like I promised."

I clench my eyes shut. "That means absolutely nothing at this point."

"I want to testify. I'll tell the police everything and the killer will get put away."

"So will you."

"Not necessarily. Maybe I can get immunity if I testify against some of the higher-up guys."

"I don't want you to take the fall."

"I can't bring Cooper back, but at least I can do the right thing now and make sure justice is served. I'm going to the police."

If Leland goes to jail, Braden will grow up like I did, humiliated and hating his dad. I don't wish that on any kid. After a long silence, I say, "No. Please don't. Ruby and Braden need you to not be in prison. Besides, it's not going to be a problem for much longer."

"Why?"

"It's being taken care of. Please take good care of Braden. Bye, Leland."

At three o'clock in the morning I receive a text from Ronnie. The message is blank.

I spring up, get dressed, and sneak downstairs.

Time to take care of business.

Chapter Twenty-Nine

My heart pounds and my breathing is rapid, but I'm not afraid. I'm jacked. Just like my dad always was when he tore out in the middle of the night after receiving a call. I leave a note for Elizabeth and Blaine that tells them I couldn't sleep and went for a Slurpee. Then I grab the keys to my car. Before I leave, I text Aiden: *TDAGF.* Just in case things don't end well.

At the 7-Eleven, I make sure to park close to the surveillance camera. I sit in my car for a minute pretending to look for something in my purse. I'm still acting distracted as I open the door and step out into the parking lot. It actually takes me by surprise when a guy wearing a black hooded sweatshirt rushes up from behind and grabs me. I scream to get the attention of the store clerk and drop my purse. Then I kick and scream as he carries me to a black Lexus that is parked on an angle so the license plate can be seen on the security camera. The store clerk has the phone pressed to his ear as he watches, wide-eyed. The kidnapper throws me into the trunk, then thrusts his arm in to make it look as if he punched me unconscious.

Ten minutes later the car stops. The trunk opens. The hooded guy lifts me out and throws me over his shoulder like a firefighter. I pretend to be unconscious because there are also exterior security cameras capturing this part. It's my television acting debut. The front door of the modern house is unlocked. The kidnapper opens it and sets me down in the foyer and removes his hood and dark glasses. I almost don't recognize Uncle Len. He is clean-shaven and wearing black skinny pants and club-boy dress shoes instead of motorcycle boots. "You look good as an Asian gangster," I whisper.

He winks, then hands me a pair of leather gloves. I pull them on and follow him upstairs. Ronnie and Terry are already standing in the hall on either side of a closed door. They open it and step in first to make sure Johnny Lee is asleep. Ronnie plants about sixty kilos of stolen cocaine and a duffel bag full of counterfeiting equipment in the room. Len tacks up a bunch of photos of me from various locations around town, along with the playbill from *West Side Story*, to make it look like Johnny's been stalking me for a while. Terry places a couple guns that were used in various unsolved crimes into the closet and between the mattresses. He hands me a gun.

I step up to Johnny's bedside and place the barrel against his forehead. His eyes open. "Hi," I say and smile.

He sits up in a panic and all three of my uncles aim guns at him. He freezes, half-crouched on his bed. "What the fuck?"

"Well," I say. "You made a grave error when you pushed that boy off the building, and now you're going to pay."

"I don't know what you're talking about."

I cock the gun. "I think you do."

He pulls his head back until it hits the wall. His lip trembles and he whines. "I'm sorry. I thought he was someone else."

"The number one rule of executing a hit is to make sure you've got the right fucking person."

"It was a mistake."

"Yes. It was a very big mistake. There really isn't any room for mistakes in this line of business, so you're going to have to pay for that."

"Please," he begs frantically, "I'll do anything. Please don't kill me."

"I'm not going to kill you. I don't believe there is any justification for taking someone's life." I jut my chin toward my uncles. "They, however, don't share the same philosophy."

He eyes my uncles, each casting a monstrous shadow on the wall.

"What I'm going to do to you is way worse than death. I want you to suffer for a long time so you don't forget that what you did was very, very bad."

Johnny tries to lunge off the bed, so Len punches him in the stomach and he falls into a fetal position, moaning. Terry takes the gun from me. I sit on the floor and Len removes my leather gloves, then ties my ankles and wrists. Ronnie hangs a black hoodie like the one Len is wearing on the handle of the closet. He sets a pair of the same club-boy shoes in Johnny's size at the end of the bed and a duplicate pair of the sunglasses on the bedside table. Then he hands Johnny a hypodermic needle and tells him to inject himself.

"No way, man."

Terry presses the gun into his temple and growls, "Do it."

Johnny injects the drugs into a vein in the bend of his arm, and it's obvious that he's done it before. Ronnie said he would use a strong enough dose to make sure I'm safe once they leave. Before long, Johnny's blinks get longer and longer until he topples over in a heap on the bed.

Terry tucks a loaded gun under the bed right near me in case I need to use it. Len drops Johnny's phone on the floor at my feet, then all three of them disappear. I wait for several minutes to let them get out the back door, where they have disabled the security cameras. My heart beats like a hummingbird on crack once they leave. My brilliant idea seems less clever now that I'm alone. Aiden is going to be livid if I die.

I fumble to turn Johnny's phone on and dial 911. "Help," I whisper with a shaky voice when the operator answers. I don't even have to act because I am terrified.

"What's your emergency?"

"I've been kidnapped." I gulp and start sobbing. "Please help me."

"Where are you?"

"I don't know. I was at the 7-Eleven on Barkley Drive. A man grabbed me and threw me in the trunk of a car. I think I'm at his house or something."

"Where is he?"

"He's passed out in the bedroom where I am. He took some drugs and he's out cold, so I stole his phone."

"You should leave the house."

"I can't. He tied my hands and feet together. Please hurry. He's some sort of psycho. He has pictures of me posted on his wall."

"Do you know him?"

"No, I've never seen him before in my life." My voice sounds panicked, and I'm not faking it. "He said he killed my brother and that I'm next."

"What's your name?"

"Tienne Desrochers. My brother was Cooper Desrochers. Please hurry. I'm scared he's going to wake up. He's so creepy and he has guns."

Her keyboard clicks, and there is talking in the background. They must be cross-referencing Johnny's license plate from the 7-Eleven security camera and verifying that it was my purse and car that were at the scene.

"Oh my God," I squeak. "He just moved. Hurry." I scoot back along the floor because he actually did move. He's groaning and trying to get up. My breath isn't going in and out properly. Shit. This was a stupid idea. Why did Randy agree to this insanity?

The operator doesn't say anything for what seems like minutes, but I can hear typing. Johnny rolls onto his side and opens his eyes. He stares right at me. I whimper. He's trying to say something. It comes out as grumbles and I'm not sure if he's pleading for me to help him, or if he's threatening to kill me. I should have let my uncles do it their way. Johnny abruptly sits up and I scream. My back is already wedged against the wall and the dresser is beside me, so I can't get any farther away from him. "He's awake!"

"I'm going to kill you, bitch." He swings his arm as if he's going to hit me, so I hold my bound hands up in front of my face. His punch misses and he falls on the ground half draped on my legs. I scream again and throw the phone at him.

I kick frantically and scoot out from underneath him. I try to worm away, but he grabs my foot. I bend both knees to break his hold, then swing my legs and smash my heels into his face. He cringes, holding his hand to his cheek. I scream and inch my way toward the door. A gun clicks. I spin around. He's sitting on his knees pointing the gun Terry left under the bed at me. Johnny blinks repeatedly as if he's trying to focus his eyes or clear the fog in his brain. His head bobs, then he growls, "Hope you're ready to die."

I squeeze my eyes shut.

The bedroom door slams open. A uniformed cop with his gun drawn fills the doorway. "Police! Drop the gun!"

Johnny glances at the cop, then at me. He blinks dopily, then drops the gun and clasps his hands behind his head. Three cops rush in. Two restrain Johnny. One scoops me up off the floor and carries me downstairs.

Once we are in the foyer, he sits me down on a chair to remove the ankle and wrist restraints. A few minutes later, a paramedic arrives, wraps a blanket around me, and escorts me outside.

I'm shaking and time passes in a strange daze. More police vehicles arrive. The blue and red lights flash hypnotically. A cop unrolls yellow tape to cordon off the street and people crowd to see what the commotion is about.

The paramedic checks me for injuries and, to sell the punch in the trunk, I pretend that my jaw hurts when he touches it. I'm trembling so badly that he guides me to sit in the front seat of a cruiser. My nose starts to bleed heavily, so he makes me lean over my knees and I watch the blood drop down to the pavement.

Eventually, a couple of cops escort a semi-conscious

Johnny out of the house in handcuffs and throw him into the back of a police cruiser. An officer takes my statement, then hands the notes to a detective in street clothes. He reads them, then walks over to me. I'm shivering under the blanket, so I pull it tighter around my shoulders to stop the shaking. "How are you doing?" he asks and searches my face, looking for something.

I shake my head to indicate that I'm not doing well.

"You're safe now. He's in custody."

The cruiser with Johnny Lee in it pulls away, and I can finally take a breath.

The detective scratches his head and makes his disheveled hair messier. "So, you never met this guy before?"

"I don't think so. I didn't recognize him. He had pictures of me as if he was a stalker or something. Maybe he works at a store or a restaurant I go to."

"I doubt it. He's involved in organized crime."

"Oh." I'm trying to sound surprised, but my voice wavers. At least the scared part is convincing.

He taps his pen on the notebook. "He's a known associate of the gang that we believe was also connected to your father's murder."

"Oh, so my brother's death and what happened tonight are all linked with what happened to my dad?"

He nods, still weighing the facts. "Looks like it."

"What's going to happen to him?"

"Well, he was already wanted on two warrants and, even if we can't prove that he was the one who pushed your brother off the building, there is enough incriminating evidence in his bedroom to put him away for quite some time."

"That's good. Will I have to testify in court?"

"Maybe. Your statement and the video evidence will probably be enough for the kidnapping and illegal confinement charges. We found drugs, weapons, counterfeiting equipment, and what looks like child porn on his computer, so it's pretty cut and dry."

"Child porn?" Oops, I might have sounded too shocked to hear that, because we didn't plant any child porn. I hope he suffers in prison.

The detective glances up from his notebook and holds my gaze for an uncomfortably long moment. "He'll likely be going to prison for a long time and you'll be notified if and when he's released."

I don't break the stare, although I'm not sure if my expression is going to reveal more than I want it to. I swallow, but otherwise remain perfectly still. I have never felt more afraid in my entire life. Blood rushes through my body like a tidal wave after an earthquake.

Finally he tucks his pen into the coil of his notebook. "You're free to go. I'll send an officer over. He can either take you home or call someone to come pick you up."

"All right." I slide the blanket off my shoulders and leave it on the front seat of the police cruiser. "Thanks."

He turns and walks away. I exhale and drop my head to hide the proud smile that is creeping across my face. That was the best performance of my life and nobody is ever going to know about it.

An officer approaches and stops in front of me. "Do you want me to call someone or arrange for a ride home?"

I lift my head and smile when I notice the bike parked down the street. "My ride is already here. Thanks." I duck under the police tape and weave through the people on the sidewalk before running across the street.

Aiden gets off the bike, ready for me to fling myself at him. He wraps his arms around me tightly and his lips touch my ear. "You could have been killed."

Relief floods through me. Justice has been served, I'm alive, and Aiden's arms are wrapped around me. A whimper catches in my throat and my eyes fill with tears. "I'm sorry."

He leans back and cradles my face. "I can't believe my dad agreed to let you do something that dangerous."

"He couldn't have stopped me."

He closes his eyes, almost as if he's thanking God or something. "I know."

"Don't let your dad convince you that you owe him. If there is a debt to pay, I'll pay it."

"There's no debt. He doesn't want me to come back."

"You talked to him?"

"He phoned to tell me where to pick you up."

"Really? Why doesn't he want you back?"

He smiles and slides his thumbs over my cheeks to wipe away the tears that dripped out. "Because he knows what it's like to love someone as much as I love you."

"Do you love me enough to forgive me?" I ask.

"Yes, but you're not allowed to go for a three-in-the-morning Slurpee run ever again."

God, he's the most amazing person. "Let's hope I never need to again." I smile and pull his face in.

He leans his forehead on mine. "We can't change where we came from, but we can choose the life we want to live. Are you ready to leave all this bullshit behind you?"

I look back over my shoulder at the real-life type of dramatic scene that I want nothing to do with ever again. I'm so glad it's over and nobody else is going to get hurt. "Yeah. I'm ready."

He leans in to kiss me, then we both straddle the bike.

I rest my chest against the familiar curve of his back. We fit together perfectly and, when he starts the engine, the rumble vibrates through every cell in my body. It is the most comforting feeling in the world. "Thanks for being here, Gylly."

His hand reaches back to slide along my thigh. "Always, babe."

Acknowledgments

I would like to especially thank my mom who has read every one of my manuscripts and given me encouraging, yet honest feedback. Her steadfast faith in my ability has always instilled the belief in me that I could achieve whatever I set my mind to.

Thank you to my husband, Sean, for his unwavering support. He is the most patient, generous, and determined person I know. He inspires me daily to be more like him.

Thanks to my brother, Rob, who designed the Noir et Bleu Motorcycle Club logo and has done a million other things to help me. To my sister, Luan, who gives me free marketing advice and is the quintessential protective big sister. To my dad, who taught me the power of language and was the voice of reason while I worked on edits.

Thank you to everyone who was kind enough to read the early drafts of One Percenter: Cory, Erica, Belinda, and my critique partner Denise Jaden. Thanks also to my Harley guy Kelly, and everyone else who has supported my writing.

I would be remiss to not thank the late Ms. McNulty, my grade four teacher, who taught me to write whatever was in my imagination without worrying about spelling or punctuation. Also, thanks to Mr. Rawlings, my grade seven grammar teacher, who on the contrary, insisted that grammar does in fact matter.

Thanks to Heather Howland and Sue Winegardner along with Debbie Suzuki, Brittany Marczak, Anita Orr, Vanessa Mitchell, and the rest of the team behind the scenes at Entangled Publishing.

Finally, thanks to the readers.

About the Author

D.R. Graham currently lives in Vancouver, British Columbia, Canada with her husband. She worked as a social worker with at-risk youth prior to becoming a youth and family therapist in private practice. She writes novels that deal with issues relevant to young and new adults in love, transition, or crisis.

One Percenter is the first book in the *Noir et Bleu Motorcycle Club* series. For more on the series, visit www. drgrahambooks.com.

Made in the USA
Charleston, SC
21 April 2015